LETHAL RAGE

BRENT PILKEY

ECW Press

Published by ECW Press, 2120 Queen Street East, Suite 200,
Toronto, Ontario, Canada M4E 1E2
416.694.3348 / info@ecwpress.com

LIBRARY AND ARCHIVES CANADA CATALOGUING IN PUBLICATION

Pilkey, Brent
Lethal rage / Brent Pilkey.

ISBN 978-1-55022-925-7

I. Title.

PS8631.I479L48 2010   c813'.6   C2009-905970-3

Cover and text design: Tania Craan
Cover images: Blood splatter © Dave Wall / Arcangel Images
Man in alley © Peeter Viisimaa / iStockphoto
Author photo: Photography by Andrew Hay
Typesetting: Mary Bowness
Printing: Friesens   1   2   3   4   5

The publication of *Lethal Rage* has been generously supported by the Canada Council for the Arts,
which last year invested $20.1 million in writing and publishing throughout Canada, by the Ontario
Arts Council, by the Government of Ontario through the Ontario Book Publishing Tax Credit, by
the OMDC Book Fund, an initiative of the Ontario Media Development Corporation, and by the
Government of Canada through the Book Publishing Industry Development Program (BPIDP).

PRINTED AND BOUND IN CANADA

ECW PRESS
ecwpress.com

For Carol,
in pursuing your dream,
you inspired me to reach for my own

Author's Note

In the spring of 2004, the officers and civilian staff of 51 Division said good-bye to 30 Regent Street and moved to their new home at 51 Parliament Street.

All would agree, the original station was too small, too run down and simply too old to carry on. The new station was better in every way. But ask any officer who worked out of Regent Street and they'll tell you, the old station was the heart and soul of the division. The old lady will be greatly missed.

Lethal Rage takes place several years before the closing of the real 51.

When you stare for a long time into an abyss,
the abyss stares back into you.
— Friedrich Nietzsche

Sunday, 30 July
2343 hours

"5106, in 9's area. See the complainant at the corner of George and Britain. He believes he's found a body in a dumpster."

The cop driving the scout car chuckled. "A body in a dumpster. How clichéd."

"Interesting, at least," the cop in the passenger seat replied. "You think it'll tie us up for the rest of the night?"

Paul Townsend grinned at his passenger, white teeth flashing in an ebony-black face. "I keep forgetting you're still kind of new to this, Jacky-boy. If it's a homicide, we'll be lucky to be out of here on time this morning."

Jack Warren, recently of 32 Division, frowned self-consciously, embarrassed he had asked such a rookie question. "Well, you don't get a lot of calls involving dead bodies up in 32."

Paul snorted. "If it's dead bodies you want, you've come to the right place. Stay in 51 long enough and you'll soon lose count of how many you see." Paul Townsend had been in 51 for three years now and some of the stories he had told Jack over the past week were hard to believe.

Jack nodded noncommittally and turned his attention to the life on the downtown sidewalks passing by the police car. Almost midnight on a Sunday night and the streets were still busy as if it was six hours earlier. But it was a different busy from what he was used to. Six years as a Toronto police officer and he had just discovered in the past week how little he knew about being a cop.

He was used to university students and young professionals out for a night of partying, young guys full of too much testosterone cruising the asphalt in their street racers, simple trouble looking for a place to happen. Oh, sure, 32 Division had its problem spots, notably the Jungle, a sprawling government housing complex in the city's north end, but nothing compared to this.

51 Division was another world entirely from the North York communities Jack had patrolled for six years. Drugs and violence, that's what his old staff sergeant had warned him he would find downtown. Nothing but drugs and violence. The old guy had been right; drugs and violence pretty much summed up the small division.

And Jack loved it.

They cruised by the large Salvation Army hostel — or the Sally Ann, as Jack had learned to call it — and Paul automatically slowed down to scan the faces by the front steps. Jack kept his attention focused on his side of the street, watching the people in front of the Moss Park community centre. That was the first new skill he had had to develop upon coming to 51. Jack had moved from an area that had little street-level crime; he had to learn how to scan a crowd for the people who casually turned their faces away, for hands sliding into pockets or behind backs.

Watch the hands, Paul had told him the first night they had worked together, the night Jack had learned how little he knew. *Watch for the exchange of drugs or money. Watch for the ones trying to hide. Look for the ones getting ready to run, waiting to see if you slow down. Watch, watch, watch.*

"Streets are busy tonight," Jack said without taking his eyes from them.

"Always are on a summer night. Busy, busy, busy."

Jack grinned and slowly shook his head in mild disbelief. "What a difference," he whispered out the open window.

"What's that, Jacky-boy?"

"Nothing, really. Just thinking how different it is down here. I mean, if this call had come across in 32, we'd be flying there, lights and sirens, and just about everybody would be jumping on the call."

"Just another dead body, man. Nothing special."

Sure ain't in Kansas anymore, Jack thought. Paul had three years less on the job than Jack, making Jack the senior man in the car. Technically, at least. But three years in 51 were a whole lot different from double that in 32. *Just another dead body.*

"That must be our man," Paul announced.

Jack snapped out of his reverie.

Paul had turned the car onto George, a small street running south off Queen. Jack saw a mixture of old buildings and converted warehouses. A man in a business suit was frantically waving at them from the end of Britain Street where it T-intersected with George. Paul pulled up short of the man to let Jack get out. *If you don't know what's going on, don't let anyone walk up to the car window,* Paul had instructed him. *Fewer nasty surprises that way.*

Jack rolled up his window, catching a faint image of himself in the glass. Dark brown hair, cut regulation short, and a clean-shaven, unremarkable face that looked its twenty-eight years. He had been told he looked like a cop, but he always figured it was the uniform people responded to, not the person wearing it. The uniform represented different things to different people and right now Jack was betting it meant safety to one hell of a nervous guy.

"Oh, thank God, you're here. It's over there," the man said, gesturing down Britain Street. With his other hand, he clutched a cell phone the way a drowning man would hold on to a life preserver.

Jack stopped out of arm's reach and casually rested his forearms on his gun butt and double magazine pouches. A nice, relaxed stance that just happened to keep his hands in front and his gun side turned away from whomever he was speaking with. The interview stance, they called it in the college, but Jack thought of it as the 51 stance. He couldn't remember ever seeing anyone, including himself, use it in 32. *Just another dead body.*

"What's over there, sir?" Jack asked as he studied the complainant. Mid-thirties, what was left of his hair dishevelled as if he'd been running his hands through it and a business suit as dishevelled as his hair.

"The body. In the dumpster." The man in the suit pointed down the street again then turned to face Jack. Big, frightened eyes.

"Why were you looking in a dumpster?" Paul asked as he joined them on the sidewalk, standing a short distance from Jack. *Never stand next to each other,* Paul had instructed. *Never present a single target unless you know who you are talking to.* The man turned to Paul and took an involuntary step backward. "Calm down, sir. We're here to help." Standing six-five with a bodybuilder's mass and a complexion he liked to call "midnight black," Paul was accustomed to making people nervous. Hell, even Jack, at five-ten and just fifteen pounds shy of two hundred from hitting the gym regularly, had been nervous the first time they met.

"Sir? Why were you in the dumpster?" Jack asked, drawing the man's attention.

"Oh, uh, I'm an architect and I was looking for some cardboard tubes to take some drawings home to work on. That's when I found them." He shivered.

On a hot summer night, he shivered, and Jack realized the man wasn't scared, he was downright terrified. "Them? I thought you had found one body."

"No, not a body," he said, shaking his head emphatically. "At least . . . I don't know. Maybe."

"Maybe? Sir, I need you to slow down, take a deep breath and tell us what you found in the dumpster." Jack spoke slowly, using his voice to calm the complainant.

It worked. For a moment. Business Suit took a deep breath, held it, then it all gushed out. "Feet! I found a pair of human feet in the dumpster."

"Feet," Paul said, disbelieving. "Are you sure it wasn't an old pair of shoes someone had thrown out?"

The man shook his head so hard Jack was surprised it didn't pop off. "Uh-uh. Feet. Bare human feet. In that dumpster over there." He turned and pointed again. Not down Britain but into a dark parking lot not a stone's throw away from where they were standing.

"Jack, you want to have him point out the dumpster while I get the car?"

"Sure thing. C'mon, sir. Show me where this dumpster is."

It was a small parking lot, between Britain and Richmond, the next street south. Despite being downtown, it wasn't paved but hard-packed dirt, but this was 51: a little east of the downtown core and a whole lot east of normal.

The lot's east side ran up against the brick wall of an old building with a single loading dock jutting into the night. There were no lights and the building was heavy with shadows. Jack couldn't see a dumpster but thought there was a darker shadow close to the loading dock.

White light swept across them as Paul pulled the scout car into the lot. He parked beside them, the headlights aimed at the loading dock, and turned on the high beams and roof-mounted takedown lights. The side of the building and part of the lot were bathed in intense light. Steps away from the loading dock, sitting harmlessly in the stark brightness, was the dumpster.

"That's it. I'm going to stay right here, if you don't mind."

"No problem, sir. Just hang tight."

Jack and Paul approached the dumpster together. Its lid was open and the remains of cardboard boxes and packaging jutted up like broken teeth from a gaping mouth.

"Just another dead body, right?" Jack said.

"Yup. Or parts of one. Watch where you step," Paul cautioned. "Don't want to trample any evidence."

They picked their way over the oil-stained dirt to the metal sides of the dumpster. One at each end, they stepped up onto the lip that ran around the bin midway up its sides. The lights from the scout car scattered sharp shadows across the contents and buried the depths in a deeper blackness. Suddenly, Jack could understand why the complainant — *Damn! I didn't even get his name yet* — was so shaken. The bin was crammed full of old boxes and Jack wasn't exactly thrilled about digging for a body. *Or just feet,* he thought.

He glanced over to make sure Business Suit was still waiting for them but couldn't see him. A spark of panic jumped up his throat. He could picture the ass kicking a sergeant would give him for letting the complainant go without getting his information and taking a statement.

First to discover a homicide and quite possibly a suspect and I let him go. I'm screwed.

Something moved beside the car and Jack saw the man's dim form beyond the lights. He blew out a relieved sigh. "Just stay put, sir," he called. "We'll be back in a minute to speak with you."

"C'mon, Jacky-boy. Quit stalling."

"I don't see you digging for the surprise at the bottom," Jack shot back, a little more sharply than intended.

"True, true," Paul conceded. "Let's get to it, then."

Both cops slipped on latex gloves before thumbing on flashlights. Jack played the beam over the garbage at his end. Flattened and broken boxes were mashed together like a lunatic's 3-D puzzle.

"No blood so far," Paul said.

"Same here. Let's move on to the next level, shall we?"

Jack pulled back the nearest cardboard flap, ducking his head to check under it before pulling it off the pile. Nothing. He shifted the next box and stopped. Dead.

"Paul," he said softly. "I've got a pair of feet over here."

He focused his flashlight on them and forced himself to slow down. *Look before you move. Note what you see. For God's sake, don't mess this up.*

The feet were bare — as the complainant had said — but the legs, what little Jack could see of them, were wearing jeans. The feet were side by side, toes pointing up and no blood. So maybe there was a body to go with the feet. The skin was dark, but from dirt or skin colour he couldn't tell.

"No blood, no shoes," he told Paul without looking up.

"Check the lowest point of the foot for discoloration," Paul instructed from his end of the dumpster.

Jack looked up. "For what?"

"For pooling blood," Paul explained. "When a body's been dead for a while, the blood settles to the lowest points and the skin looks purple."

"Right. I knew that." He did too. He was just a little too freaked out to remember it. "No, no discoloration, I think. It's hard to tell; the skin is too dark or dirty. Hang on a sec, Paul." Jack turned off his flashlight, jumped down from the dumpster and pulled out his portable radio. "5106, call radio."

"5106, go ahead," the dispatcher came back.

"Yeah, dispatch. We've definitely got a body here. We're going to need extra units, a road sergeant, and could you notify the CIB, please?"

"10-4, 5106. What's your exact location?"

"Parking lot south side of Britain, just east of George. They'll see our car."

"10-4, 5106. Units on the way."

Jack slid the radio into its pouch and climbed back onto the dumpster. He clicked his flashlight on and looked at Paul.

The big cop nodded. "Okay, nice and slow. Let's see what we've got."

Together, slowly and carefully, they started pulling cardboard away from the feet, trying to get a clear look at the rest of the body. Jack's blood was pounding in his ears. His first homicide, and Jack was first on the scene. The boxes and shadows shifted in the lights, folding in on themselves, never revealing what lay beneath. He was reaching into darkness, groping blindly.

Oh, God, I don't want to put my hand in — his hand touched something warm.

"Paul, I think I've —"

And then the body sat up.

Jack screamed and leaped backward. His feet hit the dirt, then his butt and then his back slammed into the ground. His breath whooshed out of him and he gasped for air, squirming on the ground like an overturned turtle in its Kevlar shell.

Dimly, he heard shouting through the roaring in his ears. He coughed and gratefully pulled in a lungful of air, then sat up and saw Paul kicking the dumpster for all he was worth.

"Get the fuck out of there! You little mother —" The rest was lost beneath the great clanging as his boot slammed into the metal bin again and again.

Still fighting to breathe properly, Jack dragged himself to his feet as a very scared-looking fellow timidly poked his head out of the bin.

"What the fuck are you doing in there?" Paul yelled.

The man cringed. "I was sleeping, that's all."

"Why the fuck would you sleep in a dumpster?" Paul shouted and Jack realized he wasn't the only one who had been scared half to death.

The man ducked into his cardboard fortress, fleeing from the angry giant's wrath. "I was just sleeping." It sounded like a desperate plea for surrender.

"Sleeping. He was sleeping," Paul muttered in disbelief. In control again, he spoke in a softer tone. "All right, buddy. C'mon out now. No sleeping in dumpsters. Someone's liable to throw you away with the trash."

The man scrambled out of the dumpster and dropped to the ground and Jack recognized him from the Queen and Sherbourne area. An old, frail black man, he came up to about Paul's chest.

"Don't you have any shoes?" Jack asked.

"No, sir. Don't need 'em till it gets cold. Can I go now, boss?" He looked at Paul.

Paul laughed. "Go on, my man. Get out of here. And no more sleeping in dumpsters," he called after the fleeing figure.

Paul sagged against the dumpster and laughed again. "I don't know about you, Jack, but I need a drink." He took two steps away from the bin and stopped. "And possibly a change of pants."

Friday, 4 August
0700 hours

"All right, everybody. Settle down and listen up."

The officers quieted down as the sergeant strode to the front of the parade room. Looking at the seven cops, he slowly shook his head. "Things are getting a little tight, manpower-wise, this week. There's only two on early days and you seven mutts, so if anyone wants T.O. for the weekend don't bother asking."

A few cops quietly muttered obscenities at the announcement of no time off, but they ceased immediately when Sergeant Johanson glared at them from beneath bushy grey eyebrows. He had been on the job for more than thirty years and had heard all the bitching before. And in more colourful language.

"We got three on holidays, two on courses, and Stiller is off getting his AIDS cocktail shots after that crack whore bit him. So quit your griping and listen up. Frederick, Holmberg, 5102, twelve o'clock for lunch. Townsend?"

"Sarge?" Paul called from the back of the room.

"Now that Carter's back from holidays, we'll give you a break and let him have the newbie. Carter, Warren, 5103, eleven o'clock lunch. And Warren?"

"Sarge?" Jack looked up from his memo book. He was sitting at the first table in front of the sergeant's podium and tried not to squirm when Johanson speared him with his eyes.

"Next time you put over a homicide and call for a road sergeant, make sure the fucker's dead." Jack felt his face heat with embarrassment as the platoon laughed. "For a fucking minute there, I thought I was going to have to go out on the road," Johanson added after the laughter died down.

"Yeah, fuck up like that again, rookie, and you'll be walking a beat down on Unwin." The voice came from the back of the room, but there was no laughter, only silence.

"And if I hear any more complaints about you gawking at the whores on Church Street while you're still marked on a call, Borovski," Johanson snarled, "you'll be walking with him. Do I make myself clear?"

"Got it, Sarge," Borovski said meekly, sounding so much like a pouting child Jack turned to look at him. Sure enough, the officer sitting next to Paul, or at least at the same table as Paul considering how Paul was physically distancing himself from the other cop, was sitting with his arms crossed defensively and a frown fixed to his fleshy face.

If you looked up sulking *in the dictionary. . . .*

"Nothing on the parade board to read out, but Detective Mason wants a few minutes. Rick?" Johanson gave up his position to the boss of the division's Major Crime Unit.

Mason was thickset, intimidating and, unlike most guys out of uniform, kept his greying hair cut short, but the goatee that hung down to his chest spoke of the years he had spent in old clothes.

"Morning, everyone. I know it's your first day of days and you're probably all eager to get out there and have your morning coffee, so I'll keep it brief." He leaned massive forearms on the podium and Jack heard the wood creak in protest. "We've got a new problem in the division. An aggressive dealer has moved in and he's trying to take over the crack trade by selling higher-quality rock at slightly better prices. And he's doing something different to promote and identify his product. He's adding a bit of food dye to the mix so his crack looks black, not the usual dirty white or dull yellow. Of course, everyone on the street is calling it Black. So if you hear someone saying they're looking to score some Black, you know what they mean.

"Now, I'm all for free enterprise and shit, but one guy controlling the crack market in 51 is bad for us. The more suppliers and dealers we have, the more they fight each other and not us."

Mason straightened and the podium sighed in relief. "We've been trying to get a fix on who's behind this new crew, but so far we've come up with zilch. All we know is that this crew is organized and violent. The last two homicides in the division are directly related to them. Seems the boss is not above more direct means of removing the competition.

"So if you find someone dealing Black, play it safe and call for another car to watch your back, 'cause chances are there's someone nearby whose job it is to keep an eye on the dealer. And word on the street is that they'll tolerate no interference from anyone. Including us.

"If you grab a dealer, give the office a call, and one of us will come down to put the squeeze on the guy and see if he'll give up his supplier. That way we can start working our way up the ladder. That's it. Thanks for your time."

"This black crack," Paul asked before the detective could leave the podium, "is it just darker than normal or really black, like me?"

"Glad you said that, Townsend, and not me." Mason chuckled with the rest of the room. "Well, I don't think anything's as black as you, but, yeah, it's pretty damn dark. You'll know it when you see it. Anything else?" He waited a beat. "Then they're all yours, Sarge."

"Thanks, Rick," Johanson said, clapping the big detective on the back as he headed for the door. "Well, what are you waiting for? Get your asses on the road."

"Jack, is it? Simon Carter. Call me Sy. Good to meet you, kid. And, yes, I have enough time on to be the platoon's old fart. Like Fish on *Barney Miller*."

They had shaken hands in the station's back lot after dumping their duty bags in the scout car's trunk. Jack figured "grizzled old veteran" was a better description than "old fart." To call his short-cropped hair salt and pepper was generous; there was a lot more salt than pepper. His face was worn and lined, and Jack wondered what he had seen to give it so many creases. His non-regulation moustache grew down to his chin, and it too held more grey than black.

Simon was a touch taller than Jack and the ballistic vest under his shirt appeared to be pulling double duty as a girdle. But any-one who mistook him for a stocky, out-of-shape cop obviously wasn't looking at the solid shoulders and the arms straining the black uniform shirt. Simon looked like he could scrap it out with a guy half his age and, judging from the scabs on some of his dis-torted knuckles, had — and not all that long ago either.

"Don't know if Paul told you, but down here we don't bother with the hats unless the media or brass are stopping by a scene." Both uniform hats followed the duty bags into the trunk.

They climbed into the car and while Jack powered up the workstation Sy flicked on the lights and gave the siren a quick blast to make sure everything was working.

"We are set. Clear us whenever you want and if nothing's pending we'll grab a coffee. Sound good to you?"

"Iced coffee might be more like it."

"Yeah, it's gonna be a hot one today," Sy agreed. "But I need my coffee. The public will not want to deal with me if I haven't had my morning shot of caffeine."

But coffee would have to wait.

"5103, in 11's area, at Street City. A male tenant has thrown bleach in another tenant's face. Use caution; staff advise the male can be violent. Time, 0727."

"And throwing bleach at someone isn't violent?" Sy heaved a sigh and headed south out of the station's lot. "So much for my morning coffee."

"What's Street City? I never had a call there on nights."

"It's a community co-op kinda thing. They built a bunch of little apartments, nothing but single rooms really, inside an old warehouse, so it kind of looks like a town or village. Basically, it's a huge rooming house with a few unlucky staff to supervise it. We get a lot of EDPs down there."

"Sounds like fun."

Sy turned onto Parliament, joining the early rush-hour traffic. "Something tells me you ain't used to dealing with our kind of crazies."

"Hey, 32 gets its share of the emotionally disturbed. Just that, when you have money, they call you eccentric, not crazy."

"Well, no one at Street City is eccentric, then. I don't know if she's still there or not, but there was one old lady who liked to hug people, especially people in uniform."

Jack figured there was more to it. "And the problem with that?"

Sy grinned. "She liked to hug you after covering herself in her own feces."

"I see." Jack nodded solemnly. "Note to self: don't hug anybody."

Sy laughed. "That's generally a good idea anywhere in 51, kid."

"5103, I just ran your suspect and he's on file for violence and weapons. Do you want another car to attend with you?"

Jack picked up the mike but looked to Sy, who nodded. "Sure, dispatch. If someone wants to drop by with us, we'd appreciate the company."

"10-4, 5103. 5109, attend 393 Front Street with 5103 for an assault." The dispatcher received no answer. *"5109, are you 10-4 on the call?"*

There was a lengthy pause before a reluctant voice answered. *"Yeah, but I'm a ways off."*

Sy snorted. "I bet he is. Lazy bastard."

"Who was that?" It would take some time before Jack could recognize everyone's voice over the air.

"Borovski." Sy spat the name out as if it was a bad taste in his mouth. "Watch your back around Boris," he cautioned. "He's always the last one at a call and he's the first to cut corners on the work. He'll come across as your best friend, but he'll sell you out in a heartbeat if he thinks it'll save his ass."

"Boris Borovski? Sounds like something out of a book."

"Boris isn't his name," Sy explained. "It's Scott or something like that. Everybody just calls him Boris."

"How come?"

"'Cause he hates it." When Jack stayed silent, Sy looked over at him. "What? Everyone in 32 was a team player? Someone you could trust?"

"No, of course not," Jack said, a little defensively. "I just know how reputations can stick to people whether they deserve them or not. There was one guy I worked with. When he came to us from another platoon, they all warned us that he was stupid. Turned out the 'stupid' label came from one mistake he had made three years earlier when he had first got on the road. He was a really good guy to work with." Jack shrugged. "I guess I just like to make up my mind about people after I've met them, that's all."

"And that's a good way to be. But all I'm saying is watch your back around Boris. Okay, here we are."

On the short trip, they had left behind the mixed residences and businesses and crossed over into a commercial wasteland. The south end of the division was a desert of abandoned warehouses and weed-choked, deserted lots and thus a desirable location for movie productions. Some buildings were still in use and the Canary Restaurant at the corner of Front and Cherry was a favourite breakfast hangout for the foot patrol and traffic cars.

Street City was in an old warehouse squatting on the corner across from the Canary. A bearded, pot-bellied man and a scarecrow of a young woman with green spiky hair were waiting out front in matching navy T-shirts. Jack figured them to be the staff. The woman waved them over.

Sy parked the car on the other side of the street and he and Jack joined the staff on the cigarette butt–littered sidewalk. "What happened today?" Sy asked the man, but it was the woman — no more than a girl really — who spoke up.

"Lloyd and Mohammed got into a fight over the TV. In the common room. Mohammed was there first and the rule is the first one gets to choose the channel. They started arguing and Bob and me," she gestured to her staff partner, "had to tell Lloyd to leave cuz he was making so much noise. Lloyd's always bullying the other tenants and hitting them. No one does nothing cuz they're all scared of him."

As she talked, Jack studied her: besides her bristling lime-green hair, he saw that each ear sported a dozen or so earrings. But it was her arms that fascinated him the most. The arms hanging out of her too-big staff shirt were twig thin. He was willing to bet her elbow joints were the widest part of her arms and how the bones didn't simply snap when she flung her hands about as she talked was a mystery to him.

"A few minutes later Lloyd comes back carrying a cup in his hand. He just walks up to Mohammed —"

"Calm as you please," Bob added.

"Yeah, just as calm as shit," she agreed. "He walks right up to where Mohammed's sitting and throws it — splash! — right in his face. I thought it was just water, but Mohammed starts screaming, really bad like, and I could smell it."

"Smell what?" Sy wanted to know.

"You know," she said, spinning her hands in front of her as if that would make the proper words come out. Jack waited for her hands to snap off at the wrists. "Ajax or something like that. You know, what you use to clean stuff with."

"Good enough. We'll need to get statements from you two later."

"Yeah, we wuz already doing that when we wuz waiting for you."

"Done this before, have you?" Sy suggested, smiling at her.

"Yeah, lots of times." She paused and cocked her head. "You gonna arrest Lloyd?"

"If he's still here."

"Yeah, he's in his room, I think. I can show you which one.

Mohammed's in the laundry room, washing that stuff out of his eyes." Her head tipped the other way. Jack figured it had something to do with her thought process. "Ain't an ambulance coming? We asked for one."

"Speak of the devil," Sy said, spotting the ambulance coming along Front Street.

"The devil?"

"The ambulance is here," Jack interpreted for her.

"Oh." She looked at Jack for the first time and smiled, showing him a full set of heavily stained teeth. "Hey, you're kind of cute for a cop. I'm Lisa."

Jack almost introduced himself out of habit but caught himself. In no way did he want Lisa knowing anything about him. "Um, thanks. You want to show us where Lloyd's room is?"

"Hang tight for a second, kid. You chat with Lisa for a few minutes while I tell the medics what we've got." Sy smiled goodnaturedly and clapped Jack on the shoulder, then walked — slowly — over to the ambulance, stranding Jack on the sidewalk with Lisa.

You're a prick, Sy, Jack thought as Lisa sidled up to him. He busied himself taking down Bob's and Lisa's information. Lisa made sure he wrote down her cell phone number correctly.

Minutes later — long minutes — Sy and Jack followed Bob and Lisa through the metal double doors into Street City with the ambulance crew and their stretcher bringing up the rear. The building was indeed an old warehouse and the roof rose an easy twenty feet or so above them. The vast interior had been laid out in "streets" with rows of single-room apartments lining both sides. Each simple wood structure had its own entrance and front window looking out onto the street. Potted plants and trees decorated the laneways.

The streets were wide, about a dozen feet across and laid out in an H pattern; the double front doors were at the bottom left corner of the H. The office was right next to the doors, with a large window so staff could see everyone coming and going. The common room was on the short centre street that connected the two long streets. A mismatched collection of couches, chairs and tables formed a social setting. An old TV blared static and a picture not much better.

Bob stopped, pointing to a man near the TV, and Lisa spoke for him. "That's Lloyd there."

There were several people in the common room, but there was a definite no man's land surrounding the lone resident watching TV.

"The one on the couch at the other end?" Sy asked, wanting to be sure.

"Yeah, that's him." Lisa bobbed her head in confirmation and Jack winced as her neck vertebrae pushed sharply against her skin.

"Is Lloyd known to carry any weapons — knives, stuff like that?" Sy was talking to both staff members, but his eyes never left Lloyd.

Lisa cocked her head in thought. "Don't think so. Bob?"

Bob shrugged.

"Bob, Lisa. Why don't you go show the paramedics where Mohammed is while we talk to Lloyd?"

As he worked his way through the maze of furniture toward the man slumped on the couch, all Jack could see was the back of Lloyd's head. He and Sy split up to circle the ends of the sofa and cut off Lloyd's escape routes.

Jack approached from the left and got his first clear look at Lloyd. He was a bulk of a human, his legs apart so his enormous gut could hang down between his thighs. His greasy hair was a rat's nest and the remains of breakfast, or possibly last night's dinner, clung to the stubble on his multiple chins. He wore old grey sweatpants and a T-shirt that probably had once been white.

The sharp smell of bleach hung in the air but did little to cover the stale odour coming from Lloyd.

"Morning, Lloyd," Sy began, positioning himself to Lloyd's right. Jack stood to the left. Lloyd couldn't see them both without turning his head. Jack watched the man's hands, which were resting limply in his lap. "Guess you know why we're here. You're under arrest for assault with a weapon, so why don't you stand up for me and put your hands behind your back?"

Lloyd rocked forward and braced his hands on his knees. He wheezed, then heaved himself up, but his ass had barely pulled free of the cushion before his left hand slipped off his knee and he thumped back down. He grinned foolishly and held out his right hand to Sy.

"You need a hand up, buddy?"

Sy was stepping forward, hand extended, when Jack saw Lloyd's left hand sneak under his thigh. His grin no longer looked foolish.

"Sy. . . ."

Lloyd grabbed Sy's hand and gripped it tightly. His left forearm flexed, as if gripping something hidden under his leg. His grin was cunning.

"Knife!"

Lloyd suddenly pulled Sy off balance and his left hand flashed a blade toward Sy's neck. Jack dove after the knife hand and rammed into Sy, knocking him onto the couch. Jack landed across Lloyd's lap, the knife arm pinned between them. There was muscle under Lloyd's bulk and he shoved Jack away, swinging the blade backhanded. Jack sprawled on the floor, hoping Lloyd's size would slow him down so he could get his Glock out of its holster.

"Drop it or die, fucker!" Sy was kneeling on the couch with his gun hard against Lloyd's temple. The fat man froze, his hands in front of him, but he didn't drop the knife.

"One twitch and I splatter your brains across the floor."

If this was a movie and Sy had a revolver, this is where he would cock it, Jack thought and wondered why he would think something stupid like that when he had his own gun aimed at Lloyd's chest.

He smiled; he didn't remember drawing the gun.

Whether it was Jack's smile or Sy's calm, emotionless words, Lloyd decided to drop the knife. His left hand opened and the blade bounced off the sofa cushion to clatter onto the concrete floor.

Jack got to his feet, his aim on Lloyd never wavering; where there was one knife, there could be another.

Sy ordered Lloyd to lie face down on the floor. The fat man had no trouble getting off the couch this time. Sy cuffed and searched him — one knife hidden in each sock — and Jack felt his hands trembling slightly.

Sy noticed. "Just the adrenalin dump, Jack. It'll pass in a couple of minutes. Let's get this piece of shit out to the car."

They each grabbed an arm and hauled Lloyd to his feet, fast-walked him out to the scout car and were none too gentle stuffing him into the back seat. Sy got the bottle of sanitizer gel from the front seat, squirted some into his hands and held the bottle out for Jack.

"Nice job in there, Jack. I think you saved me a trip to the hospital," Sy admitted. "Or worse. Thanks."

"I'm just glad we didn't get hurt." Jack started washing his hands with the gel and hissed when pain stabbed through his right hand.

"What is it? You hurt?"

Jack held up his hand. On the edge of his palm, just below the last knuckle of his little finger, was a short but deep cut. "Bastard got me after all. That'll teach me not to wear my gloves."

"Son of a fucking whore," Sy breathed. "That's going to need a couple of stitches."

"I guess. Why don't we get the medics to tape it up for now? We can take buddy into the station and head to the hospital later. Besides, we'll have to get pictures of the cut before it's stitched up."

Jack's hand was wrapped, Bob's and Lisa's statements taken and Mohammed transported to hospital. There was still no sign of Borovski.

"See? Completely unreliable."

"Yup. I get your point," Jack conceded, then advised the dispatcher they were "heading into the station with one." After a brief pause, he keyed the mike again. "5109 on the air?"

Borovski came back right away. "Sorry, guys. I got tied up. You need a hand with anything?"

"Fucking unreal," Sy muttered.

"No thanks, '09. We took care of everything. You can disregard . . ." Jack paused to look at his bandaged hand ". . . Boris."

Friday, 4 August
1234 hours

"You know, Jack, you could have taken the rest of the day off IOD. Hell, no one would say anything if you waited until the stitches came out before coming back."

"Yeah, I know, Sy, but what can I say? I'd miss your cheery smile."

They had booked Lloyd into the station, briefed the detectives, photographed Jack's cut and then headed to the hospital. All in all, Jack was surprised they were ready to clear so soon. He knew some senior guys, and unfortunately some not so senior guys, who would have milked that arrest for the whole day.

"How would it have looked if I went off injured on duty my second week here? Besides, it's only two stitches."

"Your choice." Sy started up the car. "An open cut on your hand down here is a serious risk. There's too many fucking diseases floating around out there. Make sure you have plenty of latex gloves on you for the rest of the week."

"Yes, Dad."

Sy grimaced. "Just because I'm old enough to be your father doesn't mean I can't kick your ass. I saw how Lloyd tossed you around. We'd better get you into the gym and put some muscle on you." He stuck out his arm and flexed an impressive bicep. "Get you some guns like these."

"Hey, I work out," Jack said, mildly offended. "My wife likes to say I'm built like Russell Crowe in *Gladiator.*"

Sy appraised him. "Hm. More like Kirk Douglas in *Spartacus.*"

"I just run more than I lift. I figure, what good are big muscles if you can't catch the bad guy?"

"What good is catching him if you can't hold on to him?" Sy countered.

"Touché. Tell you what. I'll chase them and somehow hold on to them until you get there and thump them."

"Ah, the makings of a classic tag team. Speed and power. Like the Hart Foundation."

"The what?"

Sy lifted his hands beseechingly. "Oh, Lord, I'm working with one of those." He pulled out of the lot and headed north on Parliament. "Seriously, though, Jack. Thanks. I owe you one."

Jack shrugged it off. "You would have done the same for me. Coffee?"

"Damn straight. See what happens when I don't get to have my morning cup?"

But coffee would have to wait again and this time it was Jack's fault.

They were heading up Sherbourne to get Sy's long-overdue caffeine when Jack twisted in his seat. "Hang on, Sy."

"What did you see?" Sy was already throwing the car into a U-turn, bouncing the wheels over the curb.

"Out front of 310 Dundas. I caught a glimpse of a hand-to-hand exchange. Some money, not sure what else."

"Could be innocent, could be not." Sy eased the car up to the corner of Sherbourne and Dundas. Jack leaned forward to see past Sy along Dundas.

"Those two there. The black guy passed some money to the skinny white guy in the blue tank top."

In front of the short apartment building on the northeast corner of the intersection, two men had just parted company. The black guy Jack had pointed out, wearing the typical baggy white T-shirt and blue jeans, took a couple of steps in their direction but staggered when he caught sight of the police car. Recovering quickly, he dropped his eyes to the sidewalk, made an abrupt turn and started to walk up Sherbourne.

"Subtle, buddy. Real subtle." Sy unclipped his seat belt. "You make the black guy the buyer?"

"Yup." Jack freed himself of his belt. Neither of them had taken their eyes off their prey.

"Then that makes Whitey our dealer. Shall we?" Sy pulled away from the curb and hit the roof lights, then slipped through the intersection on the red light. Their possible dealer was ambling along the sidewalk, his back to the approaching cruiser. Like so many 51 residents, he was skinny to the point of scrawny and his dull blue tank top hung on him like a limp sail.

Sy accelerated, wanting to cut off the dealer before he reached the laneway that ran north from Dundas along the east side of the apartment building. But whether their man heard the revving engine or some instinctual predator awareness alerted him, he looked over his shoulder as Sy cut across oncoming traffic, mounted the curb and stopped the cruiser's front bumper inches from the skinny man's legs. The car was a hand's breadth from the building, cutting off access to the laneway.

Jack expected the dealer to bolt the way he had come. Instead, from a dead stop, he bounded onto the hood of the cruiser and over the car. He landed hard on the sidewalk and staggered a couple of steps but caught his balance and in seconds was up and running for all he was worth.

When Sy threw the cruiser into reverse, horns blared.

"Shit! Get out of my fucking way!" he bellowed at the cars behind him, but Jack barely heard it, jumping from the car and sprinting after the dealer.

Skinny or not, the guy could run. He flew along the sidewalk, elbows and knees pumping frantically, and Jack — suddenly thankful he had trained chest that morning and not legs — had to push himself to keep up. The heat wrapped itself around him. By the time he hit Seaton, a little residential side street not a hundred yards from the laneway, he was soaked in sweat and every breath felt like it came through a wet gag.

And the dealer kept running.

Son of a bitch, you ain't losing me, Jack swore and doubled his efforts.

They crossed Ontario Street. Half a city block and Jack was dying. Running for exercise was one thing, but an all-out sprint in this heat wearing a black uniform — mostly polyester, thank you — a vest and a gun belt was simply hellish. He thought he might puke.

By the time they reached the next street, the dealer was starting to falter. He dropped from a sprint to a run and when he cut north on Berkeley he was down to a quick jog. Jack was right on his tail, but his legs were burning.

The dealer made it about three houses up the street before staggering to a halt, hands on his knees, labouring for breath. Jack stopped short of him, fighting the urge to double over as well.

"Get ... get on ... your knees," he gasped.

The dealer raised his head, drawing deep breaths, and looked at Jack.

Jack wiped sweat from his eyes. "Get on — fuck!"

The dealer took off again and Jack forced his screaming legs back into a run.

The side streets in this area were all residential, with older homes, mature trees and well-travelled laneways. The dealer cut into the first lane, doubling back on himself. Jack was past the point of pain, running on anger and determination. Neither of them was moving very fast and Jack would be damned if he was the first one to give up.

The lane cut across Ontario, but the dealer never reached it.

Sy screeched the cruiser to a halt across the lane, plugging the dealer's escape route. The dealer stumbled the last few steps to the cruiser and put his back to the passenger door. He started to squat down but jerked upright when he heard Jack's footsteps approaching. His running footsteps. The dealer's eyes widened in alarm and he raised his hands, whether in surrender or protection Jack didn't know and didn't care.

Jack plowed into the dealer. The man's body made a very satisfying thud against the door of the scout car and they tumbled to the ground, Jack landing on the dealer's back.

He wanted nothing more than to lie still and rest, but lying across a drug dealer's back was not the most professional position to be seen in and, besides, the guy stank like he hadn't showered since the start of the heat wave. As Jack straight-armed himself up, the dealer showed signs of wanting to get up. Jack dropped his knees on the dealer's back and the air woofed out of the man. His face made an agreeable smack on the asphalt.

"Stay . . . down . . . this time."

Jack slowly climbed to his feet and collapsed against the car. Black dots swam across his vision and his head spun wildly. Gasping hot air, he fought the urge to heave.

If I do puke, I'll make sure I puke on him.

Sy sauntered around the rear of the car. "Nice tackle." He squatted and dragged the dealer's unresisting arms behind his back. Snapping on the cuffs, he asked Jack, "He piss you off or something?"

Jack shook his head, still gasping. "First time . . . he stopped. . . ." He held up a hand and took several deep breaths. "Okay. First time he stopped I told him to get down and he took off again. I didn't want to have to chase him a third time."

"Ah, I see. You tackled him because he was getting ready to run again."

"I wasn't gonna run," the dealer protested, trying to lift his face from the hot pavement.

"I wasn't talking to you, Mumblee." Sy shoved the man's face down. "Damn, this guy's soaked. Jack, get the hand cleaner, would you?"

Jack opened the car and grabbed the bottle of gel sanitizer that all cops carried in the car. He squirted some for Sy and then himself. Once their hands were clean, they both slipped on their search gloves.

"All right, buddy, up you get." Each grabbing an arm, they hoisted the dealer to his feet. "What's your name, bud?"

"Uh, Mike."

"Mike what?"

Pause. "Smith."

"Mike Smith. How original. Now, Mike Smith, before I search you, do you have anything sharp on you that I might cut myself on? Knives, needles, razor blades. Anything like that?"

"No, nothing like that," he answered quickly.

Too quickly for Sy's comfort, Jack noticed.

Sy gripped him by the neck, thumb and middle finger resting lightly on the nerve centres behind the jawbone. "Think before you answer. Do you have anything sharp on you?"

"No, man. Nothing. I swear —"

Sy squeezed the nerve centres briefly but long enough to cut off Smith's oath in midsentence. "Don't swear. Just think, then tell me. If I find anything sharp on you that you didn't tell me about, I'll put you in the fucking hospital. You understand me?"

"I have . . . I think I have a knife in my pocket. One of those box cutters. In my back pocket."

"That's better. See what a little co-operation does? It keeps me happy and you healthy." Sy patted the pocket before slipping his hand inside. He pulled out the utility knife and held it up for Jack, thumbing out the blade. "Not long enough to stab with, but it'll cut you to the bone or slash open your neck easily enough." He retracted the blade and handed the knife to Jack. "Never take these pieces of shit at their word. Their word means less than nothing." He turned his attention back to the dealer.

"That everything? Remember, think before you answer."

Smith was quiet, then, "Yeah, that's it," he said, licking his lips.

"Uh-huh. Let's see, shall we?" Sy continued his search, slow and methodical. Except for a wad of cash — tens and twenties mostly — he came up empty-handed.

"See, man? I told you I didn't have anything on me." Mike Smith had a tentative grin on his face.

"Then why'd you run?"

"I was scared, man. The way you pulled up, I thought you was gonna jump me or somethin'."

"See, Jack? This whole misunderstanding was our fault."

"Hey, man, no problem. You was just doing your job. I understand." Smith was all but bouncing on his toes, eager to be out of the handcuffs and gone.

"Damn, stupid me," Sy said with a silly grin. "I forgot to check one area." Still holding the man by one arm, Sy reached for Smith's waist and the man tried to turn his hips away. Sy straightened him out. "Hold still, this won't take long." He lifted the tank top and loosened the man's belt.

"Hey, man, what are you? Some kind of fag?"

"If I was, I'd have better taste than you." Sy shoved his gloved hand down the front of the pants. "What's this, Mike?"

"My dick, man."

"If that's your dick, you'd better see a doctor, 'cause that don't feel right. Oops, what's this?" Slowly, teasingly, he slipped his hand out, tugging a plastic bag, then holding it for Jack to see.

It was a small sandwich bag with about two dozen small pieces of crack. Jack may have been new to 51, but he had seen crack already. Hell, his first night here he'd made two arrests for the narcotic. Smith's crack looked like it was all twenty pieces — the size you could buy for twenty dollars — individually wrapped in plastic. And every piece was black.

"Yup, that's P for P, Mike. Time to go to jail."

Mike cranked his head around to look at Jack. "What's that?"

"Possession for the purpose of trafficking." Sy snorted. "Like you didn't know." He opened the back door of the cruiser. "Get in, Mike. And by the way —" he paused before closing the door "— you may want to think of a new name before we get to the station."

He slammed the door shut, then clapped Jack on the shoulder. "Nice pinch, Jack. Major Crime will be interested in talking with him." Sy headed to the driver's side. Over the car's roof, he asked, "He pissed you off, didn't he?"

"Yeah."

"But you tackled him 'cause he was going to run again."

"Yeah." Jack grinned.

Sy grinned back. "You're learning, Jack. You're learning."

A brief but thunderous rain shower had done little to drag the humidity down. Now, just shy of four o'clock, the sun ruled once more in a cloudless sky and steam rose from the rapidly drying asphalt. Sy and Jack had conveniently missed the storm while processing their small-time drug dealer and were on the road again, hoping the last hour of the shift would be kind to them. From Jack's point of view, things were definitely looking good.

"Hm, nice legs."

"Where?"

"You blind?" Jack asked. "Right there, on the bike."

Two CRU officers were biking along the street, not hurrying, just cruising the crack area of Queen and Sherbourne. With Moss Park on the northwest corner of the intersection, the Sally Ann just up the street, a couple of run-down bars nearby and a rat's nest of laneways, the area was perfect for the sale and use of crack.

Simon slowed behind the bike coppers, matching their pace, and Jack took the opportunity to enjoy the view Sy was providing. The external vest carrier and the gun belt obscured much of her figure, so Jack focused on admiring her legs. Long and tanned, her thighs and calves flexed nicely as she pedalled.

"I hope you're talking about Jenny and not her partner."

Jack glanced at the other cop. "His are nice, too, but too hairy for my liking. I'll stick with hers."

"I thought you were married," Sy teased.

"I am, and happily. But there's nothing wrong with looking."

"Uh-huh. And your wife is in full agreement with this attitude?"

"Of course she is." Jack took one more wistful look at Jenny's legs. "You won't tell her, will you?" he asked in his meekest voice.

Sy laughed. "I don't know. You buying tonight?"

"If that's the price of your silence."

"Then my lips are sealed."

"It's good to see some bike cops out and about. The Community Response up in 32 did more of the community-based policing stuff. You know, mostly flipping burgers and playing sports against the schools."

"Our foot patrol does those things as well, but when they're not playing Officer Friendly, most of them are out chasing the assholes, either on foot or bike."

"I could think of worse things to do than follow those legs around all day."

"Am I going to have to hose you down?"

"I can control myself. It's you I'm worried about. You're getting on in years and I'm wondering if your old heart can take the sight of those young legs."

"Old, my ass," Sy snorted. "I could whip your butt in the gym anytime. But don't be discouraged. A few more years of working out and you'll be big enough to be the before picture."

"Haw, haw," Jack muttered. "Fuckhead."

Sy laughed again. "Language, language."

The bike cops were stopped for the red light at Sherbourne, and Sy cruised up beside them. He thumbed down Jack's window and leaned across the seat. "Hey, Jenny! Al! You guys coming out tonight for beers?"

"Fucking right we are. Fuck, I could use one right now." Al

unclipped his water bottle, took a long pull, then emptied it through the slots on his helmet. He grinned as the water dribbled down his face. "Too motherfucking hot to be riding a bike, but I have to be working with a fucking masochist."

"I'm not a masochist, Al. I'm a sadist," she said sweetly. Jenny leaned down on her handlebars to look into the scout car. "Hey, Sy, you sexy old man. You buying me a drink tonight?"

"As many as you want, sweet cheeks, 'cause Jack here is buying."

"You're the guy from 32, aren't you? I'm Jennifer Alton. This slug is Al."

They shook hands all around; then Jenny and Al headed south to find some shade before Al passed out. Sy pointed the car north, up Sherbourne.

"Sexy old man?"

"Hey, what can I say? She digs my action."

"That's the stuff of nightmares," Jack commented. "Too bad she had the helmet and sunglasses on. From what I could see, she must be a knockout."

"Yeah, Jenny's a sweet one, all right. And the price of my silence has just gone up."

"Thought I'd find you out here." Jack gave Karen a quick kiss before settling in on the lounge chair beside hers on their back deck. When they had moved in last summer, the deck had been a pathetic little square outside the kitchen sliding doors and Jack had spent the summer building an extension that spanned the entire rear of the house. Now the original deck held the barbecue, and steps led down to the lower and much larger tier. There were plans for a hot tub and pool. The hot tub first and the pool when the kids they were hoping to have were old enough to enjoy it.

For now there was the deck attached to the home in the new development outside the city. And his wife lounging oh so provocatively on that deck. At twenty-six, Karen was just two years his junior and the woman of his dreams made flesh. Her dark blond hair, with natural, sun-kissed highlights, was loose around her shoulders tonight. She was wearing one of his old light-blue police shirts, which covered her to mid-thigh. She stretched languorously and the shirt pulled tightly across her breasts. He could tell — as he knew he was supposed to — she wasn't wearing a bra. His eyes slid down to her tanned legs and he wondered what else she wasn't wearing.

Her lounge chair creaked softly as she rolled onto her side, facing him. "How was work?"

"Good."

Her shirt had ridden up on her hip. He hadn't turned on any lights when he'd come out, but there was enough twilight left for him to see a faint tan line. Just the shirt, then.

"Hey, you," she whispered, "I'm up here."

"Sorry, I got distracted." He let his eyes linger on the curve of her hip and the swell of her breasts before he looked at her smiling face. He loved it when she teased him, and she knew it.

"Anything interesting?"

He took a slow sip from his beer bottle. "I got into my first foot pursuit today." He held the bottle out to her.

"No, thanks, I'm good. You chased someone? What for?"

"Spotted him selling some crack." He sipped some more, then told her the story, playing up the effect running in the heat had on him. She murmured a "poor baby" in the appropriate spots, then burst into laughter when he told her how the dealer had taken off on him again.

"I'm glad my physical misfortune gives you so much pleasure," he commented dryly.

"I'm sorry," she said, giggling and wiping away tears. "It's just something you never see in the movies."

"That's for sure." He tilted the bottle again. He was learning there was a lot more to policing than what was in the movies. Unfortunately, before she met him, Karen's only exposure to policing had been movies and television. There was her friend Barb, who worked in 32, but Barb was so incompetent she made the more laughable TV cops look serious.

"Did you catch him?" Karen asked when her giggles had finally dried up.

"Yup. Sy cut him off with the car and when he went to deke around the car I caught him with a beautiful tackle." The altered version — a lie, he supposed, if he wanted to be honest about it — slid effortlessly off his tongue. Karen wouldn't understand what had really happened. She wouldn't understand that Jack had delivered a lesson for that little fuckhead not to run next time. She'd call it police brutality and they'd spend the rest of the night arguing. Better to keep some things to himself.

"And what was better, when Sy searched him, he found a bunch of crack on him. And it was new stuff, called Black. The boss of the Major Crime Unit told us about it on parade this morning. . . ." His voice trailed off as Karen slowly sat up, swinging her feet down to the deck.

"Did you have a good time after work with the shift?" She stretched again and the old police shirt, mostly cotton and worn thin, did little to hide her erect nipples.

"Yeah, it was a good time." Sounding casual, uninterested, he stared at her breasts. All part of the game. "Had a couple of beers, some wings. Got to meet the rest of the platoon." *Didn't have to lie about the tackle to them. Shut up, Jack.*

"You like it in 51?" she asked, standing up.

"Yeah, I do."

He sipped at his beer as she straddled his chair and slowly lowered herself onto his lap.

"You like working with Simon?" Slowly, oh so slowly, she began undoing her buttons.

He swallowed. "Yeah, Sy's great. He asked me if I want to pair up. Be permanent partners."

All but two buttons were undone. "Is that like going steady

with him?" She plucked the beer bottle from his hand, pulled the shirt open with one hand, then ran the cold glass over her nipple. She shivered at its touch.

"Um, kind of."

She changed hands, passing the bottle over her other nipple, leaving a wet trail between her breasts.

"More like being married, I guess," he added, his voice suddenly hoarse.

She drank, tilting her head back, her glistening breasts exposed to the warm night air. She pulled the bottle from her lips and waggled it at him. "Want some?" He had no voice to speak, so he simply nodded. She tipped the bottle and let the last of the beer pour over her breasts, moaning at the liquid's cold caress.

Jack wrapped his arms around her and pulled her to him, his tongue lapping at the drops on her nipples. His hands slid down and beneath the shirt to find her firm ass bare to the touch.

Their house was on the outside of a curve in the road, curling the neighbours' backyards away from theirs; he'd hate to have to pause to go indoors. Karen seemed to agree.

Her lips and tongue kissed his ear. "Fuck me, Jack," she whispered.

"Out here?" His voice was hoarse with desire.

She ground her hips on his lap. "Right here. You want to, don't you?"

He most certainly did.

Sunday, 6 August
0900 hours

"Now, she's out early."

"Who? And what do you mean early? It's nine o'clock," Jack said, checking his watch. It felt like it should be later. In the past hour and a half, they'd done six radio calls: two house alarms, which turned out to be false, three medical complaints and an unwanted guest. To Jack it felt like theirs was the only car on the road, even though he could hear the other cars getting just as many calls as they were.

"Her." Sy pointed at a woman standing on the corner of Dundas and Pembroke. "Usually, the only hookers out this early are the crack whores and she ain't no crack whore."

The woman in question was slender but without a crack addict's wasted scrawniness. Her long blond hair, white tank top and blue miniskirt looked clean. She was leaning down to peer into every car that slowed as it passed her.

"Shall we see what brings her out in off-peak times?" Sy pulled the car out of the small parking lot at the corner of Sherbourne and Dundas and headed toward her. She saw them coming and, oh so casually, started to stroll away from the corner, northbound on Pembroke.

"Silly girl," Sy chastised. "Going up a one-way street isn't going to save you."

But it did, temporarily. A moving van rolled to a shuddering stop on Pembroke and Sy had no room to slide past it. Their hooker glanced back at them and kept walking north, a little quicker, putting a little more distance between them.

Sy drove off along Dundas Street at a sedate pace. As soon as they were hidden by the barbecue chicken place — where so many cops and criminals ate — Sy hit the gas. He darted the short distance to George Street then hammered the brakes and sped north. He flicked on the roof lights as they raced the wrong way on the one-way street. They flew past Seaton House, the city's largest men's hostel, then slowed as they approached Gerrard.

There were two east–west laneways connecting George and Pembroke, one near the north end of the block and one near the south end. Sy killed the lights and crept the car along the northern laneway. Halfway along, a third alley ran north and south.

Jack would have to learn the division's ants' nest of main

streets, residential streets, alleys and dead ends. Good thing 51 was so small.

"There she is," Sy said. "No use running, sweetheart. I can see you," he cooed softly.

As if sensing the scout car, she made an abrupt about-face, heading back the way she had come with as much speed as she could manage while trying to appear casual.

"I love how they do that. Like we don't realize they're trying to avoid us."

"Maybe she's just out power-walking," Jack suggested.

"Yeah, and maybe she's not charging forty bucks for a blow."

"Forty? That seems kind of cheap. Not that I'm speaking from experience, you understand."

"Forty for a blow in this area is actually on the high side. I was giving her the benefit of the doubt 'cause she looks clean." Sy powered down Jack's window as the car drew abreast of the woman. She was still clipping along at a good pace, determinedly not noticing them. "We can keep this up all day, honey. We have air conditioning, you don't," Sy announced.

She hung her head and waited for them to get out of the car. Sy stood in front of her; Jack took up a position to her right, just out of her peripheral vision.

"What's your name?" Sy asked.

"Julie Lee," she answered and Jack was impressed. He figured her blond hair was either a very good dye job or an even better wig. From in the car, he had taken her dark skin for a good summer's tan, but now he could see it was more natural than that. He moved to get a look at her face.

"Lee doesn't sound like a Filipino name to me," he said.

"Who says I'm Filipino?" she shot back, a little too defensively. Her accent was slight, but "Filipino" came out "Pilippino."

"Your name?" Sy asked.

"I told you, Julie Lee. You can't stop me like this. I haven't done anything wrong." She took a step.

Sy blocked her. "Your name, now." Impatience hardened his words.

"Jul —"

"Quit fucking around," he snapped. "What's your fucking name?"

How can he be so sure she's lying? Jack could tell the hooker was nervous, and Sy wasn't backing off. *What am I missing here?*

"Marquez." She sounded resigned. "Jason Marquez."

"Thank you." Sy's tone was back to normal.

Jason? But that's — And then it hit him. *Oh, crap! It's a guy.*

"I don't get it. Why was she — why was *he* — avoiding us? He wasn't wanted, wasn't breaching any conditions."

Sy shrugged. "Who knows? Force of habit maybe. Or maybe he's had bad experiences with cops. Some coppers have a real hate-on for the trannies."

"Trannies?"

"Transsexual or transgendered. Whichever one means someone going through the surgical process of becoming the other sex. I forget which one it is. I know calling them trannies isn't politically correct, but if you want political correctness you're working with the wrong guy."

"How could you tell she was a guy?"

Another shrug. "Just got a feeling with that one. Usually, it's not too hard to tell. The easy ones are six foot two with shoulders wider than mine and a five o'clock shadow. The Oriental ones are hard. For some reason, Filipino trannies are the worst, or best, whichever way you look at it."

"That was scary," Jack admitted, shaking his head. "If I'd seen him in a bar, I would've bought him a drink."

Sy laughed but without much humour. "Don't kid yourself. It happens. That's why I warned him about hooking that far south. Usually, the trannies work on Maitland and the johns know what they're getting. If some guy finds out he's getting blown by another guy, Jason's gonna end up in the hospital."

"I guess he's hooking to pay for the operation?"

Sy nodded. "A lot of them do. They get the hormone shots and boobs first. I guess getting the genitals altered costs a shitload of money."

"Hell of a life." Jack turned to watch the streets go by. They had the AC on and the windows up. Not even nine-thirty and it was stinking hot. Humid, too. Welcome to summer in Toronto.

"If we're working together on evenings, we'll do some 208s on the trannies up on Maitland and you can get an idea of what it's like. Some guys don't like talking to them, but if you treat them nice they'll be nice back to you."

"It's easier to start out nice and move up to asshole level with someone than it is to start as an asshole and then have to work down to being nice."

"Very good, grasshopper. You did learn something up in 32."

"Blow me."

"Not even two weeks in the division and he thinks he's a tough guy." Sy shook his head. "What's 32 like? I belong to the 51 quarter-century club. I've never been that far north."

"Quarter-century club?"

"Yup." Sy nodded. "There's a plaque by the front desk for coppers who have spent more than twenty-five years in the division." He puffed his chest out. "I'm the most recent addition."

"Congratulations . . . I think." Jack thought about the two divisions. "First off, 32's bigger. Hell, each patrol area is the size of 51, so it's about ten times bigger. Lots of residential. Mostly middle class, I'd guess, but lots of money in some areas too. Some industrial spots and two big parks. Yorkdale Mall is always busy with shoplifters, frauds and the odd shooting. The division even has some Ontario Housing, but the Jungle is nothing compared to Regent Park."

"So, not a lot of street-level crime?"

"God, no." Jack laughed. "Some, but nothing like down here.

I honestly think I've learned more in my two weeks here than I did in six years in 32."

"I wouldn't doubt it, grasshopper. You sure ain't in Kansas anymore."

Sunday, 13 August
1745 hours

"We missed you at church this morning, Jack. I thought you weren't working this weekend."

Jack swallowed his bite of salmon and wiped his lips before answering. Manners were very important at these Sunday dinners with Karen's parents. "I had a paid duty this morning, Mrs. Hawthorn."

"A paid duty? What in the world is that? And, please, call me Evelyn. How many more times will I have to tell you?"

"Sorry. Force of habit." *A habit you drilled into me while I was dating your daughter.* "A paid duty is extra work you can do on your time off. Companies hire police officers —" not *cops*, not with the Hawthorns "— when they need security or traffic control. Not exactly exciting stuff, but this morning's was six hours, so it was a nice piece of cash."

"Missing church for money. That's not very Christian of you, Jack." Leaning back in her chair, Evelyn Hawthorn sipped her wine and managed to look both reprimanding and disappointed. But the look wasn't wholly for Jack. A good piece of it was directed at Karen, who pretended not to notice.

Both women had had lots of practice with "the look" when Karen and Jack were dating. Karen's mother never bothered to hide her belief that Jack was far beneath her daughter's status. After two years of marriage with no signs the union was weakening, Evelyn only tolerated Jack. Her manner was chilly rather than civil.

"Oh, lay off the boy, Evie. With his salary, I'm sure he can't afford to turn down any opportunities to raise some additional income." While Evelyn tolerated Jack, her husband, *Doctor George Hawthorn Senior,* thank you, had no use for his son-in-law and rarely missed an opportunity to highlight Jack's failings. And at the top of that list was Jack's profession.

Karen's father — Jack had no doubt the only reason he named his son George was so he could add that pretentious "senior" after his name — taught political science to open, impressionable minds at the University of Toronto. George Senior was a famous educator, lecturer and author; Evelyn was a retired social worker turned social activist, well known among the anti-poverty groups and at City Hall.

These idealistic and connected parents would have expected Karen to pursue a career in education or politics. *How disappointed they must have been when she chose to be a grade-school teacher in the public education system,* Jack thought with a touch of perverse pleasure. But a teacher, even a grade-school teacher, was still an educator, and a police officer was just a civil servant. A job that didn't require much academic achievement.

Jack admitted his in-laws made a good-looking couple. Karen's mother had a mature beauty that embraced her age, flaunted it, in fact. And George. . . . Well, slip a tweed jacket on him and hand him a pipe and he'd be the stereotype of a professor from the 1960s. Full black hair with just a touch of grey at the temples — very distinguished — probably made him the object of first-year-student fantasies.

"What does a first-class constable pull down these days, Jack? Seventy, seventy-five?"

"Around that." *You arrogant prick. You probably know to the penny what I make.* "But now that I'm downtown, I hope to make an extra ten or fifteen on top of that with court and overtime." Jack pushed his plate away, leaving his dinner, his very expensive dinner, half finished.

The Hawthorns were done with their entrees; it was time for the post-dinner Let's Bash the Son-in-Law.

After a long and busy week, the last thing he wanted, or needed, was another bout of character assassination at the hands of his in-laws. Why couldn't he and Karen have ordered in? Because family is important, she'd say.

And we wouldn't want to deprive the parents of the evening's entertainment.

"I can imagine so, what with the crime rate and all." Hawthorn motioned for the waiter to clear the table. At least he had waited for Jack to indicate he was finished. Karen had ordered a salad and had been the first to finish. She knew the rules of the game all too well.

"When Karen told us you were transferring down to 51 Division, I did some checking." George crossed his legs and brushed at his jacket. He cradled his wineglass, an almost exact imitation of his wife's pose.

Jack snagged the waiter for a refill of his coffee. The restaurant might be out of his comfort zone and the meals on the small size, but the coffee was excellent. Damned if he was going to be abused with an empty coffee cup.

"I must say, Jack, what I learned about your new precinct was far from encouraging. It has an extremely high crime rate and an equally high number of complaints lodged against the officers." George sipped his wine, looking satisfied. "It seems you'll be surrounded by criminals wherever you turn."

"Well, first of all, Mr. Hawthorn —" Hawthorn never insisted Jack call him by his given name and there was no way Jack was going to call him *Doctor Hawthorn* "— it isn't a precinct, it's a division. Precinct is an American term."

Hawthorn's lips twitched ever so slightly on his wineglass. He hated to be corrected. Score one for Jack. A small one, but Jack had learned to enjoy any victory, however small, against his father-in-law.

"And, yes, there are a fair number of complaints against officers."

"I imagine," Hawthorn slid in, not giving Jack a chance to elaborate, "that is an indication of the quality of officers in the ... division." There was a pause. "Present company excluded, of course."

Jack didn't miss the jab and neither did Karen. "Dad, that wasn't nice."

Hawthorn gave his daughter a disarming smile. "I'm sorry, sweetheart. Jack knows I didn't mean anything by it. Don't you, Jack?"

"Of course." Jack met Hawthorn's eyes over the rim of his coffee cup.

Two natural enemies eyeing one another over disputed territory. In this case, Hawthorn's daughter and Jack's wife. When it had become apparent that their relationship was progressing beyond casual dating, Karen's parents had started playing Let's Bash the Boyfriend. Karen had defended Jack, but she hadn't confronted her father head-on. Jack sometimes thought her choice of career and husband were unconscious acts of defiance.

Jack knew he would never be accepted by his in-laws and really didn't give a flying fuck. But he did care about Karen and how the game, the constant slams, affected her. Nothing about him was right or good enough for the Hawthorns' daughter: his job, his education — he had gone to university but hadn't graduated — his upbringing, his taste in clothes and music, and his house. Karen had paid half of the down payment and was paying half of the mortgage, but to George and Evelyn it was Jack's house, probably because it was in a middle-class commuter community.

Jack always told Karen not to worry about it, that he could endure their petty snipes. He could gain a small measure of revenge by doing their prim and polite daughter on the back deck, where neighbours might see, or in the bathroom when they were forced to attend one of the Hawthorns' snooty parties.

For now, all he had to do was endure the game and hope no one ordered dessert.

"There's a saying down in 51: if you don't get complaints, then you're not doing your job. Since so many of the criminals down there are repeat offenders, a lot of them lodge complaints when they're arrested so they can use the complaint as a bargaining chip later on in court."

"I can see how that might explain some of the complaints," Hawthorn admitted. There was another deliberate pause. "But not all of them."

"What I don't understand," Evelyn said, "is why you would want to go to work there. From what George told me, it sounds perfectly horrible." Her perfectly painted lips puckered in distaste.

Jack nodded. "It can be. But it can also be very interesting and educational. I'm learning a lot." It was his turn for a deliberate pause. "I'm surprised you're not familiar with the area, Mrs. Hawthorn. A lot of the people you fight for live there."

Evelyn smiled and twirled her wineglass between perfectly manicured fingers. "I don't get out of the office too much these days, Jack. The government is determined to drown our efforts in paperwork."

"What I'm worried about is Jack's safety," Karen put in, taking his hand. "He hardly ever mentioned guns or knives in 32 and now he runs into them almost every day."

Hawthorn wasn't worrying about Jack's safety. "Learning? What could you possibly be learning there? As I understand it, the policing is relatively straightforward. The drug trafficking is out in the open, so you simply go and arrest the . . . perps, is it? Or is that another American term?"

"It is. We say suspects." Jack took a sip of coffee and again hoped no one ordered dessert.

"So what are you learning in such a . . . challenge-free environment?"

Challenge-free? Jack almost gagged on his coffee. "I'm learning to be a cop," he said, almost snapping.

Karen squeezed his hand and he forced his anger down for her. Hawthorn gazed at him calmly, a small, sly smile playing across his lips. He knew Jack had almost lost his temper and he wanted Jack to know it.

"If I want to get into a squad like Holdup or Drugs, I need the street-level experience 51 can give me."

"But I thought being a police officer was only a temporary occupation until you finished your degree and found a bet . . . new job."

"No, Mrs. Hawthorn, that was never the plan. I don't want a different job and I can't honestly imagine a *better* job either." Just a slight emphasis to let her know he had caught her slip and what he thought of it.

No one wanted dessert, thankfully, and when the bill came Jack reached for it, but Hawthorn beat him to it. "It's on me, Jack." He plunked down his credit card without looking at the bill. "Evie and I chose the restaurant and I know this isn't exactly your normal dining experience. It would be unrealistic of me to expect you to pay for the meal." His smile was as smug as it was gracious.

Along with his professor's salary, Hawthorn banked a nice amount from his lectures and book sales. Add in that he came from a family of old money and Jack could never even hope to compete with Hawthorn's credit limit.

"Thank you, sir. It certainly was an . . . experience."

Hawthorn waved away Jack's gratitude. "Don't mention it, Jack."

Especially now that I already have. Jack hid his grimace behind his coffee cup. It was their wedding all over again. He and Karen had planned a nice, intimate ceremony with close friends and family. Then Hawthorn had opened his chequebook. Jack wanted to tell his future father-in-law where he could shove his money, but he saw the longing in Karen's eyes. She denied it, but Jack knew he could never give her the fairy-tale wedding she really wanted. So, with a flourish of a pen, Karen's parents seized control of the wedding and two hundred additional guests, a horse-drawn carriage, a string quartet and an eleven-course dinner later Jack was indebted to his father-in-law. To be fair, Hawthorn rarely mentioned the cost. Just when there were people around to hear.

The humidity had finally broken and after the stuffiness of the restaurant the warm night air was a relief. Everyone said their goodbyes — strained on Jack's part, condescending on Hawthorn's — and then Jack and Karen started the long walk to the car. She hugged his arm as he loosened his tie and popped the top button on his shirt. *Who in hell enjoys wearing a suit and tie to dinner?*

"Thank you, Jack. I know these dinners are hard for you."

"When we have kids, I'm going to teach the babies to splash food on him. Accidentally, of course."

He felt her shake her head against his shoulder. "I don't understand why he picks on you so much. I thought he would stop when we got married."

"Face it, hon. Your dad doesn't like me and he doesn't like his only daughter being married to a cop. I'm sure he wanted you to marry the son of one of his colleagues. Probably still does."

She giggled. "Or someone I met at a political rally."

"Rally sounds too radical for your father. Maybe a political convention or a lecture."

"That's where he and Mom met."

Jack had heard a glorified and detailed version of the story at his wedding reception, when Hawthorn had given a half-hour toast. Hawthorn, the ambitious doctoral student, and Evelyn, the freshly graduated social crusader, had met and fallen instantly in love at a political demonstration on the hills of the nation's capital.

"Love and political upheaval. Who could ask for a more romantic beginning?"

"Oh? And our meeting was more romantic?"

They had reached the car and Karen leaned against the passenger door. She took Jack by the hips and pulled him close.

"What's wrong with meeting at the gym?" He leaned in to kiss her nose. "Okay, so we weren't expressing social ideologies, but that doesn't mean I wasn't impressed by your . . ."

"My what?" she asked with a smile.

"Your discipline and dedication to a healthy lifestyle."

"Really?"

"Well, that and the way your ass looked in Spandex."

"Speaking of my ass, I think it's wasting away. I don't know about you, but I'm still hungry."

"What my lady wants, my lady gets," Jack declared, opening the door for her.

Before he could close the door, she snagged his tie and pulled his head level with hers. The kiss she gave him made the night air cool by comparison. "Thank you, Jack, for putting up with my parents."

"I'm used to it." He freed his tie and darted around the car. "Besides," he added as he dropped into the driver's seat, "whenever you speak up for me, your mom starts quoting scripture."

"And you're such a naughty sinner."

"Damn right. And I intend to prove it as soon as we get home."

"But dessert first."

"Dessert, then sex," he confirmed, pulling out of the parking lot.

"How about we get something to go and have dessert with sex?" Karen asked, toying with the buttons on her blouse.

"I knew there was a reason I married you." He grinned at her and stomped on the gas.

"Fucking bloody seat." Sy muttered expletives as he threw his shoulders back against the driver's car seat, which refused to budge from its upright position. "How the hell does anyone drive like this? My chest is over my fucking knees."

"Are you using the seat lever?"

Sy glared at Jack. "Yes, I'm using the seat lever. Smartass." He pushed once more and the seat back smacked into the Plexiglas partition behind the front seats. The headrest was missing and Sy smacked his skull on the glass. "Fuck!" He sat up and glared at his partner again. "One word, smartass, and you're riding in the trunk."

"Far be it from me to laugh at my partner's misfortune." Jack swivelled the dashboard computer so he could see the screen and began logging them on. He couldn't help snickering.

"Smartass," Sy repeated. It seemed to be his new word for the day. "At least the fucking seat's working now." He fiddled with it some more, then started up the car and cranked the air conditioning on.

It was another hot day and the humidity had crept back up after the weekend. Jack and Sy were on the first day of evening shift and the air felt like an old rag doused with hot water.

"Mason grabbed me after parade for a quick talk." Sy was fiddling with the seat as he drove.

"Mason?"

"Rick Mason. Fucking seat. The Major Crime boss. Got you, you little son of a whore." The gears beneath the seat gave a final, mortally wounded whir before falling still. Sy wiggled his ass and sighed contentedly. "Finally."

"Mason?" Jack prodded.

"Oh, right. Remember that dealer you grabbed last week? The one with the Black?" Sy cruised through the parking lot and pulled out onto Regent Street.

"Yeah, I remember him. Karen laughed her ass off when I told her about how he took off on me the second time."

It was Sy's turn to snicker. "Good girl."

"But I won't tell you what she did with the beer bottle after that."

Sy glanced at Jack, his eyebrows peaked in curiosity. "I have got to meet this wife of yours. Well, Mason —"

"5106, in your area. 279 George Street. See the complainant in room 3. He was assaulted earlier by the tenant in room 2. Suspect still on scene. Time, 1721."

Sy turned onto Shuter Street, then eased to a stop for the red light at Parliament. While they waited for the light to change, they wrote down the call in their memo books.

"So, Mason told me the dealer was more than willing to co-operate once he talked with the MCU boys." The light changed and Sy accelerated through the intersection.

"What, um, incentive did they use?"

Sy laughed. "Despite what you may have heard about us 51 coppers, we don't get confessions using phone books or pepper spray. Instead of Show Causing him, they cut him loose on a Form Ten."

"Isn't trafficking an automatic Show Cause? I thought it was a reverse-onus charge."

"Yup, it is." Sy nodded. "But Mason cleared it with the booking sergeant. So instead of spending the night in jail and heading to court in the morning, the dealer got cut loose with a shitload of conditions, one of them being he's not allowed in the division. So, if we see him again, we can pinch him for that."

"I take it they got some useful information from him?"

"Yup. They've been working on it and they're doing a search warrant day after tomorrow."

"We invited?" Jack asked hopefully.

"Damn straight we are."

"Excellent!" Jack was ecstatic.

Sy grinned, catching his exuberance. "It's a thank-you for the pinch. Also, they like to have some uniforms along with them so if the shit hits the fan the assholes can't say they didn't know it was the police."

"Oh, great," Jack moaned sarcastically. "They want to use us as targets to draw the gunfire."

"Something like that. We start at two on Saturday."

"Cool. Meet for a workout first?"

"Sure, but not legs, in case we — I mean you — have to chase someone."

Sy cut up Pembroke Street, then drove along Dundas to George and up the one-way southbound street. It seemed Sy didn't pay much attention to one-way arrows. An odd collection of buildings lined George Street. The west side was heavy with residential buildings. New apartment buildings occupied the south end of the street and old homes the north. Between them was the back entrance to the youth courts and detention centre.

On the east side was the Schoolhouse, a little-known exclusive men's hostel with strict rules and small occupancy numbers. It catered to a better-behaved, more sober class of homeless men. Next to the Schoolhouse was Seaton House, the Schoolhouse's behemoth of a cousin and Toronto's largest shelter for men, which took up almost half the block. The four-storey institutional building offered clean beds, warm showers, food and counselling. Despite the best intentions of the staff, many homeless men were afraid to sleep there because of the shelter's human predators.

South of Seaton House was their destination, a brief line of townhouses sandwiched between a run-down apartment building and Filmore's, the strip club at the corner of George and Dundas streets. 279 was the last unit in the line and the decrepit townhouse appeared to sag in the heat, an old and forgotten relative waiting to die.

Sy and Jack mounted the cracked concrete steps and entered

a dim hallway that seemed even hotter than outside. The warped floorboards under the threadbare carpet creaked beneath their boots. Sy pointed at the second door in the hall and Jack nodded. According to the radio call, room 2 belonged to the suspect. Jack eyed the door as he passed. There was no peephole and the door was firmly shut. If the suspect was expecting the police, he wasn't keeping an eye out for them. At least not from his room. Sy and Jack moved on to room 3, and Sy rapped on the door.

"If you're lookin' for Phil, I'm out here."

A stooped figure stood silhouetted in the door at the end of the hall, backlit by early evening sun. To Jack, he was nothing more than a solid shadow, but his raspy voice and broken-down posture suggested he was too old to be their suspect. The back door led out onto a fair-sized deck a few steps above a small yard of dead grass and dried mud. Mismatched lawn chairs and ashtrays heaped beyond capacity with old butts crowded the deck space. Phil, their victim, shuffled over to one of the chairs and slowly, carefully lowered himself into it. Jack put Phil's age somewhere between seventy and ancient. Knuckles swollen with arthritis gripped the armrest of his chair.

Jack had started sweating the moment he had stepped out of the air-conditioned car, yet Phil was wearing a long-sleeved denim shirt and jeans. There wasn't much to him. His breastbone and collarbones were visible in the open neck of his shirt and his jeans hung limply on stick-thin thighs.

Why would someone want to beat on an old guy like him? But Jack could see that someone surely had. The dark skin under Phil's left eye was swollen and scraped. Jack was looking forward to meeting this someone.

Sy dragged over a chair and eased down as though not sure its old webbing would take his weight. It protested but held.

Jack stood so he could watch the back door.

"That's a nasty bump you got there, Phil," Sy commented as he flipped open his memo book. "You want to tell us who did that to you so we can go and arrest his chickenshit ass?"

"Damn right I wanna tell you." Phil might have been old enough to be called ancient, but his voice, cigarette rasp or not, still had some strength to it. "Damn bastard in room 2 did this to me, not more'n half an hour ago."

"Do you know his name?"

"Damn right I do. Jake Carlsberg, like the beer."

"Easy enough. How old is Jake? Any idea, Phil?"

Phil laughed, or coughed, Jack wasn't sure which.

"Younger'n me, that's damn sure. Otherwise, I'da smacked the little shitter right back. He's 'bout this feller's age." Phil pointed a crooked finger at Jack. "You laughin' at me, young feller?" he asked, daring Jack to answer yes.

"No, sir," Jack replied, not hiding his grin. "I just admire your attitude. But why did this guy hit you?"

"Says he don't like niggers. Right to my face, he says that! Damn little shitter. If I was ten years younger, I'da smacked him good." Phil worked a rumpled cigarette pack from his shirt pocket. Jack felt sorry for him, watching him concentrate on making his gnarled fingers slide a cigarette out of the pack. Once he had it wedged firmly between his fingers and the pack safely in the pocket, Phil asked, "You fellers mind if'n I smoke?"

"Not at all, Phil; it's your home. Let me get that for you." Sy produced a lighter and held the flame out for Phil's cigarette.

Phil leaned forward to meet the flame and Jack wasn't sure which creaked more: his back or the chair. The cigarette tip danced erratically around the flame until Phil steadied it with a second hand. After several weak drags, the tip began glowing to his satisfaction and he eased back in the chair gratefully.

Sy was patient through the cigarette-lighting ordeal. When Phil blew out a pitifully small plume of blue smoke, sighing contentedly, Sy continued with his questions. As he took down Phil's particulars, Jack used his radio. "5106 for a check on a male."

"5106, go ahead."

"Surname, Carlsberg, like the beer. Given, Jake. No date of birth, so run him between twenty-five and thirty-five. 10-4?"

"10-4. Stand by."

Jack listened to the dispatcher hand out a couple of calls to other units. Then he heard, *"5106, I have your return. Is the party nearby?"*

"Negative, dispatch. We haven't gone to talk to him yet."

"Carlsberg, Jacob. DOB '68-07-12. On file for mental instability, violence and suicidal tendencies. Accused: assault times two, awaiting disposition. 53 Division case. 10-4?"

"Got it, dispatch. Any conditions to go with the assault charges?"

"Must reside 35 Thorncliffe Park Drive; not to possess or consume alcohol. That's it."

"Thanks, dispatch. Could we also have a SOCO attend here for victim photos?"

"Is there a SOCO on the air in 51?" she voiced out.

They waited, then, *"5103, I'm just clearing the station. Who needs a SOCO?"*

As the dispatcher began to give 5103 details, Jack replaced his radio and turned to Sy and Phil. "Looks like our boy just moved into the division. We can add a fail to comply to the assault."

"The more the merrier."

"What's soccer got to do with that little shitter?" Phil asked, squinting at Jack.

"Soccer? Oh, SOCO. *Saw-koe.* Scenes of crime officer," Jack explained. "An officer's going to come by and take some photos of that lump under your eye."

"You fellers did'n say nothin' 'bout me posin' for no pictures." Phil tapped ash from his cigarette into one of the heaped trays. "Shee-it. And I did'n shave or brush my hair or nothin'." He ran a hand over his bald scalp and laughed. Or coughed. Or maybe both.

"Don't worry about that, Phil, you're beautiful as you are. Now," Sy began, his pen poised over his memo book, "while we're waiting for the soccer, I'm going to take your statement. After that, my partner and I will go drag this Carlsberg coward off to jail. How's that sound?"

"Sounds mighty good t'me."

Jack listened with half an ear while Sy jotted the old man's words in his book. According to Phil, Carlsberg had moved in a few weeks earlier and enjoyed terrorizing the other tenants, especially the man he called "the nigger." Jack hated that word and wished he could solidify it and shove it down the throat of anyone who used it, especially against someone as defenceless as Phil. Jack was looking forward to meeting Carlsberg. Maybe the piece of shit would decide to fight.

"So, I was havin' a smoke out here with Bear when that little shitter — don't write that, it don't sound too good — when Carlsberg comes up t'me and says, 'I've got something for you, nigger.' Then he up and smacks me."

"Who's Bear? A friend of yours?" Sy asked.

"Friend? 'Course he's my friend. Best friend I've got." Phil looked around the deck, perplexed. "Now where'd that little bugger get to? Bear?" He cocked his head and aimed a shout at the yard. "Bear! C'mere, Bear!"

There were shuffling and clicking noises at the back of the deck and a grey-haired and arthritic little dog hobbled into view, then shuffled over to Phil, his nails clicking on the wood of the deck. His legs may have been well past their prime, but his stubby tail beat enthusiastically as Phil reached down to scratch him tenderly behind the ears.

"This here's Bear, my best friend. He's been with me nigh on fourteen years." A tear glistened in Phil's eye as he introduced his cherished companion.

"Nice to meet you, Bear." Sy reached out, but the dog shied away.

"He's a little timid 'round new folks," Phil explained.

"Me, too," Sy said. "Let's finish up this statement."

While Sy wrote, Jack squatted and softly coaxed Bear out from under Phil's chair. The little guy — he had to be no more than fifteen pounds — hesitantly approached Jack's hand and gave it a tentative sniff, then nuzzled Jack's hand, asking for an ear scratch. Jack obliged gently.

Phil looked shocked. "You must be special. Bear don't normally take t'people like that."

"I've always had a way with dogs," Jack answered, smiling down at Bear. "Why is he trembling, though? Is there something wrong with him?"

"Oh, no. That little shitter took a kick at him. That's why he's shakin' like that."

Sy's pen and Jack's fingers stopped simultaneously.

Jack slowly looked at Phil and very carefully, very clearly, asked, "Kicked *at* him or *kicked* him?"

"Kicked him," Phil clarified. "When that shitter hit me, Bear went for his leg, but his teeth ain't what they used t'be. That's when that shitter kicked him."

Without looking at each other, Jack and Sy stood up. Sy tucked away his memo book and Jack pulled on his leather gloves, then flexed his fingers eagerly against the Kevlar lining. They headed for the hall. Over his shoulder, Sy said, "Wait here, Phil. We'll be back in a minute."

They flanked Carlsberg's door and Jack put his ear close to the wood. Faint sounds came through the door, footsteps and muffled words, but Jack heard only a single voice. He held up one finger and Sy nodded, then gestured for Jack to check the doorknob. It was locked.

Jack unholstered his collapsed baton and slammed the butt against the wood several times in rapid succession. "Police! Open the door!" There was sudden silence from the apartment and Jack raised his stick to knock again.

"What do you want?" a voice asked from the other side of the door.

Sneaky little bastard. "Police. Open the door. Now."

"Open the door, Carlsberg, or we'll fucking kick it in." Sy looked pissed enough to chew through the door.

Locks clacked and the door cracked open, stopped by a security chain. Through the hand-width gap, a suspicious face peered out at them. "What do you want?"

"You," Jack snarled and slammed his shoulder into the door. It flew open, striking Carlsberg in the face, and Jack kept going into the apartment with Sy right behind him. Carlsberg backpedalled, his hands clasped to his face. Sy and Jack each grabbed a wrist and wrenched Carlsberg's arms down, then flung him to the floor.

"What did I do? What did I do?" Carlsberg bleated as Jack snapped on the handcuffs.

"Punched the old man and kicked his dog. Now shut the fuck up." Jack hauled Carlsberg roughly to his feet and, while Sy held him, searched him quickly. He was a beefy enough guy to be intimidating, but there wasn't much more than flab under his dirty T-shirt and jeans.

"That dog attacked me! It's vicious!" Carlsberg may have been a big man physically, but his voice squeaked like a coward's. "The old nigger sicced it on me."

Sy's open hand smacked off the back of Carlsberg's head. "Use that word again, asshole, and I'll put you in the fucking hospital."

Carlsberg stared at Sy, wide-eyed, probably imagining numerous injuries that could require a trip to the emergency. "You wouldn't," he whispered.

Sy smiled.

"No, he wouldn't," Jack said and Carlsberg looked relieved until Jack added, "we both would. Welcome to 51, fuckhead."

"So you just broke down his door?" Karen asked incredulously.

She had waited up for him — an advantage of having a wife who had summers off. They were sitting on the deck again, but his old police shirt was in the wash and there were no cold beer bottles for her to play with. She still looked fantastic to him, dressed in jeans and a sweatshirt — amazingly, the night air had a slight chill to it — with her hair pulled back in a ponytail.

They were enjoying the coolness — no need to sleep with the AC on that night, thankfully — and a cup of tea before calling it a night. Karen was on a lounge chair with her legs stretched out; Jack sat on the stairs leading to the lawn. His free hand was casually rubbing her bare feet. He thought she would be happy, maybe even proud, about them arresting Carlsberg, but she wasn't.

"It's not like we broke the door, Kare, just the chain." *Trust her not to see the positive side of the job.*

"I realize that." He heard a hint of irritation in her voice. "But don't you need a warrant or something before breaking into someone's home? Even if it is just the chain?"

"Technically, yes. But if we left to get a warrant, there's no telling what he would have done while we were gone. And there's no way a sergeant would have authorized us to guard the door until a warrant was obtained."

"It still seems wrong to me." Karen drew her knees up to her chest, sliding her feet away from his touch.

Great. Now she's really pissed. He ran a hand through his hair, thinking. How to make her understand? "You should have seen this guy, Kare. Eighty-three years old, built like a toothpick, not bothering anyone, and this ..." He searched for the right words to express his utter contempt for Carlsberg and decided blunt was best. "This fucking gutless coward comes out and sucker-punches him for no reason. Just because he knows Phil can't fight back."

"I understand, but —"

Jack held up a hand. He needed her to *really* understand. "After he knocks Phil down, and we're lucky he didn't break a hip or something, Carlsberg draws his foot back to lay the boots to him, and Bear defends his owner. Kare, you should have seen this dog. Fourteen years old, twenty pounds tops, so arthritic he can barely walk, and he goes after this guy to protect his owner." Jack felt himself tearing up. Bear had made quite the impression on him. "If not for that dog, Carlsberg could have stomped Phil to death."

"Why did he stop?" Her voice was softer. Maybe she was beginning to understand.

"Phil's good luck. After Carlsberg kicked Bear across the deck, a couple more tenants came out, and I guess he didn't want an audience. He beats up a defenceless old man and his dog and then hides behind his door when we arrive. I'm learning there's a huge difference between what's illegal and what's wrong. So, please, don't tell me what we did was wrong."

She sat quietly, her bottom lip caught between her teeth. He knew she was thinking it over, trying to overcome the logical, straightforward, black-and-white world she had been raised in. He admired her, sitting quietly, sipping his tea while she reached a decision.

Finally, she got up and sat beside him on the steps. She wrapped an arm around his waist and leaned her head on his shoulder. "Sorry. Guess I've still got a lot to learn about being a policeman's wife."

He laughed. "Not as much as I have to learn about being a cop." He slipped an arm around her. "Want to hear some more news?"

She straightened, a comically horrified look on her face. "It doesn't involve you breaking down a door, does it?"

"No." Jack laughed. "Well, maybe. Remember the drug dealer I chased back on day shift?"

It was her turn to laugh. "You mean the one who got away from you twice?" For some reason, she still found that story amusing.

"Yes," he replied dryly. "And, technically, he only got away from me once. Anyway, he was dealing that new crack, the black stuff, and when the Major Crime boys talked to him, he gave up some information. So, Saturday they're doing a search warrant, and Sy and I are going with them."

"It isn't dangerous, is it?"

Jack shrugged. "Guess we won't know till we get there. But don't worry. There'll be plenty of us and these guys know what they're doing. Sy says they're bringing us along as a thank-you for the arrest and to have a uniform presence there. That's all. I bet we won't even be allowed in the house or whatever it is we're going to."

"So you're not the one breaking down the door?" she persisted, really concerned.

"I wish, but there's no way they'll let that happen."

"Good. Not that I don't think you could do it." She felt up his chest. "The way you've been working out with Simon, you could probably push it open with one hand." The caressing hand started poking his chest. "You're not going to get all big and bulky like a bodybuilder, are you?"

"Again, I wish."

"I'm serious, Jack. I don't want you getting too big. I like the size you are now. You're more of a Stallone than a Schwarzenegger."

"Wow, you didn't sleep through those movies when we were dating after all. I'm shocked. Next you'll be telling me you enjoyed them."

"Let's not go that far." She stood up, stretching. "Come on, Rocky, let's call it a night."

"Right behind you, babe." Following her across the deck, he added, "You know, I've always seen myself as more of a Terminator than a Rocky."

Saturday, 19 August
1400 hours

"Terminator, huh? Did you tell her 'Ah'll be back' when you left for work today?"

"Nah. I don't think Karen would have gotten the reference."

Sy snorted. "Typical woman. No taste in movies."

They were sitting in the station's basement parade room, down the hall from the change rooms. The room held five rows of metal tables and chairs facing the sergeants' wood lectern, but Jack and Sy were the only ones there. The lights were off, but sharp summer light slanted in from the windows near the ceiling, fighting the air conditioning for control of the room.

"I hope we don't end up standing outside somewhere while the Major Crime guys search the building. It's too damn hot out there."

"I wouldn't worry about that if I were you," Sy commented. He had his feet up on a table and was reclining comfortably in one of the few decent chairs in the room.

"Oh? What do you know that I don't?"

Sy snorted again. "That list would take years to read, grasshopper. But if you're referring to the warrant —"

"Hey, sexy! No one said I was going to get to work with you today." Jenny strolled into the room and Jack forgot about the warrant. Even in the unflattering uniform shorts, her legs looked good. Long, tanned and nicely curved with feminine muscle, they had him thinking about what she would look like out of uniform. Completely out of uniform.

Jenny was tall for a woman. Jack figured she would look him straight in the eye were she ever to hug him. Slender but not skinny, she carried herself well as she crossed the room. Hopping up on the table next to Sy's feet, she flashed Jack a smile that was even better than her legs. The first time they had met, down at Queen and Sherbourne, she had been wearing sunglasses and a bike helmet and he hadn't gotten a good look at her face. Now he soaked it in from only two tables away. Her eyes were a sharp, crystal blue and her hair, done up in a French braid, was raven black, a vibrant contrast to her eyes.

Damn. If I wasn't married. . . . Then he noticed the gold band on her ring finger. *Lucky bastard.*

"You should know I'm pissed at you," Sy announced, glaring at Jenny but not bothering to sit up.

"Me? What did I do?" She looked completely innocent and shocked.

"Don't give me that look. I taught it to you, remember? You were supposed to come out for beers on day shift, but you never showed. I was even going to buy you one."

"Actually, I think you said Jack was going to buy me one for you."

"That's right. So we're both mad at you."

"I'm sorry, honey. I went home to look after the kids —" *Damn! Kids too!* "— and was planning to head down, but I was just too tired." Jenny slid off the table provocatively — Jack never knew anyone could move provocatively in a police uniform — and swayed her way behind Sy's chair. She traced her fingers up his arms, then began to knead his shoulders. "What can I do to make it up to you?" she purred.

"I'll think of something," Sy grumbled. He wilted under her touch.

It was too much for Jack. "Hey," he protested. "Don't forget I'm mad at you too."

"Forget it, grasshopper. She's mine. You can work on your own today."

"Don't get him too excited, he's liable to have a heart attack." Detective Mason came into the room and headed for the lectern, sparing only a glance at Sy and Jenny.

"I can think of worse ways to go."

Sy reminded Jack of an old bulldog lying in a sunbeam, luxuriating in the warmth. "Like getting shot by some crackhead 'cause you slept through the briefing?"

"Oh, bloody hell." Sy patted Jenny's hand. "We'll have to finish up another time, love."

She walked to a chair, shaking her head. "Typical man. Gets what he wants and leaves me hanging."

"If I may interrupt this little lovers' tryst . . ." Mason said.

"Wasn't I supposed to get four of you from the Foot?" The big detective's brow furrowed beneath his cropped hair as he gave her an accusing look, as if the missing officers were her fault.

"The guys are upstairs finishing lunch."

Muttering to himself, Mason crossed to the wall-mounted phone and punched the code for the PA system, then spoke loudly into the receiver. "Any lazy bastards who are supposed to be in the parade room for a briefing better get their asses down here before I decide to replace them with some competent officers." He slammed the phone down.

Seconds later Jack heard rapid footsteps on the stairs. Jenny's partner, Al, and two other bike cops casually strolled into the room, but when they saw Mason's glare they quietly took a table at the back of the room.

"I guess we can get started now."

"You the only one from upstairs coming on this?" Sy was sitting up straight now but still looking relaxed.

"My guys are loading up the car. They'll be down in a minute. So let's get this started," Mason said. "Last week, Jack nabbed a guy dealing Black and we squeezed him. He told us where he picks up his stash — 259 Sumach, corner apartment, ground floor — and we've spent the week doing obs on the place."

Mason turned to the room-wide chalkboard and drew a quick outline of the building. Roughly shaped like a squared-off dog bone or a squat capital I, the six-storey building was in the northeast corner of Regent Park, a large housing project in the division. The building had four main entrances, each in a corner of the I. Mason circled the top left corner of the bottom cross-piece. "That's our target. From what we've been able to determine, the crack isn't made there, but it's a central pickup spot for the street dealers. We figure the crack is delivered whenever they're running low, day and night, and the dealers pick up at the back windows. There's usually a delivery between noon and two. We're going to catch them right after that."

"Any idea how many people in the apartment?"

"No idea, Jenny." Mason dropped the chalk and wiped his hands on his jeans. "The windows are all covered with heavy drapes, so we've never been able to get a look inside. But we can assume enough people and guns to protect the place." He ran his fingers through his long goatee, then added, "I won't lie to you. We're going in blind and it could get messy. Anyone having second thoughts, let me know now."

No one spoke up.

Mason nodded and Jack was sure he looked pleased. "Whoever's running the Black knows what he's doing. He's quickly pushing out the other suppliers or buying them up. I'm hoping we can hurt him a bit today and maybe work our way up the ladder a few more rungs."

"Any idea who's at the top?"

Mason looked at Sy a moment before shaking his head. "No, not yet."

Sy accepted the answer without comment, but Jack thought he caught a knowing look pass between the two old-timers.

Then the rest of the Major Crime crew clomped into the room. They were an odd assortment of officers. Some cops looked like police no matter how hard they tried not to; others could shed the image as easily as the uniform. Jack thought these three would have a hard time looking like cops even in uniform.

He hadn't formally met any of them, but in a station as small as 51 you get to know people by reputation. First through the door was Kris Kretchine: average height with a seam-straining physique. A competitive amateur bodybuilder for the past five years, Kris was aiming for a pro card in the next few years and her sergeant's stripes. Kris was short for Kristine.

Behind her came Jason "Tank" Van Dusen, the division's one-man riot squad. He was the biggest short person Jack had ever seen. Claiming to be the illegitimate love child of a Viking berserker and a female Sumo wrestler, he had enough mass on his five-foot-six frame for two men. Two big men. His massive bald head sat squarely on equally massive shoulders. Where Kris was lean with veins roping her forearms, Tank was sheer bulk. But anyone who thought there was no power in the mass was in for a world of hurt. Jack had once seen Tank in the gym doing dead lifts with four hundred pounds. For a warm-up.

John Taftmore was tall and lanky, his acne-scarred face framed by nondescript shaggy brown hair. He looked young enough to cruise the university bars. There was nothing notable or memorable about Taft until he opened his mouth.

"Sweeeeeet!" he crowed. "The party girl's here." He headed straight for Jenny's chair, which she had turned away from him as soon as he had stepped through the door. That didn't deter Taft. He gripped her shoulders and started humping the back of her chair. "C'mon, Jenny, just a quickie for good luck."

She shrugged his hands away. "Fuck off, Taftmore."

Taftmore would not be denied. He grabbed her shoulders again and resumed his chair humping, more vigorously this time, chanting, "Jenny, Jenny, Jenny."

Jack was surprised no one did anything about his behaviour. He quickly learned Jenny didn't need anyone's help. She freed her shoulders, then exploded from the chair, driving it back on its rollers with her straightening legs. The top of the chair back caught Taftmore squarely in the groin. Every male in the room winced as Taftmore doubled over.

He shuffled to the closest chair and gingerly folded himself into it. Looking quite pleased with herself, Jenny reclaimed her seat and high-fived Sy.

"If you're finished being beaten up by a girl, Taftmore, maybe we can continue the briefing," Mason said.

Taftmore, still hunched over, actually had the balls — sore, no doubt, but still there — to wave his boss to go on. "Sy, you and Jack are with us. The rest of you uniforms will be out on the perimeter."

That caught Jack by surprise. Never had he expected to be at the initial entry. He looked at Sy, who nodded and gave him a conspiratorial wink.

"Sy, you and I are first through with the shotguns. That way we have two pipes and a uniform going in the door first. Tank, you've got the key, as usual."

"Whoa, hold on a minute, Mase." Kris was bristling under her spiky blond hair. "You said I was first through the door at the next warrant. So that makes it me and Sy."

Mason looked like he had expected this argument. "Yeah, but that was before you started dieting for your competition and you know how bitchy you get when you're dieting. You'd probably shoot the first person you saw just to make a point. Or worse, if you're shot and can't work out, you'll fucking shoot me. Next time."

"That's what you said last time," she argued.

"If you start eating like Tank," he countered, "you can go first."

Tank perked up. "Did you say she can go first if she eats me?"

As the room laughed, Kris rolled her chair next to Tank and cuddled in. "Any time you want, big boy."

"Better be careful, Kris. I've seen Tank in the shower and you may have a bigger dick than him." Taft stopped laughing when Kris and Tank glared at him. "Easy there, big fellas. Just joking."

"You're an ass, Taftmore."

"C'mon, Kris, I was just kidding. I'm sure you don't have a bigger dick than him."

"That's it, you little fucker." Kris was out of her chair and from the set of her shoulders she looked ready to go through the metal table that separated them.

"That's enough!" Mason barked. "Kris, settle down. Taft, shut the fuck up."

Kris reluctantly sat down but not before shooting Taft a look that promised retribution. Taft blew her a kiss.

Mason calmly surveyed the room, his face expressionless, until all fidgeting stopped. Hell, when he looked at Jack, Jack was afraid to breathe.

"All right, then." He turned his attention to the foot officers. "Did you get a car?"

The two coppers at the back of the room who had — rather wisely, Jack thought — kept quiet throughout the briefing nodded.

"I want you two to sit on Gerrard east of Sumach. The north end of the building and the townhouses along Gerrard will keep you out of their sight. Make it look like you're writing up your memo books or having a coffee or something." The two coppers nodded, still quiet. "Jenny, Al. Head over on your bikes and wait behind 260." 260 Sumach was the twin of the building they'd be entering and directly west of it across a small parking lot.

"The four of you stay out of sight until we take the door, then move into the parking lot to cover the windows on both sides of the apartment. And for fuck's sake, don't stand in the open. Use the cars for cover. If someone starts coming out the window, yell at him or whatever it takes to keep him inside. I don't want any needless foot pursuits.

"The rest of us will enter the building through the southeast door. We'll let you know as soon as we hit the door. Tank takes the door, Sy and myself in first, then Kris and Taft, then Tank and Jack."

Mason sketched the apartment's layout on the chalkboard. "It's a typical Regent Park two-bedroom. The door opens onto the living room, with a little kitchen off to the left. Sy, when we go in, you cut into the kitchen, then down into the dining area. I'll go to the right to cover the hall. Kris, Taft, cover the living room. Tank, go where you're needed. Once they're all in, Jack, you join me and we'll clear the bathroom and bedrooms. Everyone got that? Good. Now remember, the plan will hope-fully last at least until we take the door. After that, it's a crapshoot. Meet in the parking lot in ten."

A few minutes later Jack and Sy were leaning against the trunk of their scout car. Sy was having one of his rare smokes and Jack swigged a Diet Coke. "I don't get it, Sy. I'm excited that we're on the entry, but why would Detective Mason have me back him up down the hall? Why not Tank?"

Sy dragged on his cigarillo and let the smoke drift lazily from the corner of his mouth. "When Rick told me about the warrant yesterday, he asked me if I felt you would be okay to come along. I told him about the guy with the knife down at Street City and how you saved my ass. How's the hand, by the way?"

"Stitches came out on days off." Jack held up his hand. "Got my first work-related scar."

"Good for you." Another drag, more lazy smoke. "I said you have a level head and you can be trusted."

"Trusted not to fuck up?"

Sy shook his head and wispy tendrils of smoke zigzagged through the air. "We all fuck up sooner or later. No, he wanted to know if you could be trusted *when* things fuck up." Sy studied Jack. "I told him you could be. I wasn't wrong, was I?"

"No, of course not. I was just thinking about how this could go wrong and hoping I'm not the one to cause it."

Sy snorted. "Like Rick said, if the plan lasts up to the door, we're laughing. Everything after that is a crapshoot. Just keep your head on straight and if you shoot anyone make sure it's a bad guy."

"I don't think I'll have any problem with that. The MCU guys are a rather distinctive-looking group."

"I think the term is 'eclectic.'"

They stood in a companionable silence, Sy with his stogie, Jack with his Coke, faces upturned to the sun, enjoying the warmth. Fall was not far off and Jack meant to savour what was left of the summer.

"You and Jenny close?" he asked, not turning his head.

"She got you, didn't she?"

Puzzled, Jack faced Sy. "Got me? What do you mean?"

"Don't give me that innocent look, partner. I've seen it before and, trust me, you won't be the last."

"What are you babbling about?"

"Jenny." He sucked deeply on the cigarillo, flaring its tip. "She has this effect on guys. They take one look at her and they're tripping over themselves to get to her. For some guys, it's her eyes, others it's her smile. Some guys just can't explain it."

"And what do *you* think it is about her?"

Sy took another drag, then watched Jack through the drifting smoke. "I think she has that effect on guys because she's just a very sensual woman. A modern-day siren."

Jack huffed an indignant laugh. Almost a Sy snort. "She's good-looking, but I wouldn't go that far."

Sy didn't bother to comment; his disbelief was plain.

"Taftmore seems a bit of a jerk," Jack commented, draining the last of his pop.

"Nice change of subject. Real subtle." Sy held up a forestalling hand. "All right, I believe you. You're not interested in her at all." He picked a piece of tobacco from his teeth and flicked it away. "Taft's all right. He can be an annoying prick at times, but he's solid when there's work to be done. Rick wouldn't have him in the unit otherwise."

"You ever work in Major Crime?"

"Few times. I was there when Rick brought Kris in. Helped train her, too."

"Why'd you leave?"

Sy smiled. "Her tits were too distracting."

Jack laughed. "You know they're not real, right? Anyone with body fat that low can't have tits like that."

"Partner, when they look that good, it doesn't matter if she was born with them or bought them."

Further discussion was cut off when Mason and his crew came out, all of them wearing their vests with POLICE across the chest and back in big white letters. Tank carried the key — a steel battering ram with four handles so two people could swing it — slung casually over his shoulder like a baseball bat.

Sy dropped the stub of his cigarillo and crushed it underfoot. "Well, grasshopper, let's get it done, shall we?"

Regent Park. A sprawling housing project divided into north and south by Dundas Street. A warren of townhouses, low-rise and high-rise apartment buildings, walkways and parking lots. South Regent had the high-rises; the northern buildings, greater in number, never climbed above six floors. A cesspool of drugs, violence and dead-end lives, Regent Park was an unfortunate mix of good, honest people and low-lifes.

North Regent was bisected by a service road — a glorified, over-wide sidewalk — running east and west through the complex. The two police cars carrying the entry team sped along the walkway and Sy pulled up sharply behind the unmarked car at the southeast entrance to 259 Sumach. The MCU team was already making for the door and Jack and Sy quickly joined them.

As they passed through the stairwell to the main hall, Jack could hear feet pounding up the stairs. So much for a quiet approach. No doubt word was flying through the building: cops were here and they had a ram with them. Someone's door was about to be punched.

Mason heard the runners as well and motioned for his team to hustle as quietly as possible. There was still the chance they could take the apartment unaware. The entry team hurried along a hall painted in what Sy called "off-white, off-yellow, off-government-cheap."

They reached the apartment door: so far, so good. Sy and Mason framed the door, shotguns at the ready. Kris was behind Mason; Jack was behind Kris. His back was to the lobby entrance, a small wasteland of discarded cigarette butts, fast-food wrappers and dried puddles of urine. The halls weren't air-conditioned and the heat had baked the entrance into a fetid desert.

The faint sounds of a TV game show murmured behind the closed door. The rest of the building was surprisingly quiet, as if it were a living thing waiting expectantly to see if this sickness, this area of rot, would be successfully cut from its body.

Behind Jack, the front door of the low-rise opened, the broken lock clicking ominously in the stagnant air. Jack twisted to face the lobby, his Glock pointed at the floor. The team froze, a collective entity with Jack now as its head, waiting to see who stepped into view. A dealer coming for a pickup would be disastrous; a shouted warning could be the difference between a by-the-numbers entry and a gunfight. Jack readied himself to knock whoever came through the lobby senseless.

He blinked sweat from his eyes. What was taking the guy so long? He could hear someone moving across the tile floor, taking his or her sweet damn time.

Seconds later — Jack would have sworn it was more like five minutes — an elderly black woman shuffled into view, her sundress with its faded orange flowers a stark blast of colour against the utilitarian drabness of the lobby. A wide-brimmed straw hat — an orange flower tucked brazenly in the band — shaded her face as she crossed to the elevators. She pressed the call button and settled in to wait, her hands folded primly before her.

Jack glanced at Mason, who gave him a palm-down gesture. *Wait.* If the entry went bad, the last thing they needed was a civilian on the edges of a gunfight. Bullets tended not to care whom they hit.

The woman removed her hat and fanned herself with it as she glanced around the lobby, looking for friends, for dangers — just because you were a Regent Park resident didn't mean you were safe from its predators — and saw Jack staring at her.

He lifted a leather-gloved finger to his lips and she nodded curtly, as if to say, *What do you think I am? Stupid?* The elevator dinged and the doors wheezed open. The lady gave them a broad smile and a thumbs-up before stepping into the elevator. Jack blew out a breath he hadn't been aware he was holding and turned to Mason, a grin fixed on his face. Mason grinned back.

Tank stood beside Sy, the two-man ram cradled easily in his arms. He nodded at Mason, who flipped the nod to Jack. Jack keyed the mike clipped to his shoulder, then whispered, "Go. We are taking the door. Go."

Jack heard a scout car squeal onto Sumach; then he saw two bike cops sprint out from behind 260 Sumach. He signalled Mason, who then gave Tank the go-ahead.

The big man squared himself to the door, drew the ram back, paused for the briefest of moments, then drove it forward, using all his considerable mass and power. The heavy metal pipe tapered to a point beyond the handles, focusing all of its devastating power into an area no bigger than a quarter. Tank's aim was perfect. The ram hit the door right beside the lock and the door exploded inward.

The pipes were in first. Sy button-hooked around the door frame, the shotgun tight to his shoulder, and cut left to the kitchen, while Mason pushed to the right, both bellowing, *"Police! Don't move!"* Kris and Taft were right on their heels, guns following eyes as they swept the living room for threats.

Tank dropped the ram with a thunderous clang and Jack bolted through the doorway, driving to his right and through the living room to back up Mason in the bedroom hall. He was dimly aware of shouting as he ran, commands of "Police! Don't move!" mixed with screams of terror and shouts of rage. He didn't stop to look.

Then he was beside Mason, not remembering having run across the living room. If he had been asked right then to describe the living room, he would have drawn a complete blank. It could have been filled with dancing hippos in tutus and he wouldn't have noticed. But the hallway he could describe. It was his area of responsibility and he was damned if he was going to fuck this up.

The hall was short, no more than a dozen feet, and he was facing a closed door. The bathroom. The left side of the hall held two bedroom doors, also closed. The hall was too narrow for two people side by side, so Jack slipped in front of Mason, crouching below the level of Mason's shotgun. They edged forward this way, guns trained on doors, trigger fingers resting easily along the weapons' frames.

"I've got the hall," Mason whispered. "The bedrooms are yours."

Still crouched, Jack grasped the doorknob, turned it and flung the door open. It banged against the wall. "Police! Anyone in this room, I want to see your empty hands, now!"

Silence.

Didn't think it would be that easy. Tucking his gun into his chest, Jack pivoted around the door frame, sweeping the room. Filthy yellow curtains filtered the afternoon sun and bathed the room in a putrid haze. A mattress, heavily stained and disfigured, lay amid the remains of countless take-out meals. The closet doors hung broken and sagging on their hinges. The closet held only more garbage.

"Clear!" was all he said as he slipped into position again with Mason.

The detective pushed himself as tightly as he could against the right-side wall, giving himself the greatest possible angle on the bedroom door. "I've got the second bedroom. Clear the bathroom."

Jack called, "Police! You in the bathroom! Open the door and show us your hands! Do it now!"

No answer. No sounds of movement.

"It's never easy, is it?" Mason echoed Jack's thoughts.

"That wouldn't be any fun." Jack stalked the bathroom door, trusting Mason to blast anyone in the bedroom to hell and gone if they stuck their nose out. There was nowhere to hide and his ass was hanging in the wind, so he figured speed was better than stealth right now. He aimed for the same spot that Tank had targeted to obliterate the front door and lashed out with his foot, putting all of his weight behind it. Bathroom doors are not the same as front doors and this one flew open with a satisfying shattering of wood.

Jack followed through on his kick and rammed his shoulder into the door, smashing it flat against the wall, eliminating that hidden danger zone while covering the rest with his gun. Empty. Of people at least. The bathroom was empty but made the bedroom look clean. The toilet was overflowing with dried human waste and it looked like the tub was pulling double duty. Jack forced down the urge to vomit.

Breathing as shallowly as he could, he turned his back on the filth — *How could people live like this?* — and faced the final door. Mason edged closer and Jack twisted his free hand, showing he would try the doorknob. Mason signalled Jack to wait. He cracked his neck to the left, then the right, settled the shotgun back into place against his shoulder and nodded at Jack. Keeping as much of himself tucked into the bathroom as possible, Jack reached out and gripped the knob. It turned easily in his hand.

Bullets ripped through the centre of the door and splinters and chunks of wood lacerated the opposite wall like grenade fragments. Jack snatched his hand back. As soon as the gunfire stopped, he kicked the door open.

In the instant it took to bring his gun up on target, Jack noted a box spring and frame; clothes littered the floor, and heavy drapes dimmed the room. The scant light silhouetted a man wearing only a pair of unbuttoned jeans. His bare scalp and black skin glistened with sweat as he frantically tried to work the action of the assault rifle he held.

"Drop the gun, motherfucker!" Mason's voice sounded strained, but his hands were rock steady. As was his shotgun. "Drop it or die!"

"Mason! What the fuck is going on down there?" Tank shouted frantically.

"We're good, Tank," Mason called back, his eyes still on the gunman. "There's no room down here for anyone else."

The gunman was frozen, his hands gripping his weapon and his eyes flickering between Jack and Mason.

"Just open your hands and let it drop. If it even twitches in this direction, you die. Just let it drop. Simple as that."

The silence stretched out. Was the gunman working up his nerve? Sweat ran down Jack's face, into his eyes. He didn't blink — he didn't want to lose his target, even for a heartbeat. His shoulders were starting to ache with the effort of holding the Glock out at arm's length. How much longer would he have to kneel here?

A lifetime was crammed into every heartbeat.

Slowly, so slowly, the gunman drew himself erect, his gun pointed down. Defiance was bright in his eyes.

"Don't," Mason warned. "Just drop the gun. Now."

With a sneer, the gunman snapped open his hands and the rifle clattered to the floor.

"One of the key rules to policing: for every minute of excitement, there's at least one corresponding hour of paperwork." Mason cast a satisfied eye across the empty apartment. "You did good work today, Jack."

"Thank you, sir."

Jack and the detective were alone in the apartment. The gunman had been cuffed and the bedroom searched; the hours of corresponding work had begun.

It turned out there had been no dancing hippos in the living room, just three guys and one busy crack whore. She was doing the guys in exchange for some Black and there was more than enough to go around; the delivery man was pumping away when the police came through the door and his merchandise was stacked neatly on the coffee table. Along with the crack and several thousand dollars in cash, Mason's team found three handguns and a shotgun, all loaded and ready to go. If the fools assigned to the crack house had not been paying attention to the whore's wasted body, the entry could have gone sour in a very bad way. But it hadn't, and the only one to get off any shots —

not including the delivery man; apparently, the sudden explosion of police officers into the apartment had triggered another, smaller, explosion — had been the one with the faulty assault rifle.

The bodies had all been hauled off to 51, where Mason and his crew would interrogate them.

"I've hopes for the whore talking. I figure she'll want to avoid being associated with a large amount of crack and firearms, but I doubt she'll have anything useful to give us. The next best bet is the gunman. He's facing attempted murder charges along with all the rest and he's looking at a long stint behind bars. Might be we can work out a mutually beneficial arrangement." Mason gave a satisfied smile. "And drop the 'sir,' Jack. It's Rick. Sy was right about you. Once you've done a year or so in the division, learned the streets, there'll be a spot in Major Crime for you if you want it."

"Absolutely. Thank you."

Taft stuck his head into the apartment. "Rick, Toronto Housing's here to replace the doors."

"That was fast, for a change. Tell them we're done. They can get to work whenever they're ready."

"Got it." Taft disappeared.

"Where's Sy, Jack?"

"He went to get the car. Said he'd meet me out front."

"Do me a favour, will you? I want to get this baby to the station —" Mason hefted the gunman's AK-47 "— and get started on everything. Can you hang tight till Housing takes over?"

"No problem." Like Mason had to ask. After the offer of a spot in MCU, Jack would have volunteered to replace the doors himself.

"While you're waiting, maybe give the place a final once-over. Make sure we didn't leave anything behind. It's embarrassing when Housing calls us to pick up a memo book or a bag of evidence we forgot."

"Sure thing."

"Tell Sy we're ordering pizza back at the office." He contemplated the weapon in his hands. "You know we got lucky today, don't you? If this gun hadn't jammed. . . ." He didn't finish the thought. He didn't need to.

"Yeah, I know."

Mason laughed. "Thank God for cheap ammunition, huh?"

"I'm sure my wife will see it that way."

Mason nodded. "See you back at the office."

Alone in the apartment, Jack drew a deep breath and let it out slowly between pursed lips. *If the gun hadn't jammed. . . .* But it had and the good guys had won and no one had got shot. Jack was the only one sporting any injuries. His left forearm had some heavy scratches and minor cuts from the splintered bedroom door. Jack had dismissed them, but Tank had insisted on calling an ambulance.

"You don't know what type of filth or disease was on that door," was his reasoning and the medics agreed. So Jack's arm was wrapped in pristine white gauze from wrist to elbow. Karen was going to freak when she saw it.

Have to remember to take it off before I get home. But it sure makes for a hell of a story. Another keeper, as Sy would say.

Jack wandered through the tiny kitchen, as filthy as the rest of the apartment, looking for anything that should have gone to the station. The whole place had been thoroughly searched, so he gave the kitchen a simple visual inspection. In the living room, he saw discarded latex gloves on the floor, little patches of blue floating in a sea of old take-out and other garbage. In the smaller bedroom, he saw nothing but garbage and used condoms. The bathroom, thankfully, had also proved fruitless.

Jack froze in the doorway to the master bedroom, at first thinking he was having some sort of post-traumatic flashback to the shooting. But the man standing in the bedroom was on this side of the bed and he wasn't holding an assault rifle. True, he was black and bald, like the gunman, but he wore shorts, a Toronto

Raptors jersey and a pair of black leather gloves.

The man seemed as surprised as Jack to find someone else in the apartment. Their faces wore identical expressions of shock and their stances — knees slightly flexed, arms held motionless away from the body, shoulders rounded — were also comically similar. They both looked like a base runner getting ready to steal second.

Jack was the first to break for second. "Okay, buddy. I don't know where you were hiding, but right now you're under arrest."

Jack stepped into the room and his movement shattered the stillness in the other man. He yanked up his shirt and Jack spotted the handgun an instant before the man grabbed it. Had the man been on the far side of the bed, Jack would have gone for his own gun, but he was so close that Jack's first instinct was to tackle him. He lunged forward, driving hard with his legs to generate as much power as he could in the short rush.

Jack was three strides from him when everything dropped into slow motion. He watched the man's gloved fingers curl around the butt, the index finger slide over the trigger.

Two strides away. Jack saw the muscles in the man's forearm flex as he tightened his grip, noted the gun was a semi-automatic as it began to emerge from the waistband, its dull black finish in stark contrast to the vibrant red of the shorts.

One stride. The gun pulled free with a final snap of the waistband — *Fuck me, it's huge!* — and Jack was amazed to see the shorts ripple like scarlet water as the waistband slapped back against the man's flat stomach. The gun rose.

Time slammed back into full speed as Jack's shoulder took the man in the gut and they both crashed back onto the box spring. The mattress lay on the floor where it had been tossed during the search like a drunk who had slid out of bed. The springs squealed in protest as they landed, Jack on top with both hands clamped around the gunman's hand, trapping the pistol between them.

The gunman's free left hand was pummelling Jack in the side of his head, but lying on his back the gunman couldn't generate any power. How long before he decided to go for Jack's throat or shove a finger in his eye?

The voice of a defensive tactics trainer from the college was suddenly in Jack's head. *Do whatever you can during the fight to distract them. Knee, stomp, bite, whatever you have to do to win.*

Jack stared down at the man's face and realized the man — boy, really — couldn't have been older than eighteen. *Sorry, kid.* Jack butted him squarely on the nose and felt something snap. The kid howled in pain and Jack took the opportunity to shift his grip on the gun hand. His left hand gripped the kid's wrist and his right hand wrapped around the hand from the back. Pulling the forearm upright, Jack leaned his weight down on the trapped hand.

It was a trick a girlfriend had taught him back in university. An ergonomics major, she had shown him how a person's fist will automatically open if it is bent toward the forearm.

Jack used it now, forcing the hand down. He would either break the grip or break the wrist. Either was fine with him.

"Let go of the gun, or I'll break your wrist. Let go now!"

The kid continued to scream wordlessly, but his hand popped open and the gun dropped onto his stomach.

Thank you, Kathleen.

Jack batted the gun away. He flipped the now unresisting kid onto his stomach and reached for his cuffs. The handcuff pouch was empty. His cuffs were at the station on his buddy with the assault rifle.

"Ow! Lemme go! Lemme go!" The kid was full-on wailing now.

"Shut up, I'm not hurting you. Just lie still."

Jack pulled out his radio and prayed Sy still had his on the tactical channel they had all used during the warrant. If Sy had dialled back to 51 band or had his radio off, then Jack would have a hell of a time retuning his radio while the kid thrashed under him.

"Sy! You out there? Sy! Damn it."

Jack holstered his radio and leaned down to speak to the kid, keeping his arm trapped. "Shut up and listen to me!" He had to shout to be heard over the kid's cries. "You have to lie still. If you lie still, I'll let you up."

The kid stopped as abruptly as an unplugged radio. "Y-you'll lemme . . . go?" he managed between sobs.

"Yeah, I will." *Eventually. What kind of gunman cries like a baby when he's arrested?* Jack was beginning to have some questions regarding the kid's mental state.

Those were the magic words. The kid's sobbing dried up almost as fast as his fight had stopped. "Okay. My nose hurts. Are you a real policeman?" This was asked with the simple, straight-forward innocence of a child and Jack finally clued in to whom he was arresting.

Oh, fuck me.

"Sorry, guys, you missed the pizza," Kris greeted Jack and Sy when they finally made it to the Major Crime office. "We were going to save you some, but Tank likes cold pizza."

Tank smiled jovially. "It's true, I do." The Sumo Viking was sitting at another desk with a mound of Black in front of him.

"You could have left some for them," Kris berated him.

"There was just a little bit left, guys. It wouldn't have been enough for the two of you."

"There was a whole pizza!"

"Like I said. . . ." Tank took cover behind the crack when she pelted a marker at him. It missed him and pinged off a filing cabinet. Tank cautiously rose. "Sheesh. She gets bitchy when she's dieting."

"It's okay. We stopped for take-out chicken on the way back." Sy headed for an unoccupied desk and Jack sat opposite him.

The MCU, like every office on the station's second floor, was too small for the unit's needs. A half dozen desks, shelving units and filing cabinets created a mini maze. RICI photos — mug shots — of various criminals were tacked up on bulletin boards and any available wall space held motorcycle or movie posters, Stallone's *Cobra* holding centre stage.

Taftmore strolled into the office, a Coke in one hand and a vending machine Danish in the other. "There he is! Hey, Warren, heard you beat up a retard. Next time someone pulls a gun on you, make sure it's real before you bust his nose."

Jack scowled, intent on his dinner.

"Hey, Taft," Sy called.

When Taftmore turned, a gun was pointed at his face. "Whoa!" he yelped, instinctively dropping to a crouch. Then he laughed. "Oh, I get it. That the gun the retard had?"

"The politically correct term is developmentally delayed," Sy informed him. "Yes, it is, and you couldn't tell the difference either. And you were a hell of a lot closer than Jack was."

Kris asked to see the gun and Sy tossed it to her, ignoring Taftmore's reaching hand. She whistled softly as she examined it. "This looks real. I'd shoot anyone who pointed it at me. The only way you can tell is by the feel of it and if you waited long enough to feel it you'd probably end up dead. Any idea why the kid was carrying it?"

"Because he's a gangsta. Or likes to pretend he is."

Kris shook her head in disbelief and tossed the gun back to Sy. "That would be a stupid way to die. Good thing he was as close to you as he was, Jack."

Jack nodded, still too busy eating to talk.

"What's his mental age?" Kris asked.

Sy shrugged. "Seven. Or thereabouts. After we took him to the hospital, we asked him why he'd been in the apartment, but the hospital was a fascinating new world for him. He didn't even care about his nose anymore. We got in touch with a cousin, who came down for him. His parents are both dead, apparently."

"What's the cousin like?"

Sy snorted. "Typical street shithead. Three guesses on where the kid gets his gangster motivation from."

Mason blew into the office, a sour expression creasing his face. "Good, you're back. Taftmore, why aren't you doing any work?"

He held up his Coke and Danish. "I just went to get —"

"I don't give a fuck. Get to work." The big detective dropped into a chair. "None of them are saying a thing and the whore doesn't know anything," he announced disgustedly. "Now that everyone's here, I'm going to bring this up once and leave it at that. I'm not even going to ask who searched the bedroom, but whoever it was didn't think about checking *inside* the box spring. Rookie mistake, people. Now, did you figure out who the kid is?"

Sy looked to his younger partner, giving him the opportunity to speak, but Jack was busy with his fries. Sy answered. "The name I gave you over the phone, Sean Jacobs, turns out to be real, but what his connection to the apartment is he wouldn't, or couldn't, tell us. And he isn't smart enough to lie." Sy flipped open his memo book. "He did call the shooter 'Uncle Jamie.' I've got the guy's name here somewhere."

"James Dwyer," Jack said around a mouthful of fries.

"That matches with the name we have for him," Mason said. "So what's his connection to Sean Jacobs? And what was a mentally slow eighteen-year-old kid doing in the apartment? And why was he the one hiding? There's a warrant out on Dwyer for aggravated sexual assault. He was in deep shit even before he shot at us."

"Maybe they're using him for transport?" Kris suggested.

"Doubtful," Sy mused. "We might overlook him, but Sean would be an easy target for competitors."

"It doesn't make sense, him being in the apartment."

"And a kid like him carrying a replica handgun does? Or wearing leather gloves in the summer?"

Mason's head snapped up. "Leather gloves? You didn't mention that."

Sy shrugged an apology. "Didn't think it mattered. Does it?"

"Maybe. . . ." Mason looked lost in thought. For a few minutes, the only sounds in the office were the clicking of computer keys and chewing from Jack and Sy. "I've got an idea. Jack, when you're done eating, I'll get you to help me."

"Done," Jack announced, tossing his take-out container in the garbage.

Sy looked up from his half-finished meal. "What did you do, inhale it?"

"I was hungry."

"Listen up." The sour expression wasn't completely gone from Mason's face, but he no longer looked like he was sipping unsweetened lime juice. "Dwyer hasn't said a word, even though he's facing a shitload of charges. He's either very loyal to whoever's in charge or scared shitless of him. I think it's a bit of both. The only time I got a reaction out of him was when I mentioned the kid."

"What did you tell him?" Jack asked.

Mason smiled an evil little grin. "Not much. Just that the kid pulled a fake gun on a cop and now he's in the hospital."

"That's nasty, Rick," Kris approved. "Tell him just enough of the truth and let his imagination fill in the rest."

"Exactly. He didn't say anything, but I could tell it shook him. Now Jack and I are going to shake him some more."

The Criminal Investigation Bureau may have been larger than the MCU, taking up the north end of the second floor, but it was still too small. The detective sergeant's office was in the corner opposite the entrance; to the left of the door were interview rooms 1 and 2. Another two interview rooms were tucked in behind the D/S's office. Bulky desktop computers seemed out of place on the ancient metal desks crammed together in the limited floor space.

Abandoned and forgotten, resting in broken pieces atop a row of filing cabinets, were the remnants of manual typewriters. They seemed to stare at their successors with hate and envy as they waited to be shipped off to their final resting spot. Sy told Jack they had been waiting for several years.

The office was quiet; the only bodies being processed were the MCU's, so most of the detectives were down in the lunchroom watching a ball game on TV.

Mason unbolted the door to interview room 1 and stepped in. Jack leaned in the door frame, trying to look unconcerned. Dwyer, still wearing only his jeans, sat on the built-in bench in the small, windowless room, his face set in a mask of resentment and defiance.

"Thought you might like to meet the other officer you tried to kill today," Mason said in opening.

"Yeah? If the fuckin' gun 'adn't jammed, I'd kilt yo' asses instead." His voice held a lingering trace of a Jamaican accent.

"Guess we'll never know, will we?"

"Whatcho wan' dis time, mahn? I tolt you, I ain't sayin' shee–it."

"No questions this time, James. This is also the officer Sean pulled a gun on."

That sparked a nerve. Anger flushed Dwyer's face. "You fucker 'urt 'im?"

"I shot him." Stone faced. Uncaring. "He's dead."

Dwyer shot up from the bench, lunging for Jack, but Mason straight-armed him down. "Knock it off," he warned, "or I'll drag you down the stairs to the cells."

Dwyer sat, but his body quivered with rage, and his eyes burned with hate. Jack hadn't moved, was still leaning in the doorway, his arms crossed in relaxed boredom. His whole demeanour taunted Dwyer, told him, *Yeah, I just shot the kid and I don't give a shit. Just another day at work.*

"'E didn' 'ave no gun." Dwyer's voice was hoarse with emotion and tears glistened in his eyes.

"Yeah, he did, James. It was a fake gun, but it looked real, and he pointed it at an officer who had no choice but to shoot him. Dead." Mason leaned in to emphasize his next point. "And you killed him. You hid him up in the box spring, you knew he had that toy gun, you left him alone, and now he's dead." Straightening up, Mason fixed him with an amused, pitying look. "I think someone's gonna be really pissed at you."

"No, mahn, not me, 'im." Dwyer thrust his chin at Jack. "'E's a dead mahn." A pause, then his eyes widened, and his mouth snapped shut.

Mason smiled. "Thank you, James. You just told me what I needed to know."

The detective left the room and Jack reached in to close the door. "By the way, Sean's not dead. I didn't even shoot him." Jack shut the door on Dwyer's shouts.

Sunday, 20 August
0130 hours

"Any idea what time we might be finished by?"

"Why? You got a hot date or something?"

"Sort of," Jack said to Mason. "My wife's coming to pick me up and I need to give her about an hour's notice."

"All right, Jacky-boy. You've got your woman well trained." Taftmore never let an opportunity for a sexist comment pass by unmolested. Kris smacked the back of his head as she walked behind his chair.

"I could have given you a lift," Sy offered, sounding offended. "Don't you trust my driving?"

"It's not you, it's your car I don't trust. That thing has more rust on it than paint. Besides, you live in the opposite direction."

"Sure, use that as an excuse." Sy returned to his paperwork, muttering something about cars and three wives.

Mason grinned at Sy's discomfort. "Give your wife a shout now, Jack. We're almost done for the night. What are our totals, people? Tank?"

Tank cleared his throat dramatically. "There were ten bags, each filled with approximately one hundred individual twenty pieces, for a grand total of just over eighty grams of crack, with an estimated street value of twenty thousand dollars."

Kris had the money count. "Forty-three hundred in the apartment and our delivery man must also be responsible for picking up the cash. He had fifteen thousand on him."

"Ouch. He'll have some 'splaining to do."

Jack looked at his partner and sighed in disgust. "Do you ever watch any TV filmed after the eighties?"

Sy gave him a withering look. "They're classics. Just like my car."

"Taft? What about the guns?"

For once, Taftmore was serious. "One AK-47 with two full clips and another missing a few rounds."

"I say again: thank God for shitty ammunition."

"Three handguns, two of them semi-autos, all loaded but no spare ammo, and one sawed-off shotgun."

"Not a bad day's work, people. And thanks to Mr. Dwyer, we know that Sean Jacobs is important to someone higher up on the food chain. Gives us a place to start." Mason opened a bottom desk drawer and started pulling out beer cans, tossing them to his people. Jack caught his eagerly; a beer would go down perfectly right now. "Cheers, everyone," Mason toasted.

Jack popped his can open and swigged the beer gratefully. Nice and cold, not icy the way he liked it, but cold enough. *I could get used to this.*

Once the beer was done — only one per person; Mason wasn't going to have any of his guys picked up for impaired driving as they pulled out of the parking lot — he told Sy and Jack to take off. "Thanks for the help today. Sy, good to have you back on the team, even for just a day."

Heading down the stairs, Sy clapped Jack on the back. "You made a good impression with Rick. Looks like the next available spot in the unit is yours."

"Aren't they supposed to go by seniority?" Jack held open the locker room door for Sy.

"Not necessarily. And since Rick took over Major Crime, it's been showing some impressive results, so the superintendent basically lets him pick who goes upstairs."

"There something wrong with that? You sound a little weird about it."

Sy paused, as if considering how much to say. "Mason's a good guy and you can learn a lot from him, but be careful around him. Let's just say nothing ever comes free from him."

"Okay, thanks." Jack dropped his gun belt. It felt almost as good as the beer had tasted. "That was a good day, wasn't it?"

"Damn straight. You going to tell Karen about being shot at?" Sy was on the other side of the centre lockers but Jack could imagine his expression: waiting to see if grasshopper had taken the old man's advice.

"Damn straight. Like you said: she's got to learn what my life is like down here." He added, "Although I may leave out the part about beating up the guy with the child's IQ."

Sy laughed. "Just tell her how you single-handedly disarmed an assailant. No need to get into the exact details."

"Good call." Jack bade Sy a good night as he headed for the showers wrapped in a towel.

"I can give you a lift. There's no need for Karen to come all the way down here."

"Thanks, but she's on her way. I just want to grab a quick rinse before she gets here. I've discovered that automatic gunfire can cause one to perspire a touch more than usual."

"It can at that. See you tomorrow."

Jack showered, changed into his jeans and T-shirt and was waiting outside when Karen pulled their Honda CR-V into the parking lot. The blue SUV was just a year old, a gift to themselves, although Karen got to drive it most of the time. Jack's old Ford was in the shop receiving another extension on its death sentence.

He popped open the passenger door and stuck his head in. "Hi, hon. Want me to drive?"

"No, thanks. I'm good."

"You certainly are," he said. He got in and leaned across the seat to give her a kiss. Her blond hair was pulled back in a loose ponytail and she was wearing an oversized T-shirt and cut-offs. He moved in for another kiss and snuck a hand up to cup a breast. There was nothing between his hand and her skin but the thin cotton.

Karen broke the kiss and gently pushed his hand away, saying, "Whoa, Romeo. I've got nothing against sex in the car but not where your co-workers could be watching."

"Such a prude." Smiling, he settled back in his seat and clicked on his seat belt as Karen pulled out onto Regent Street.

"You must have had a good day."

"It's been an amazing day . . . so far." He drank in the sight of her long legs and made no effort to hide his interest.

"Down, boy," she reproved him. "You can wait until we get home. Tell me about your day."

"You know we did a search warrant with the Major Crime Unit, right? Well, you should see the cops we worked with." As they drove up the sinuous length of the Don Valley Parkway, he described Mason and his team of mismatched coppers.

"Her arms are really as big as yours?" Karen asked incredulously when he described Kris.

"Well, mine might be a bit bigger, but I wouldn't want to break out a tape measure to see."

By the time she was merging with the eastbound traffic on the 401, Jack was entering the apartment again. He purposely drew out the story of how he and Mason approached the second bedroom door. Despite her disapproval of the police, he could tell Karen was enthralled by his tale, because she kept stealing quick glances at him. Then bullets ripped open the bedroom door.

"He shot at you?" The SUV swerved as her hands jerked on the wheel. A horn sounded behind them and she quickly righted the CR-V. "Are you hurt?"

Jack held up his left arm, proudly displaying the wood shrapnel scratches. "That's as close as it got to me. And he didn't shoot at *me*, he shot at *us*, Mason and me."

"What did you do? Call for the SWAT team?"

"Hell, no!" He laughed. "And it's called the ETF, hon. Emergency Task Force."

"Whatever." She waved away his explanation. "What did you do?"

"I kicked open the door and we both drew down on the guy in the room. He was holding an AK-47, a military assault rifle, but it had jammed. He was trying to clear it."

"You didn't shoot him, did you?"

Jack laughed again, this time without humour. "No. If we had, I probably wouldn't be leaving the station until sometime in the afternoon, if I was lucky. No," he repeated. "He finally decided to drop the gun. A good decision on his part."

"Wow! Jack, that's amazing. It sounds like something out of a movie. Weren't you scared?"

"You know, I wasn't." He held up his hands to pre-empt any objections. "I know how it sounds, but I wasn't. If you had told me before we broke down the door that there was a guy inside with an assault rifle waiting to shoot at us, yeah, I would've been shitting bricks. But when it happens like that, you just . . . do what you have to do."

"My hero," she said, not joking, and reached over to squeeze his thigh. Her hand lingered, then lightly brushed his crotch before she pulled it away. "Is there any more?"

"Not much. Well, there is a little bit more. . . ."

"Jack! I can't believe it," she exclaimed when he finished describing his fight with Sean Jacobs. "You tackled someone who had a gun!"

"Remember, it wasn't real." He heard the heat in her voice

and tried to diffuse her anger at him for acting so recklessly.

"But you didn't know that," she countered.

"There was nothing I could — where are you going?"

Karen was exiting at the Port Union Road off-ramp. "I thought we could take the back roads from here. Go on, I want to hear the rest of the story."

"Well, there isn't much left," he admitted hesitantly. He was confused by the mixed emotions radiating from Karen. She seemed excited by his story but royally pissed at him at the same time. This trip home by the back roads could be really enjoyable or . . . not.

Jack described the trip to the hospital as lightheartedly as he could, emphasizing Sean's childlike wonder in the emergency room and his leather gloves so he could be like his "big brother Tony." He was describing the undesirable cousin they had to turn Sean over to when Karen turned onto Twyn Rivers Road and headed into the valley.

The street snaked down a steep slope into darkness, the light of the street lamps left behind. Trees darker than the night sky crowded the road, swallowing the low rumble of the Honda's engine. Jack had always loved this stretch of road; in daylight, it seemed miles outside the city. At night, it was another world.

Jack turned his face to the open window to feel the night air on his skin, savouring its touch and the scents borne on its warm currents. They crossed a single-lane bridge, the tires trundling on the wood planks. A shallow river wandered beneath the bridge, carrying the shimmering moonlight into the darkness before the waters passed away behind them and they were once again beneath the trees.

An unlit dirt parking lot opened on the right and Karen turned in without hesitation. There were a few other cars in the lot, each enjoying privacy in the dark. Karen found a secluded corner, wheeled around and backed in. She cut the engine and in the sudden stillness Jack could hear the river gurgling not far from them.

Karen unclipped her seat belt and turned to face him. He could see her in the moonlight, but it was just dark enough to shadow her face and hide her emotions from him. Jack freed himself from his belt and waited.

"My hero deserves a reward." With that, Karen peeled her shirt off over her head and tossed it onto the dash. Her shorts and sandals fell to the floor. Naked, she slunk across the seat to straddle his lap. She gripped his hair and pulled his mouth to hers. The kiss was hard and passionate, frantic even. She ground her hips against his pelvis and panted in his ear, "Fuck me, Jack. Fuck me now."

Jack reclined the seat and together they pushed his jeans down to his knees. She impaled herself on him, riding him at a desperate pace. She reached behind him to grip the headrest, drawing her breasts up to his mouth. "Harder," she hissed as he sucked first one, then the other, nipple into his mouth, his teeth nipping at the tender flesh.

The force of her thrusts built with an ever-increasing urgency until she exploded in climax. She arched her back, gripped by the intensity of her orgasm. Her hips continued to buck against him, the seat slamming beneath him with every thrust. At length she calmed, a final shudder rippling through her before she collapsed on his chest. "Oh, my God," she whispered. "That was fantastic, Jack."

"You did all the work, hon, not me." He smiled and slid his hands down her back to cup her sweaty buttocks.

"Your turn." Karen smiled wickedly and, not without some awkwardness and giggling from both, managed to twist beneath him. She was still wet and took him easily. "Don't be gentle," she urged.

Jack slowly pulled out, then drove himself back in. Karen grunted in pleasure. "Again. Harder," she moaned and he did. Again and again until he was thrusting into her as hard as he could. As hard as he fucked her, still she wanted more. Wrapping her legs around him, she all but screamed, "That's it, Jack. Give it to me, baby. Give it to me!"

She bucked beneath him, riding the crashing waves of another orgasm. She raked his back with her nails and he cried out in painful ecstasy. Seconds later he erupted inside her, coming with such force he felt he might black out. Spasms racked him, firing nerves throughout his body. At last he fell still.

Karen pulled him to her and they lay wrapped in one another's arms.

I should get shot at more often.

Monday, 21 August
1731 hours

After getting their morning coffees — Sy considered coffee bought at the beginning of shift, regardless of the time, morning coffee — they cruised into Allan Gardens. The park was a city block square, sitting on the western edge of 51. It boasted beautiful flower beds circling a central domed greenhouse. Paved pathways, wide enough for service vehicles and scout cars, criss-crossed the park.

Sy crept the car along at walking speed and rolled to a stop in front of a crowded park bench. Sitting quietly on the bench, enjoying the shade from a towering oak, three grubby old men peered at the police car with dull eyes. Jack figured Sy meant to check them out and opened his door.

"Don't bother," Sy said, never taking his eyes off the men. "This won't take long. Now listen, fellas," he continued, his words for the men on the bench. "What have I told you before about drinking in my park?"

"No drinking in the park," came the hesitant reply.

"That's right. So unless you want to lose your beers, go drink 'em in a laneway where people can't see you. I catch you drinking here again, you lose the beer. Got it?"

"Yes, sir," they mumbled in near unison. Murmuring "Thank you, officer," and "Have a nice day, officer," they shuffled off to the nearest laneway.

"You just send them on their way?"

"Sure. Why not? They're just a bunch of local boozehounds. All they've got in life is their buddies and drinking. They weren't causing any trouble, so why take away one of the few things they have in life?" Dropping the car into gear, Sy glanced at Jack. "Would you have given them tickets and confiscated the beer?"

Jack thought about it for a minute. "Don't know. I guess I'm just used to handing out tickets whenever I can to keep the sergeants off my back."

"Trust me, Jack. You're gonna run into enough assholes down here just through answering radio calls to write as many tickets as you want. No need to fuck over the general public or poor old hounds like them."

Sy drove to the centre of the park and backed up the concrete ramp in front of the greenhouse. He killed the engine and kicked open his door to let what little breeze there was flow through the front seat. Jack propped his door open as well and took in the surroundings as he sipped his coffee.

The ramp was wide enough for three cars abreast and lined with concrete planters. The ramp gave them a clear view of the eastern side of the park. It was a busy place, with dogs being walked, people heading home from work and even the odd sunbather.

"This is my hangout. I like to have my morning coffee here and I drive through the park as many times as I can during the shift."

"How come?" Jack asked, curious.

"The park is my special project. It used to be overrun with drunks and crackheads. It took us a while, but we finally cleaned it up and I intend to keep it that way. Just because you live in this hellhole doesn't mean you shouldn't have a nice place to walk your dog."

They drank their coffee and the radio remained silent. Occasionally, someone passing near the car would wave to Sy and he would raise a hand in return. It was a peaceful and surprising start to the day — evening shift usually started with a backlog of calls the day shift couldn't get to — but Jack wasn't about to complain. The lack of radio calls was a welcome relief. And needed. The chest workout Sy had put him through had exhausted him.

Sy drained his coffee and dumped the empty cup behind the front seat. "Remind me later to throw that in the garbage. How'd you and Karen meet?"

"Where'd that question come from?"

"Humour me."

"We were a set-up, actually. A friend of Karen's — they knew each other in school — is a cop at 32 and she introduced us. She's also the one who tells Karen all the horror stories about 51 and the —" Jack paused, making sure he got the quotation right "— 'knuckle-dragging, heavy-handed, cheating bastards that aren't in jail because they have a badge.' I think that's how she put it."

"Let me guess. Karen's friend was married to a 51 copper?"

Jack laughed. "You'd think so, but not that I'm aware of. I don't think she's ever been south of Lawrence Avenue, let alone in 51."

"Unfortunately, a lot of people think that way about us. They just don't know, or don't want to know, about the shit we deal with. Remember when we got called to Street City a few weeks ago? It's a perfect example. One guy throws bleach in another guy's eyes, almost blinds him, over an argument about the TV and then when we go to arrest him he tries to stab me. That's shit the general public doesn't deal with. They never even hear about it. Yet they judge us."

Jack finished his coffee and Sy started up the car. "By the way, did you ever tell Karen how you got that cut?"

"Why?" Jack asked as they left the park and pulled out onto

Gerrard Street. "Why shouldn't I protect Karen from the real 51?"

"Because it'll fuck you in the end." Sy sounded serious. "Dealing with criminals every day, the shit of humanity, can get to you after a while. It can change you. Sometimes a little. Sometimes a lot. Karen has to understand what you're experiencing, otherwise all she'll know is that you're changing and she won't know why."

Jack nodded in agreement. "Sounds reasonable."

"Think about it," Sy went on. "Let's say you've had a really bad day. A really messy suicide, or maybe you arrested a guy who beat the snot out of his wife and kids, or some nut goes for your gun and you end up fighting for your life. How is she going to help you when you get home if she doesn't know what your job is like?" Sy held up a hand to forestall Jack's comments. "Worst-case scenario: you shoot someone. Perfectly justified, but now you have to handle the fact that you just killed someone. That's something no civilian ever thinks about: how being forced to shoot someone affects the cop. Not to mention that you're being investigated by the SIU, a bunch of incompetent civilian investigators whose mandate is to charge cops even if the evidence proves the cops are innocent."

"I never thought about that," Jack admitted quietly.

"So take it from me, someone who's on marriage number three. She has to hear about it. She may not want to, but if she's going to be a copper's wife, she needs to know."

"Thanks, Sy. I really appreciate it." They drove in silence; then Jack asked, "You really think the SIU is incompetent?"

"I imagine some of them are okay." Sy braked for an Asian family crossing Gerrard Street at Sackville. The parents pointedly ignored the police car, but the two little kids waved. Sy and Jack waved back. Cruising along Gerrard, Sy carried on. "Don't get me wrong. I've got no problem with a civilian body checking up on us. But a lot of them don't have a policing background, so how can they understand what we do? That'd be like putting you and me on a hospital's board and telling doctors how to do their job."

"You're just full of good points today."

"Hey, it's your fault," Sy accused, sounding slightly embarrassed. "You asked about the SIU. But I'm finished now. So endeth the lesson for today, grasshopper."

"5103 in 6's area. 230 Sherbourne. See the doctor there. He has a male who needs to go to the hospital on a Form One."

"Well, Jack, you're about to find out how bad 51 can be."

"Why? It a rough place?"

"Oh, not rough. Just . . . smelly." The wicked grin Sy shot his way should have warned Jack, but then maybe nothing could have prepared him for the call.

Number 230 Sherbourne was an old Victorian-style building that had long ago been converted into a rooming house. The once grand, elegant building was now just another shithole in a row of shitholes. An ambulance was parked out front and Sy pulled in behind it, leaving enough room between the vehicles to manoeuver a stretcher.

Sherbourne Street and Dundas Street East, the intersection the *Toronto Star* had labelled "Crack Central," was a hodgepodge of buildings. The church on the southeast corner hosted a drop-in centre for the homeless, addicts and the rest of society's discarded and rejected people. Across the street from the church was the building in front of which Jack had spotted the Black dealer, the arrest that had led to the search warrant.

Diagonally across from the church was a two-storey commercial building that changed businesses as frequently as crack whores tended to bathe. Monthly. There was a fifties-style diner on the ground floor, where the food was surprisingly good, considering the area. Jack and Sy had eaten there a few times.

Then there was a tiny plaza with a 7-Eleven on the last corner and one building south of it was 230 Sherbourne.

Jack got out of the car and surveyed the area, noting who was doing what on the sidewalks. The heat kept pedestrian activity to a minimum, but some people, looking like wilted plants, sat out on front steps and porches, preferring the oppressive open air to their stagnant apartments.

"Hey, Sy. Check out the guy across the street."

Sy glanced at a figure huddled on the church steps. "What about him?"

"A little warm for a sweatshirt and ball cap, isn't it?"

"Yup, but once you get on that crack diet, it burns the fat right off of you. Throw in some malnourishment and that guy's probably lucky he hasn't frozen to death." Sy headed up the steps to the front door of 230. "If he's still there when we're finished with this call, we'll check him out. Now, let's go see what this doctor has for us."

Jack cast a final eye at the man across the street, his arms wrapped tightly around his knees, rocking in a jerky motion. Shadows hid his face and the dark skin of his hands gave no clue to his age. Jack shook his head. On a day when most people would be willing to barter with the devil for air conditioning, that poor bastard was freezing even with a sweatshirt and ball cap. Crack was a wonderful thing. Jack joined Sy at the double doors on the front of the old Victorian building.

When they stepped inside, the stench slapped Jack in the face. His eyes started to water and he staggered. Then his hands flew to cover his mouth and nose. "What the hell is that smell?"

Sy, grinning, looked as if he was still breathing fresh air. "Years of unwashed bodies and no housecleaning." He clapped Jack on the back. "Don't worry. A few years down here and your sense of smell will be burnt out of you permanently. Let's go find the ambulance."

The front hall was an immense, two-storey affair with a grand staircase leading up. Jack stopped, mesmerized. "My God, Sy. Look at this place."

The hardwood floors were warped and hadn't felt a touch of

care in decades. The intricate detailing on the banisters, trim and moulding was all but lost beneath countless layers of cheap paint. Huge rooms, built to entertain dozens of guests, had been portioned off with slapped-together two-by-fours and drywall into cheap, one-room apartments.

"I know," Sy said wistfully. "It breaks my heart every time I come in here."

A narrow hall on either side of the staircase led deeper into the house and Sy headed down the left side. Jack followed, careful not to let his bare forearms touch the walls. He couldn't tell what colour they had been painted years ago, but now they were a brownish grey shade he had never seen before. It matched the stench perfectly. He slipped on his Kevlar-lined leather gloves.

Two paramedics and an out-of-place business-suit type — he had to be the doctor — were standing outside the last room down the hall. Jack figured his awareness of the stench should be waning, but the reek grew stronger the deeper into the house they went. By the time he and Sy joined the medics, Jack was ready to gag. At least one of the paramedics was looking as queasy as Jack felt. *What on earth could smell that horrible?*

"Afternoon, everyone. Whatever we've got, let's get it done quick before we have to burn our uniforms to get rid of the stink." It was the first concession Sy had made to the smell.

The queasy medic nodded enthusiastically and motioned to the suit.

"I'm Dr. Watson. I came by today to check on Mr. Hirsch. His caseworker advised me he has a serious foot problem that needs to be looked at."

Jack thought his voice suggested it was a very serious problem.

"I didn't think doctors did house calls anymore."

If the doctor took offence to Sy's comment, it didn't show. "I usually don't, but Mr. Hirsch is a special case. He's a bit of a shut-in. In fact, his worker can't remember the last time he left his room."

"And you've issued a Form One?"

"I have." Watson produced the mental-health form from his jacket pocket and handed it to Sy. "Mr. Hirsch is in no condition to care for himself, as you shall see." He gestured to the closed door and stepped back. Well back.

Sy exchanged a puzzled glance with Jack. Obviously, the doctor wasn't concerned about Hirsch being a direct danger to himself or anyone else. Otherwise, he'd have opened the door to keep an eye on his client or waited outside for a police escort.

"What's his first name?" Sy borrowed a pair of latex gloves from the medics.

"You may want to put these on, too," the medic said to Jack, handing him a pair. "Leather just absorbs fluids."

"I'm not liking where this is going," Jack muttered as he changed gloves.

"Bernard. His name's Bernard," the doctor called from down the hall.

"Hold your breath," the medic cautioned and toed open the door.

It was probably his imagination, but Jack would later swear he had *seen* the smell waft out of the room like a noxious fog bank. Even Sy recoiled. Jack had to fight to keep from vomiting. His eyes stung, then burned.

Can a smell physically touch you? Oh, God, I'm breathing it in!

"Ber — oh, fuck, that's disgusting — Bernard?" Sy managed to say.

"He's right in front of you," the non-queasy medic said.

His partner was bent over and looked closer to puking than Jack felt.

If Sy can handle this, so can I. Jack forced himself to straighten up and survey the room. It was tiny, no more than ten feet square and windowless. To say it was dirty was to call the Great Wall of China a fence. Grey and brown . . . stuff . . . clung to the walls. Except for the quarter circle where the door opened against the wall, the floor was buried beneath years of garbage:

old newspapers yellow and black with age and rot, fast-food containers overgrown with mould, shit. Human shit. The doctor was being literal when he said Bernard didn't leave the room.

Bernard was a human-shaped mound on top of a cot growing out of the floor's wasteland. The foot of the bed was inches from the door and Jack couldn't make out where Bernard ended and the cot began. All he saw was a congealed mass of garbage and shit. From what he could tell, Bernard was skin and bones. A beard matted with filth covered his chest, but Jack could still see the ribs standing out painfully against the too-thin skin.

"What's . . . what's wrong with his feet?" Jack asked.

"Yeah," Sy agreed. "Before we go touching him, let's find out what the worker thought was worse than the living conditions."

The non-queasy medic spoke. "The doctor said it was some kind of fungus."

"No fucking kidding."

The medic reluctantly moved into the room. "Bernard, I'm just going to take a look at your feet. Okay?"

"Sure." Bernard's voice was surprisingly strong coming from such a wasted body.

Jack couldn't help himself. He had to know. The medic was squatting in the arc of clear floor next to the door to examine Bernard's feet and Jack leaned over him, bracing himself against the door with one hand.

The medic peeled back the bedsheet and the cloth cracked in protest. Bernard's feet were bare and as dirt-matted as the rest of him. The toenails were thick and yellow, the colour of pus, but that was not the worst. They had grown so long they had curled under the toes and were in danger of growing into the skin. The medic gently pried the toes apart and that's when the cockroaches that were nesting in the curl of the nails ran out across his fingers.

That was also when Jack lost the fight and puked.

Jack stepped onto the tiny square of warped, sagging boards that passed as the building's front porch and sucked in a lungful of dirty, humid city air. God, it was beautiful. But then, anything would be beautiful after the stench of Bernard's room. *How anyone could live in that filth. . . . And the cockroaches.* Jack shoved the image aside as his stomach lurched.

"Well, that was kind of nasty, wasn't it?" Sy asked, coming out to stand beside his partner.

"Nasty?" Jack asked incredulously. He spat into the weeds beside the steps, trying vainly to cleanse his mouth of the taste of vomit and embarrassment. "It was a lot fucking more than nasty."

"Ah, grasshopper. You have so much more to experience down here." Sy stepped aside as the paramedics wheeled Bernard out on a stretcher. Once they were down the stairs, Sy eased beside Jack and pretended not to notice as Jack spat into the weeds again. "You ever see the movie *Labyrinth*?"

Jack wiped his mouth. "No."

"Cool movie. David Bowie plays a warlock or something. Anyway, in the movie they talk about the Bog of Eternal Stench and how, if you get even a drop of its water on you, you stink for the rest of your life. I truly believe the bog is somewhere in 51."

"And Bernard got some of it on him?" Jack asked with an amused smile.

"Nope. I do believe Bernard's been fucking bathing in it."

Jack laughed. Trust Sy to find a movie reference for a guy with cockroaches nesting in his toes. The laughter gurgled to a stop as his stomach heaved.

"Well, well, well. Look who we have here."

Jack straightened. The ambulance was pulling away — the good doctor would meet them at the hospital but had declined to ride in the back with Bernard — and Sy was watching the street with a pleased expression.

"What —"

There, crossing the street right in front of them as if he was coming over to chat, was Mike Reynolds, also known as Mike Smith, their small-time Black dealer turned snitch. He was shuffling across the busy street, keeping his eye out for cars and completely oblivious to the two cops watching him.

"He has conditions not to be down here, doesn't he?" Jack inquired pleasantly.

"That he does," Sy answered just as pleasantly. "Why don't we talk with him and see if he has any more information he'd like to use as a get-out-of-jail-free card."

They moved to the sidewalk and waited patiently for Reynolds, who was standing on the faded yellow centre line, his attention turned to the southbound traffic.

"I can't believe he doesn't see us."

"No one ever said you have to be smart to be a criminal in 51," Sy commented. "I'm betting he makes it to the curb before he sees us."

"No bet. I wonder what he's doing down here?"

"Didn't he give us a home address from around here?"

"Yeah, I think. . . ." His words trailed off as something caught his eye. The crack addict jonesing on the church steps was up and moving with a purpose. Gone were his jerky, sickly movements. He stepped onto the street behind Reynolds, moving like he wanted to reach Reynolds before the police did. He'd pulled up the hood to the sweatshirt and with the ball cap and a large pair of sunglasses Jack couldn't make out a single distinguishing feature.

He might as well be wearing a fucking mask.

The addict had his hands tucked into the hoody's pockets, but as he neared Reynolds he reached out with his left hand; his right hand was down at his side, tucked close to his leg.

"Reynolds!" Sy yelled.

Jack went for his gun, but it was too late. Far too late.

The addict stepped up behind Reynolds and with his left hand wrenched the dealer's head back and to the side. His right hand came up, flashing silver in the heated air. Jack watched as a blade bit hard and deep into Reynolds's throat. The metal sliced through skin and muscle, spilling Reynolds's life into the open air.

The blood jumped from the wound, splashing against the windshield and side window of a passing car. The driver screamed — Jack could hear it through the closed windows — and slammed hard on the brakes. The car, a Honda that had seen better days, screeched to a halt, only to be slammed into by the car behind it.

The supposed addict shoved Reynolds against the second car, a Ford, and its driver screamed as blood splattered through his open window.

"Don't move!" Jack hollered at the addict, his gun aimed over the roof of the second car.

The addict backed away from Reynolds and the dealer slowly collapsed to the pavement, the flow of blood from his throat sputtering out as he slid down the car's far side. The addict held his hands out to his sides, not in surrender, but in mockery, daring the police to shoot him as he backed away. A comfortable casualness showed his arrogance.

A straight razor, not a knife, dangled carelessly from the addict's right hand. The metal shimmered in the sunlight as Reynolds's lifeblood dripped from the blade.

"Don't fucking move!" Jack ordered as he began to sidle around the back of the second car.

The addict raised his left hand and Jack saw that he was wearing black leather gloves. The addict smiled and happily gave Jack the finger.

A sudden squeal of tires snapped Jack's focus and he instinctively leapt backward. When he looked up again, the addict was hopping into a blue Nissan that had skidded to a stop behind him.

The car tore away, the tires shrieking against the pavement. Jack sprinted hopelessly after it as it swung onto Dundas and accelerated into the distance. His feet plodded to a stop as he was left standing in the road, his gun held impotently in his hand.

He holstered the gun and pulled out his radio, but he heard Sy on the air giving a description of the car and the addict. Casting a final and useless glance down the street, Jack turned to help Sy with two hysterical drivers and one cooling corpse.

Tuesday, 22 August
1700 hours

"Sit down and listen up, everyone." Sergeant Rose waited impassively behind the sergeant's podium. She didn't have the ability to glare a parade room into silence, but she was working on it. A big woman with short-cropped blond hair, she seemed to enjoy her growing reputation as a man-hating lesbian or, at least, did nothing to refute the rumours. "Sergeant Johanson's booking in a prisoner, so let's get this done." She read out the day's assignments at a steady drill-march pace, as if she had more important matters to discuss and was eager to get to them.

Done with the assignments, Rose set the sergeant's clipboard aside and leaned on the podium, surveying the room. All the officers recognized the look — it was a look most veteran supervisors had — and waited soundlessly for her to speak. Only the rattle of the overworked air conditioner dared to challenge her and even it sounded hesitant.

"First, Homicide wanted me to thank everyone for a job well done at the scene yesterday. You shut the area down quickly and got hold of witnesses before they could wander off. Good fucking job.

"Second, we've got a fucking serious problem. There's an asshole out there who isn't afraid to kill someone in front of two uniformed cops."

"So what, Sarge? As long as they keep killing each other, what do we care?"

"Do you have any fucking brains in that head, Borovski?" Rose snapped, her words heavy with disgust and disbelief. "If he's that cocky now, how long until he thinks he should do a cop just to prove how bad he is?" She let that disturbing thought sink in for a minute, then went on. "I want this asshole stopped and I mean now, today. Take down his description and find this prick."

While Rose read out the description — for what it was worth — Jack struggled to keep his eyes open. It had been a long night. He and Sy had been the last to leave the station. Jack had driven home with the sun well above the horizon. Homicide had interviewed him, reinterviewed him and then started all over again. He'd had time for a short nap, then had dragged his ass back to work less than six hours after he had left it. The joys of shift work.

And, of course, he'd had to tell Karen what had kept him at work. She had listened, horrified, then had given him a curt good-night and an even briefer kiss and left Jack to shuffle up the stairs alone. If he hadn't been so tired, her abrupt dismissal would have kept him awake. As it was, he had nodded off with his toothbrush still in his mouth.

"Anything to add to the description, Sy?"

"Nothing to the description, but —" he turned in his seat to face the rest of the platoon "— watch your backs with this guy. Jack spotted him first. He was sitting on the steps of the church across from 230 Sherbourne acting like a crackhead needing a fix. Hiding in plain fucking sight." He shook his head. "Ballsy, very fucking ballsy. He was waiting to ambush Reynolds and he didn't give a fuck that Jack and I were there." Sy paused, then added, "There was a backup shooter in the Nissan. I saw the barrel sticking out of the rear window. I think if Jack or I had gotten any closer to our boy. . . ."

Jack had left that little detail out of the version he had told Karen.

There was an ominous silence. Sergeant Rose knew when and how to break it. "You find this guy, be careful and remember: it's better to be judged by twelve than carried by six. Now go get 'em."

Jack waited for everyone to clear the room before asking, "Better to be what?"

Sy looked at him, openly shocked. "You're telling me you've never heard that expression before?"

"I wouldn't be asking if I had," Jack replied defensively.

"What did they teach you up in 32?" He rolled his eyes as he stood and stretched. "Aw, fuck, I'm tired." He dropped his arms with a huff and adjusted his gun belt. "C'mon, Mason wants to see us. If you get into a jackpot, your job is to make sure you and your partner go home at the end of the day, so it's better to be judged by a jury of twelve than —"

"To be carried by six pallbearers. Got it." Jack smacked his forehead. "Kind of obvious once you think about it."

"Don't be too hard on yourself, grasshopper. I imagine you're tired 'cause that sexy little wife of yours was just happy you made it home alive and kept you *up* all day long proving it. If you know what I mean."

"Don't I wish," Jack grumbled as they plodded down the hall to the stairs.

"Trouble at home? Fuck, this place needs a fucking elevator."

"Well, let's see. When I got home, Karen gave me shit for not calling to tell her I'd be late, although it never bothered her before. Apparently, now that I'm in 51, I'm supposed to call. Would have been nice if someone had told me about the new rule."

"You told her your cell was dead and we were stuck at the scene and the hospital till three?"

"Yup. Doesn't matter that I didn't want to wake her. I was supposed to call. Stupid me for not knowing, right?"

"Absolutely," Sy said, grinning as if he had heard and lived through this all before.

"Then, when I told her what had happened, she got all quiet and left."

"Left?"

"As in left the house, and she wasn't back when I came in to work."

"Any idea where she went?"

"Probably her parents'. That's where she goes whenever we have a fight."

Sy thumped on the Major Crime door and waited for someone to answer before walking in. Mason was alone in the office, slumped behind his desk. His face was as saggy as his clothes were wrinkled.

"Long night, Rick?" Sy asked, dragging a chair over to Mason's desk and dropping into it.

Jack perched on a nearby desk. If he sat in a chair, he might fall asleep.

"Yeah. I can't remember what my bed looks like." He scrubbed his face vigorously with his hands, then slapped them down on the desktop. He shot Jack a murderous look. "I don't know whether you're a blessing or a fucking curse. Every time you get involved in something, it means extra work for me."

Jack shrugged. He was too tired to care what people thought of him.

"Any leads?" Sy stretched his legs out and snuggled back into the chair.

"Fuck-all. My guys have been out since yesterday afternoon trying to dig something up on our straight-razor boy, but if anyone knows anything they ain't talking. At least not to us."

"No fucking kidding." Sy yawned and both Mason and Jack unconsciously echoed him. "Anyone who'll slit a guy's throat in front of the cops wouldn't hesitate to do someone who talks to us. Fuck, Reynolds was proof of that."

"Obviously, he wasn't planning on you two being there, but the fact that he still did it just adds that much more to his reputation."

Jack asked, "If this guy is so ballsy, why didn't he have the shooter in the car open up on us?"

"I've been thinking about that." Mason checked the collection of coffee cups on his desk, found them all empty and began tossing them into the garbage. He theorized as he tossed. "If the weapons we found at the search warrant are any indication, this guy is well armed, so it wasn't because of insufficient firepower. I'm thinking this guy may have steel balls, but he isn't stupid. He knows if he shot at you, whether he hit you or not, we would have dropped on him a lot harder than we are. A murdering drug dealer is one thing, a cop killer is something else entirely."

"Smart, fearless and well armed. Well, ain't that just fucking peachy." Sy wiggled in the chair, but gun belts just weren't designed for lounging. "And no idea who he is? A guy like that can't stay off the radar indefinitely."

"Nothing solid. There's one guy we're looking at, but it's more wishful thinking on my part than anything concrete. Not a big player. Got busted for low-level dealing a few years back, but he's been clean since then."

"Actually clean or just hasn't been caught?"

"That's why it's wishful thinking on my part, Sy. His name keeps coming up when someone gets whacked or there's a major play amongst the dealers, but we've never been able to get anything stronger than rumours." Mason shifted his gaze between the partners. "I've read your notes but, off the record, is there any chance either of you could identify yesterday's guy?"

Sy shook his head sadly. "Not a chance. With the baseball cap pulled down and those huge sunglasses on. . . . Fuck, we'd've seen more of his face if he was wearing a Batman mask. And the hood of the sweatshirt was so big it was like a medieval monk's cowl. Like something out of *Name of the Rose*."

Mason looked at Jack.

"Sorry," Jack said. "I agree with Mr. Movie on this one."

"You guys are sure he was wearing leather gloves? Like the kid at the search warrant?"

Sy nodded.

Jack asked, "You're not suggesting it was the same guy?"

"Fuck, no. That kid couldn't do something like this. But it's too much of a coincidence that they were both wearing gloves.

There's a connection there. We just have to find it." Mason dry-scrubbed his face again. "And you're sure it was a straight razor and not a knife?"

Sy motioned to Jack. "He had the better view."

"Definitely a razor. He made no effort to hide it."

"Leather gloves and a straight razor. It ain't much, but it's more than we had before. Now, fuck off," he said with a weary smile, "I've got work to do. And if you want to earn some brownie points, you could grab me a jumbo coffee when you get yours."

"Coffee? Fuck that," Sy declared. "I'm going to the hospital to see if they'll give me a shot of adrenalin."

Wednesday, 23 August
1200 hours

Jack heard the car doors slam shut and knew he was trapped. He had left it too late and now they had him cornered, the Honda in the driveway proclaiming he was inside and at their mercy.

Karen and her parents were home from lunch.

At least Karen had let him sleep in instead of insisting he join them. Now that extra sleep was biting him in the ass. If only he had gotten up even ten minutes earlier. . . .

"Son of a whore," he muttered, smiling.

If Karen or her mother heard him, he would be admonished for his language and Her Highness Hawthorn would no doubt tack on a lecture about how his vulgar expressions were a clear indication he was missing far too many Sunday mornings in church.

"Son of a fucking whore," he said, louder.

"What was that, hon?" Karen called from downstairs.

Oops. Stifling a sudden fit of giggles, Jack shouted, "Nothing. Be down in a minute."

Karen and her mother were in the kitchen preparing a pot of

tea — Earl Grey, undoubtedly; for Evelyn Hawthorn, any family meal was not complete until, regardless of weather, circumstances or illness, tea was poured — when Jack reluctantly made his way downstairs. Small blessing, her dad was out on the back deck, probably inspecting the quality of workmanship. Jack gave Karen a quick kiss and his mother-in-law an even quicker hello on the way to grabbing his lunch and post-workout shake from the fridge.

"Gotta go, hon. Duty calls." He planted another kiss on her lips and was heading down the hall to the front door, thinking he had made good his escape, when Karen called after him.

"Jack, wait. I want to talk to you about something."

Damn! He turned but held his ground, the perfect picture of a man with places to go. Any place, actually, where his in-laws weren't.

Karen was standing in the kitchen doorway, looking as anxious as he felt.

"Can it wait, hon? I'm running late as it is." *Don't do this to me, Karen. You know I don't want to be here.*

"I thought Karen said you didn't start work until four. Surely it can't take you four hours to drive into the city." Karen's mother had moved beside her, a united front he had little hope of defeating.

"Actually, on the last day of evenings we start at two and I promised my partner I'd meet him for a workout first." It was the truth and the only excuse he had, but he knew it wasn't enough. When the Hawthorn women wanted to talk, you talked. Or, more rightly, listened.

"This is important, Jack, and I'm sure your little gym routine can wait a few minutes." Mrs. Hawthorn — no "Please call me Evelyn" today — withdrew to the kitchen without waiting to see if he was following. Obedience was expected.

Jack hated it when she did that. He was tempted to give Mrs. High and Mighty a taste of her own medicine and announce that his "little gym routine" could not, in fact, wait a few minutes and get the hell out of there, but Karen's expression stopped him. She looked worried and upset. About what? Ever since the night of the search warrant, she had been rather frisky and even the news of Reynolds's murder — minus the backup shooter in the car — hadn't upset her that much because she'd felt he had never been in danger. All that had happened between then and now was . . . her parents.

Son of a whore.

"Where the fuck are you getting this energy? You're not stealing Tank's 'roids, are you?" Sy joked.

"Who needs steroids when you have in-laws?"

"Oh? Do tell."

"After your set, old man. Quit stalling."

"Bastard." Grumbling obscenities, Sy dipped his shoulders under the barbell and hoisted it off the rack.

"Eight reps, no less," Jack ordered.

"Eight?" Sy squawked. "You trying to kill me?"

"Shut up and squat."

Still protesting, Sy squatted with the 185-pound barbell resting on his thick shoulders. By the third repetition, he had no breath left for protesting. By the sixth, his face was red and on the eighth and final push his knees were quivering and Jack could see his scalp turning purple through his cropped hair.

After the final rep, Sy took a wobbly step forward and let his legs buckle, dropping the barbell onto the rack. He hung from the bar, supporting himself more with his arms than his legs, heaving great gasps of air.

When he could stand without support and had his breathing under control, he glared accusingly at Jack. "You're just doing this to me 'cause I embarrassed you bench-pressing yesterday. Spitefulness does not become you, Jack."

"What can I say? In many ways, I'm a petty man."

Like a lot of guys who worked out, Sy loved to train his upper body but neglected his legs. He could bench-press three plates a side for multiple reps and took childish joy in Jack's efforts to press up 225. But now it was the day for training legs and although Jack overall was not as strong as Sy he did train his legs regularly.

They were in the station's gym, a small L-shaped room crowded with racks of dumbbells — the 150-pound dumbbells bought specifically for Tank were on the floor — benches and assorted machines. A wood plaque proclaiming the space as BIFF'S BULLPEN hung in a place of honour on the wall. It was usually a busy place, regardless of the hour, but this afternoon Jack and his partner had the place to themselves and Sy had a CD with a mix of Guns 'N' Roses, AC/DC, Metallica and Nightwish blaring out of the small stereo system. The acoustics were shit and he had the volume up to near-distortion level.

"So what did the in-laws do?"

"Karen wasn't overjoyed about everything that happened at the search warrant and then on the street with Reynolds, but she was beginning to realize that shit happens and we're careful about what we do." Jack slid an additional forty-five-pound plate onto the bar. "And then she had brunch with her parents." He rammed the plate into place. "She told them the whole story and by the time they finished eating —" another plate on the other end "— she was convinced that it's only a matter of time before I die down here." Slam!

"And?"

"Hang on, let me do my set." Jack cinched up his weight belt and got under the bar.

"Need a spot?" Sy asked less than enthusiastically from his seat on a bench.

"Nah, I'm good." Jack straightened up to free the bar from the rack and stepped back. He readied his stance, sucked in a couple of deep breaths, then started cranking out the reps. His quads were screaming at him by the eighth rep, but he ignored them and forced out another two, shouting out his frustration and anger loudly enough to challenge "Welcome to the Jungle."

"You're a fucking animal today," Sy declared after Jack had racked the bar. "They must have pissed you off something fierce."

Jack loosened his belt and dropped to his knees, wiped out by that final set. It had been an intense workout. Just what he needed after the little "discussion" in the kitchen.

"Part-way through the conversation — although it felt more like a fucking lecture to me — her father comes strolling in from the deck like he owns the place and adds his fucking two cents. After telling me, mind you, that my deck could use another coat or two of stain and not that cheap stuff I had obviously used."

"You're not going to ask me to help you bury a couple of bodies, are you? I mean, I will, but you should have told me before the workout so I could have saved some strength."

Jack laughed. "No bodies, but I won't tell you I didn't think about it." He stood up with a satisfied groan and began stretching his thighs. "You should stretch, Sy. It'll cut down on the soreness."

"I can't fucking stand up, let alone stretch, right now. I'm good right where I am." He patted the weight bench affectionately. "Keep going."

"So, they're all telling me it's too dangerous down here and it's selfish of me — *unbelievably* selfish of me — to stay here when I know Karen worries about me. Do I want to cause her a nervous breakdown? Fuck." He switched legs, pulling his foot up behind his butt. "But, hey, let's not stop there! While we're at it, why don't we ask Jack when he's going to stop playing at work and get a real job? Something where I'm home in the evenings and Karen doesn't have to wonder if tonight's the night I don't make it home."

"Whoa, they really dumped on you. Did Karen agree with them?"

Jack shook his head. "Only about it being too dangerous here. She'd like to see me transfer back to 32 or maybe work behind a desk somewhere safe."

"What did you say?"

"Unfortunately, I told her she was married to a 51 copper and better get used to it." He wasn't happy about what he had said and he knew his face showed it.

"Ouch. That's going to take some smoothing over. Trust me, I know."

"Yeah, you're right. But I was just so fucking ticked off at her parents. First I'm not good enough for their daughter, then my job's not good enough, the house isn't good enough, the deck, the car. Then her mother starts in with the church crap. I'm missing too much church because of work, I'm falling away from my faith, I'm going to end up being one of those police officers who beats people just because of their skin colour, I'm heading to hell and I'm dragging her daughter with me. Fuck!"

"'Sometimes even angels must do evil to fight evil,'" Sy quoted.

"What's that?"

"A line out of the Bible. Basically, it says sometimes even the good guys have to get their hands dirty in order to fight the good fight."

"Cool." A devious smile twitched Jack's lips. "I'll have to find out the chapter and verse so I can throw that at her mother next time she starts quoting scripture at me."

"Don't go picking fights for the sake of picking fights. Her mother might be right, in a roundabout way."

Jack gaped at Sy, flabbergasted. "Now you're agreeing with her?"

"Take it easy, Jack. All I'm saying is that you have to be careful down here. 51 has a way of affecting people. Changing them. I've seen guys who put saints to shame start working here and a few years later it's hard to tell them apart from the criminals out on the street."

"You think that's happening to me?" Jack was getting defensive, not liking what Sy was saying.

"For fuck's sake, man, relax. Listen, we had a great day yesterday, we just had a good workout and, if we're lucky, we'll get into a scrap or a pursuit tonight. All right?"

"Yeah, sorry. Guess I'm still pissed."

"Understandable. But take it from a man who's had three sets of in-laws —" Sy pushed himself upright, groaning as if he still had a barbell across his shoulders "— it ain't worth it. Let it the fuck go."

Jack nodded.

"We good?"

"We're good," Jack confirmed. "Come on, old man. We've got time for some calf work."

"Oh, fucking joy."

"5102, 138 Wellesley. Possible domestic in apartment 302. Complainant can hear a male and female yelling. Buzz 304 for entry. Time, 2037."

"Something happening on Wellesley?" Sy asked.

"'02's heading to a domestic by the sounds of it."

They were walking to the car with coffees in hand. A light rain, no more than a drizzle, was steaming off the Baker's Dozen parking lot.

"Who's on it?"

"Hang on and I'll tell you. Sheesh, relax, old man." Jack settled in his seat and stored his coffee safely in the cup holder. "Whoever finally decided to equip police cars with cup holders was a genius. Too bad it took years of the computers getting spilled on before someone thought of it." He pulled the call up on the screen. "Looks like Boris and Manny."

"That's just down the street. We could back them up."

"I thought you didn't like Boris."

"I don't. But Manny's an okay guy," Sy explained. "And working with Boris, it's like he's solo. Don't volunteer us yet. If Boris is driving, he'll make sure we get there first."

Boris wasn't driving and he and Manny were heading into the building when Jack and Sy pulled up. 138 Wellesley was in a row of old three-storey apartment buildings across the street from Jarvis Collegiate. Normally, not a great source of trouble. But domestics have a tendency to pop up wherever two or more people try to live together.

"Hey, guys. Thanks for the backup."

"No problem, Manny. Wouldn't want you going in there by yourself." It was a casual remark. Sy looked at Boris when he said it.

Manny must have been the odd man out that day to get stuck working with Borovski and Jack couldn't help but feel sorry for him. Boris was everything Jack disliked about stereotypical cops, globbed into a fat, flabby, lazy, power-tripping asshole. Some heavy guys carried their extra weight in a firm, unrepulsive way, but Boris had loose folds of bulk hanging over in spongy bunches. Jack could imagine Boris as a child: fat, sullen and friendless, the type bullies dream of. He pictured that poor child harbouring a deep resentment toward society and vowing to be a police officer when he grew up "to show all of them."

Well, here he was: a balding, friendless man who extracted his righteous revenge on society at large through his radar gun and ticket book, who gained sustenance through others' suffering and solace in fast food. Supersized, no doubt. Some of that drive-thru food and its stains — many appearing well entrenched — decorated the front of his shirt. As bad as the black shirt was, Jack shuddered at the image Boris had presented to the public in the old light blue shirts.

Here's your ticket, ma'am. Would you like to choose a snack from my shirt to go with that?

"What's so funny?"

"Hm?" Jack realized he was biting his lip to keep from laughing. He schooled his features, not without an effort, and told Sy, "Nothing. Tell you later."

They headed inside. Boris helpfully held open the door for the others, which — surprise, surprise! — allowed him to fall in at the back of the group.

It'd serve him right if we got ambushed from the rear.

The old stairs creaked their annoyance as the four cops trudged upward.

"How do you want to handle the call, Sy?" Boris asked between gasps. He let everyone know that climbing stairs was an occupational hazard as far as he was concerned. He had been known to have the dispatcher instruct some complainants to meet him in the lobby if their building lacked an elevator. "You and Warren want to speak with the couple while Manny and me check the rest of the apartment to make sure they're not hiding evidence of an assault or something?"

That lazy sack of —

Manny cut Jack's thoughts off abruptly. "Forget it, Borovski," he snapped, turning on him so suddenly that Boris was forced to stop in mid-step on the stairs. He teetered on the edge of imbalance, not used to such a strenuous position. He took a hasty step down. "This is our call. They volunteered to back us up and we are not going to dump our work on them. Got it?"

"Yeah, sure. I was just making a suggestion, that's all." From the way Boris acquiesced to Manny, it was hard to believe he had twelve years on the job to Manny's three. But that was just the way he was.

Manny — properly known as William Armsman — was the type of guy you either loved or hated. His strong convictions about what was right and what was wrong had led to numerous clashes on the platoon, with both PCs and supervisors. Jack had once heard Sy tell Manny, "There is no such thing as 'off the record' with a staff sergeant."

Despite a reputation as a fuck-up — from those who fell into the "hate Manny" side of things — Jack thought Manny was a solid guy, the type who, when he gave his friendship, gave it without reservations or conditions.

And, from what Jack had heard around the change room, Manny was also near the top of the list of coppers you wanted at your side during a punch-up. Manny was a big guy. Standing about six-two, he was ... beefy would be an apt description. He was a regular in the Bullpen and didn't slack off when it came to lifting heavy, but he was also a regular at the vending machines in the lunchroom.

They lined up by 302, a set of partners on either side. Or, in this case, one set of partners and Manny with his assigned escort. Sure enough, they could hear a male voice, not yelling but certainly sounding pissed, and a female crying in the background.

Manny turned the knob and pushed on the door. Locked. He shrugged and banged on the door. No polite knocking required. "Well, if no one answers, at least I get to kick a door in."

"Who is it?" the male voice barked through the door.

"Police!" Manny barked back. "Open the door!"

Locks rattled and the door opened, but not in invitation. The owner of the voice stood in the gap between door and jamb. Mid-twenties, five-ten with an average build and both hands out of sight, one beyond the frame, the other behind the door. His face was flushed and carried a thin sheen of sweat.

"What do you want?" He looked left and right. "Four of you. Jesus Christ!"

The crying was louder with the door open.

"Got a complaint of a domestic," Manny stated as he stepped forward. "Got to check to make sure everyone's okay." Manny pushed past the man and into the apartment.

Jack was right behind him and made sure the man's hands were empty when they came into view.

The apartment was a neat one-bedroom with old wood floors, tastefully decorated but lacking what Karen would call a "feminine influence." There was a young woman sitting on the black leather couch crying softly but trying to stifle her tears as she viewed the police with a mixture of relief and apprehension. Manny took the male off to the side to speak with him and Jack headed toward the woman.

Sy stopped him. "It's their call, Jack. Let Boris talk to her."

Boris waddled over to her with a greasy smile on his face. "Come on into the kitchen with me, sweetheart, so we can have a private chat." Smooth as congealed margarine.

Sy motioned Jack down the apartment's short hall. While Sy checked the bedroom, Jack poked his head into the bathroom to make sure no one was hiding.

Sy tapped Jack on the shoulder and crooked a finger for him to come into the bedroom. Grinning, Sy quietly slid open a drawer in the dresser and reached into it. He came up with a small bag of white powder. He put a finger to his lips and waved Jack out of the room.

"No one else in the apartment," Sy announced when they got back to the living room.

"I could have fucking told you that." The man didn't seem happy about having four cops in his home.

"Hey, you're talking to me." Manny rapped his memo book on the man's head to gain his attention. "And there's no need to use foul language."

The man opened his mouth, then snapped it shut. He glared at Manny and rubbed his forehead.

As if Manny hit him that hard.

"Now, Mr. Thompson, who is this woman?"

"Just a friend," the man muttered.

"Uh-huh," Manny muttered back, completely unconvinced. "And her name is . . . ?"

Thompson didn't answer. He glanced about his apartment as if he hoped to find an exit he was previously unaware of. There wasn't one, just four cops, and the big one in front of him had a *Don't fuck with me* expression on his face.

"I don't know her name," he confessed. "She's just some fu — a hooker I just picked up. I don't care what she says, I didn't lay a hand on her."

"Then why is she crying?"

"I don't know." He sounded defensive. "We had a disagreement about the price, that's all."

"And that red mark I saw on her cheek? You wouldn't happen to have anything to do with that, would you?" Manny put his book away and his expression had progressed to *You're pissing me off.* Most coppers had a special loathing for men who beat on women and unfortunately for Thompson the three facing him — like most but not all — considered prostitutes women.

"I don't care what she says," Thompson repeated. "I didn't do anything. You going to take some skanky whore's word over mine?"

"That skanky whore is somebody's daughter, buddy, and my mother would be disgusted with me if I let some gutless coward get away with hitting a woman." Manny appeared ready to mete out his version of justice right there and then.

Apparently, Thompson could read body language and wisely decided to keep his mouth shut. He checked the room once more for that misplaced exit. Still just the one, and Jack and Sy were between him and it, Jack standing with arms folded and Sy in a casual parade rest stance, his hands — and the baggy of white powder — behind his back.

Boris and the woman came out of the little kitchen. Her tears had stopped, but her red, puffy eyes matched the fading mark — it looked like a handprint to Jack — on her left cheek.

"She doesn't want to proceed with charges," Boris announced and managed to look disappointed.

"Uh-huh," Sy grunted with little conviction. "I'm sure you did your best to convince her to."

"Hey, not my fault if she doesn't want to." Boris shrugged, rippling the fat in his jowls.

The woman had her head down and edged past Sy and Jack to escape the apartment. Sy gently placed a hand on her arm. "Miss, are you sure you don't want to charge him?"

She nodded, a sharp little head bob. "I'm sure." Her voice was no more than a whisper.

"All right, then." Sy stepped aside and she fled into the hall.

Jack darted after her, catching up to her just outside the door. "Excuse me, miss. Can I talk to you for a sec?"

The woman — more of a girl now that he saw her up close — stopped but kept casting distressed looks down the hall to the stairs. Her hair was a reddish blond, cut short to frame her gentle face. Her clothes — short shorts and a white tee tied beneath her breasts — were clean and new.

"You're new at . . . the profession, aren't you?"

His tone held no accusation or threat and she must have taken this as a good sign. She stopped eyeing the stairs with desperate hope and faced him, not quite meeting his eyes. She nodded.

"Look, I'm not going to give you a lecture or any grief, okay? Just some advice. There are guys out there who will spot you as new and take advantage of that, like this piece of shit did. Never go back to a john's place. It's too dangerous; you don't know what you're walking into. All right?"

She nodded again, this time meeting his eyes. "Sure."

"What's your name?" He smiled disarmingly, then raised his hands when she gave him a suspicious look. "Just asking, that's all."

"Star." She hesitated, then, "Cindy."

"Well, Cindy, there are some hotels in the area that'll rent out rooms by the hour. There's also a sex workers' phone number you can call. They can probably give you better advice than I can. And that's it."

"Thanks." She turned to go, then stopped. "What's going to happen to him?"

Jack smiled again. "Oh, I'm pretty sure he's not going to get off all that lightly."

She touched her cheek and winced. "Good." She took a few steps, then stopped once more. "Can I ask your name?"

"Jack. Nice and simple. The name, that is."

She smiled and the sight of it saddened him. He figured her smile wouldn't be that open and innocent for long. "Thank you,

Jack," she said and walked away.

Jack went into the apartment.

"So, you're saying she never left the living room, not even to use the bathroom?" Sy had taken over questioning Thompson. Manny looked interested; he knew Sy was up to something. Boris looked bored.

"No, never," Thompson answered irritably. With Cindy out of the apartment and the chances of assault charges gone with her, he must have been feeling pretty secure and impatient to get back to whatever it was he did when he wasn't beating on hookers. "What difference does it make?"

Sy shrugged, just a good-old-boy, not-too-bright copper. "Seems strange to me, that's all. You didn't take her into the bedroom? That's what you brought her here for, wasn't it?"

Thompson was disgusted at the suggestion. "I didn't want her in my bed." He sighed melodramatically and lifted his eyes skyward as if to ask what he had done to be plagued by such stupid cops. "No," he stated definitively. "She never went into the kitchen, bathroom or bedroom."

"So, I guess that means this is yours." Sy produced the bag of powder from behind his back and Thompson's face went sickly pale beneath his fashionable tan. "I'll take that as a yes. Manny, would you do the honours?"

"You bet." A grin split Manny's face as he popped open his handcuff pouch.

"You can't do this!" Thompson protested even as Manny snapped on the cuffs. Realization dawned in his eyes. "You fucking prick! You didn't have a warrant. That's illegal."

Sy got into Thompson's face and Manny had to hold him so he couldn't backpedal. "So's hitting a woman," he snarled. "Count yourself lucky you don't have to go to the hospital first."

Jack didn't know if Thompson considered himself lucky or not, but he didn't utter a single word on the way to the station.

"That little crybaby cokehead you brought in says you searched his place without a warrant." Sergeant Johanson blew cigarette smoke into a lavender sky.

Summer twilight in Toronto could linger so long it sometimes felt like it was going to stay around to watch the sun come up. Tonight the sun had burnt the western sky a fiery gold and the underbellies of the clouds were deepening from indigo to purple. It was a beautiful colour, somehow comforting and serene.

"Probably because I did." Sy had joined the sergeant for a smoke, enjoying one of his infrequent cigarillos. He didn't seem concerned that he had just confessed to committing an illegal search and arrest to a supervisor.

But on the other hand, Johanson didn't seem at all surprised by the admission. "How come?" he asked after another drag.

"The little fuck brought a young hooker home and smacked her around. She just wanted to get the fuck out, so we couldn't charge him for the assault. I found the coke, so . . ." He shrugged. *Business as usual.*

"Figured it was something like that." Johanson crushed out his cigarette. "Take it easy, Sy. Warren, you listen to what this mutt says and you'll do okay. 'Night, guys."

"That's the friendliest I've ever seen him," Jack commented after the door had closed behind Johanson.

"Darcy's okay, just a man of few words. You can trust him."

"I gather."

Sy snorted. "Don't go thinking I tell every sergeant when I cut some corners. Hell, as far as Boris knows, the coke was sitting on Thompson's dresser like he planned to have some after doing the hooker. I don't trust that fat fucker as far as I can piss." He gazed at the darkening sky. "Going to be a nice night. Darcy and I worked together down here before he transferred out. When he got his stripes, they shipped him back to the old homestead. Normally, I wouldn't tell you to go to a sergeant if you fuck up, but you can go to Darcy. Just be honest and he'll try to help you. Try to con him. . . . Well, there's worse ways to die, but I can't think of any right now."

Jack belched out some Diet Coke while Sy blew smoke.

"You know, all that artificial sweetener crap isn't good for you."

"And those things are?"

Sy studied the cigarillo smoking between his fingers. "Probably not, but who gives a fuck, right? You only live once, so you might as well enjoy it."

"Cheers to that."

A few moments later, in the car and cruising up Jarvis Street, Sy had to clear something with Jack. "You know how I mentioned during the workout about 51 changing people?"

"Uh-huh. Whoa, she's nice."

Sy followed his partner's lead and copped a stare at the prostitute working at the corner of Gerrard. The tall blonde in a miniskirt and halter top twiddled her fingers at them. Jack waved back.

"Yeah, she's one of the better ones," Sy agreed. "In the winter, she'll wear a full-length fur coat with just a bikini on underneath and flash you as you drive by."

"Cool. That's one reason to look forward to winter. What were you saying about 51 changing guys?"

"Oh, right. Fuck, I see a nice pair of legs and I forget what I'm saying."

"It happens to people your age."

"Fuck you, grasshopper. What I was saying was that 51 can change you. I don't know if the division attracts this type of copper or creates it, but a lot of guys see all the shit that goes on down here and take the attitude that, since the criminals don't have to follow any rules, why should we? Now, I'm the first one to admit that sometimes you have to cut corners, bend the rules, however you want to say it, in order to get the job done."

"Like today with the cocaine," Jack suggested.

Sy nodded. "Exactly. Are you okay with that?"

He gave Sy one of his own snorts. "Absolutely. That guy deserved it. I mean, I wouldn't be doing that all the time, but I guess sometimes the ends do justify the means."

"The problem is some guys start to handle every call, every arrest, that way. Some are lazy and don't want to bother with all the paperwork and some just work that way. As far as I'm concerned, there's a huge difference between snooping around some asshole's room and planting the evidence."

"You've seen guys do that?"

Sy was quiet for a while, then said, "There was a time, Jack, when I was one of those guys."

He fell silent again and Jack didn't push him. If he wanted to talk, he would. Eventually, he did.

"I let the division and the work change me. I didn't know it at the time, though. I thought I was just being efficient at policing. Why spend hours, days or even weeks building a case against a dealer just to have it fall apart in court because he didn't happen to have the crack on him when you pinched him? So much easier to make sure the evidence is going to be there. And while you're at it, might as well give the asshole a bit of a tune-up 'cause the courts sure as hell aren't going to punish him enough."

Jack didn't know what to say. This was a new side to his partner and he wasn't sure what to make of it.

"Yeah, I know," Sy said, catching Jack's look. He shook his head sadly. "I ended up in a pretty bad place. As far as I was concerned, if you weren't a cop, you were an asshole. I'm not sure if that attitude cost me my first marriage, but I'm damn sure it killed the second." He laughed bitterly. "Made a shitload of money, though, in overtime and court. I was in court constantly; every arrest I made went to trial 'cause I had a reputation for . . .

fabrication. Trust me, Jack, once you lose your credibility in court, it's almost impossible to get it back."

Sy glanced at him and Jack still didn't know what to say. What could he say?

Sy seemed to understand. "All I'm saying is keep an eye on yourself. If you get to the point where you have more in common with the assholes than the cops, it's time to get out. 'When you look into an abyss, the abyss also looks into you,'" he quoted.

"'Whoever fights monsters should see to it that in the process he does not become a monster.'"

Sy smiled at Jack. "I'm impressed."

Jack shrugged. "I took a philosophy course in university."

"You get what I'm trying to say, though?"

"I do, Sy, and thanks. So endeth the lesson?"

"So endeth the lesson."

And just in time. *"5106, 5108, I need you to head over to 52 Division to help out with a stabbing on Richmond east of John. 52 has cars attending the scene, but they need units to check the area for the suspect. Time, 2204."*

Sy hit the lights and swung through a red light onto Wellesley before Jack had time to answer the dispatcher. "10-4, dispatch. Can we get a description?"

"Suspect is a male, black, shaved head, wearing a silver shirt and black pants. Last seen running southbound through the parking lot. Suspect possibly armed with a knife. Use caution."

"A silver shirt? Sounds like the guy was out clubbing."

"Yup. Probably an argument over a girl." Sy sped down Church, roof lights bouncing off store windows, freezing pedestrians in brief flashes of illumination. Just after ten, traffic was still heavy and Sy wove nonchalantly around cars when the drivers were too stupid to get out of the way.

"C'mon, move!" Jack shouted at the driver of a BMW who figured making his left turn was more important than giving room to a police car. "Can't these morons see the lights or hear the siren?"

"Ah, grasshopper. You're assuming the drivers are intelligent enough to be driving in the first place." He braked hard and laid on the air horn as a pedestrian bopping along to whatever was on his iPod stepped in front of the scout car. The pedestrian — buffed, tanned and wearing a mesh tank top to display his buffness — let out a girlish scream Jack could hear over the siren. Mr. Buffness dove to the sidewalk; Sy was on the gas instantly and as the scout car accelerated, Jack made eye contact with the man and shook his head at his idiocy.

"A buddy of mine once made history's greatest proclamation," Sy cited offhandedly, unperturbed he had almost flattened Mr. Buffness. "Kevin said, 'Never underestimate the stupidity of the general public.'"

"Your friend may have been on to something."

Sy snorted. "Someone proves him right every day."

"Units attending the stabbing in 52, please see the text of the call for an update."

Jack pulled up the call and scrolled through the details. "Looks like it's been upgraded to a homicide. Victim had his throat cut open and bled out at the scene."

"Nothing like too much alcohol and testosterone to ruin someone's evening. Where on Richmond was it?"

"In the parking lot on the south side just east of John. Suspect was last seen running south through the parking lot."

Sy squealed around the corner onto Richmond and goosed the car along the four-lane, one-way street. "If you had just offed someone and needed to disappear, where would you go? Assuming you didn't have a car parked somewhere."

"Some place where my silver disco shirt wouldn't stand out. Another club?"

Sy nodded agreement. "Or at least down to a club area where I could blend in with a crowd as I got the hell out of the area."

"King Street?"

Sy agreed. "King Street."

Richmond to University, University to King. Sy killed the lights and siren and merged with the other cars. The street and sidewalks were heavy with traffic, people enjoying a night of partying in the city's entertainment district. The area was a money-making hodgepodge of theatres, dance clubs and restaurants. Traffic was moving at a crawl, giving Jack and Sy ample opportunity to scan the hordes for their suspect. Sirens wailed to the north of them, but to the masses on King Street that was a world away.

"The patios are packed tonight," Sy observed. "Ah, to be sitting outside, enjoying a beer." He sounded wistful.

"Are you saying you'd rather be drinking on a patio than in a smelly police car searching fruitlessly for a murderer?"

"Hm. Let me think. . . ."

"Holy shit, Sy. I think we just passed him."

"Where?" Sy took his foot off the accelerator and cranked the rearview mirror to scan the north sidewalk. "I don't see a silver shirt."

"It's black now." Jack was hunching down in the seat and using the side mirror. "He's walking east and he just shoulder-checked us. It's a black short-sleeved dress shirt, but when we passed him it flapped open and the inside is bright silver. The rest matches: shaved head, black pants."

"Definitely worth a look. Good eyes, Jack."

At John Street, Sy pulled a quick U-turn without using his lights, earning him more than a few rich expletives from other drivers. They backtracked on King, watching both sides of the road in case their man had crossed over. Jack pulled on his Kevlar gloves and dropped the seat belt. His heart was thumping and he found himself grinning with excitement.

Getting to be quite the adrenalin junkie.

"That him?" Sy pointed to the left and ahead of them.

"Yup," Jack confirmed. "Walking a bit faster now, too. What do you think?"

"I think it's a shitty place to confront someone armed with a knife. Too many fucking people around."

Traffic ground to a sudden halt. The Princess of Wales Theatre had just let out, dumping its mass of patrons into the street. The sidewalk ahead of their suspect was clogged with people.

"Fuck it," Sy snarled, jamming the car into park. "Let's take him on foot. See if we can nab him while the crowd's holding him up."

They jumped out of the car and dodged around cars to the sidewalk. Jack was on the portable, advising radio of their situation.

"We just walk up quickly, each take an arm and it's done. Nice and neat. No one gets hurt and if it's not our man, no harm done."

"No problem," Jack agreed as they closed the distance.

Their target was about forty feet ahead of them, trying to work his way through the crowd, and his efforts seemed a little too anxious for someone just trying to pass through. The throng slowed the cops, as well, but not as much; people tended to move for a police officer a bit more quickly than just another face in the crowd. It also helped that they weren't being all that gentle in their efforts to move people.

They were within twenty feet when the suspect glanced over his shoulder. And bolted. He plowed through the crowd like a running back breaking sloppy tackles. Jack and Sy were right after him, moving fast in the wake of displaced bodies.

"Move! Move!" Jack shoved people out of his way as he tried to close the gap.

The suspect didn't look back again; he knew the police were close. He kept his head tucked between his hunched shoulders and simply bulled his way through the crowds. Then, suddenly, like that determined running back, he broke free.

Jack was right behind him, lunging free of the clinging mob. His gloved fingers swiped the back of the suspect's shirt — he noticed the raised seams of the inside-out shirt — and then the suspect was sprinting away from him. Jack lurched forward several steps, pinwheeling his arms to save his balance, and managed not to go down, but the suspect built a lead. Jack righted himself and took off in chase.

"Get him, Jack! I'll put it over!"

Cool. With Sy alerting the dispatcher, Jack could forget about the radio and concentrate on the chase. His legs were already starting to burn, the muscles protesting a sprint so soon after a heavy leg workout. He was going to need all he had.

The suspect widened the gap.

Damn it, I'm losing him!

Jack didn't hear any sirens, the copper's modern version of the cavalry bugle, and wondered if Sy still had his radio on 51 band. If he did, then any information he gave had to be passed over to this division's dispatcher before it got to the cars. It would slow things down; it could prove dangerous.

The suspect blew along King, steadily pulling away from Jack, but then the good guys caught a break. There was a sudden blast of a car horn and the sharp screech of tires locking up on asphalt as the suspect raced across a narrow street that T-intersected with King. The southbound car braked so hard the front bumper almost touched the road.

The suspect threw himself onto the braking car's hood, then slid across — Jack would have been impressed if it didn't piss him off so much — but the car's sudden stop dumped him onto the road and he tumbled out onto King Street. Jack hoped he'd get mashed by another car. No such luck. He rolled a couple of times, then was back on his feet and moving like a bat out of hell.

Jack had made up some ground, but he was still nowhere near to grabbing the bastard. Sirens were now wailing in the night, coming closer, but if anything, the sound of approaching police support only added to the suspect's speed.

Fuck, he's fast!

Jack's legs wanted to stop, threatened to cramp, but he pushed on. No way was he going to give up on a murder pinch. He'd collapse first.

Then the suspect disappeared, cutting through a parking lot squeezed into a tiny space between buildings. Jack followed and saw the suspect almost through the lot and heading for the next street. Jack ripped out his radio. Sy was too far back to know Jack's location. "Suspect . . . north in a parking lot . . . not sure of . . . exact location." Why couldn't this chase have been in 51, where he knew all the streets and laneways?

Jack pounded along, feeling the weight of the belt and vest with every stride. His legs were done, beyond pain. Each breath he drew burned his lungs. And still he ran.

The suspect cut east and seconds later Jack burst onto a little one-way road, hardly more than a driveway, lined by the ass ends of old commercial buildings and a tiered parking lot. The suspect was still in sight — the gap was probably fifty feet — and nearing the next major cross street. University? No, too soon for that.

Fuck! I wish I knew where I was!

Again the suspect vanished, again by cutting sharply from his course. A few more quick changes in direction and Jack would lose him for sure. Finally, he reached the spot where the suspect had turned: a laneway that opened onto King Street. Jack could see Roy Thompson Hall gleaming artistically in the streetlights. The suspect was nowhere to be seen.

Fuck!

Jack held up at the mouth of the laneway. The suspect might not be in sight because he had already reached King, or he might be hunkered down somewhere ahead of Jack. Running blindly down the laneway could get Jack killed.

"Suspect . . . now . . . southbound . . . through alley . . . to King." God, it hurt to breathe, let alone talk. "Sy . . . might be . . . coming your . . . way."

The laneway was a black pit between two tall buildings, the

darkness broken only by intermittent lights high up on the walls. Jack tucked his radio in its pouch and drew his gun.

The mouth of the alley — a driveway, he realized — was narrow, barely wide enough for a single car, but the wall on his left quickly opened up into a loading dock. He kept his right shoulder tight to the wall and took the dock quickly, his gun tracking with his eyes. The bay was only about knee high and except for a square metal box — tool bin? vent hood? — at its far end, it was empty. Nowhere for anyone to hide.

At the end of the dock, fifteen or twenty feet south, the driveway sprouted parking spaces and a trio of dumpsters. A lonely car sat next to the bins like a forgotten cousin. Between the square metal box and the dumpsters was a shitload of hiding places. Two lights high on the wall, watching over the area like sentinel gargoyles, slashed the deep shadows with geometric precision.

Jack reached for his flashlight with his left hand. Cradling his gun hand in the crook of his forearm and the back of his hand, he thumbed the compact light on. Its intense beam stabbed at the shadows, ripping away their secrets. Slowly, he edged down the lane, sure he was chasing nothing — but not sure enough.

"5106, are you still in foot pursuit?"

Jack swept the dumpsters a final time as best he could from his present angle before trading his flashlight for his radio. "Negative, dispatch. Suspect last seen southbound through a laneway toward King Street. Chances are he's heading east on King. That was the direction he was going when we started chasing him."

"10-4, '06. 5207 is investigating one at King and University. Can you head over there to see if it is our suspect?"

Cool! "You bet, dispatch. Let them know I'm heading over. PC Carter on the air? Sy, if you're out there, I'll meet you at King and University." He holstered his radio and gun and trotted down the lane.

Clang!

Jack whirled left, drawing smoothly as the brief metallic echoes died away in the man-made canyon. "Police! Don't move!"

Laughter from the gloom. "I think I will move, ass-wipe. Let you see the shit you just stepped in."

A bulk of darkness, not fifteen feet from Jack, detached itself from the shadows between the dumpster and the car. The man Jack had been chasing was holding Sy, using him as a shield. Sy's left arm was behind his back and from the way his back was arched in pain, the suspect must have had it wrenched up in some sort of arm bar. With his other hand, the suspect held a knife against Sy's throat.

Jack's vision collapsed into a tunnel focused on the suspect and Sy. Details leapt out at him: the suspect hunched down behind Sy's right shoulder; a single eye peering out beneath a bare scalp glistening with sweat; a flash of silver as his shirt collar flickered in an errant breeze; a black latex glove on the suspect's right hand; the thin blade of the butterfly knife along Sy's throat, the blade gleaming in the stark light; Sy's gun in its holster, his right arm at his side; Sy grimacing in pain, but his eyes calm, confident in his partner.

"That was stupid, piggy, kicking the bin like that. Scared me so much I almost cut you open." Then, to Jack, "Your turn not to move, ass-wipe. If you reach for your radio, I'll slit open his throat quick as can be." Jack kept both hands on his gun. "That's good. Now drop your gun. Drop it, ass-wipe, or I cut him." A slight pressure and blood seeped onto the blade, dark as death in the shadow, vibrantly alive as it spilled into the light.

"You do that and I splatter the wall behind you with your brains. Drop the blade, do it *now!*"

"How you going to do that, ass-wipe?" Silver Shirt pulled Sy closer and all but disappeared. Sy groaned and rose up higher on his toes. "Don't you be reaching for your gun either, piggy, or I might have to slice me some ham."

This guy must be strong to keep Sy in such a hold. Jack didn't recall him being big enough to manhandle Sy. *A trained fighter, then. Dangerous.*

"Tell you what, man. I'll make you a deal. Let him go and I'll let you take off. You outran me before, so you know I can't catch you. Just go."

Silver Shirt's laugh was sharp, abrasive. The laugh of a man wound too tight, a man capable of murder. Again.

"I don't think so, piggy. 'Course I can run faster'n you. But you'll just shoot me in the back. Fucking pigs always shooting brothers in the back."

It was Jack's turn to laugh. A bare snicker, but he had to convince this madman. "This is Canada, bud, not L.A. We're not allowed to shoot at people who run away from us." *And as soon as you let Sy go, I'll drop you before you have a chance to move.* Jack kept the thought from his face, but Sy would know what Jack was thinking. He just had to make sure Silver Shirt didn't.

As he bargained, Jack eased to his right and Silver Shirt mimicked his movement, which put his back to the north end of the lane.

"See, man? Take off up the alley. Nothing in your way. You heard my dispatcher. They think they have you over on University, so there's no one up that way to stop you. I swear to you, man, I won't chase you." Jack lowered his gun, the barrel aimed near Sy's feet. At this range, he wouldn't need sights to put three in the guy's chest.

No answer. Silver Shirt's face, what little of it Jack could see, was in Sy's shadow. The left side of Sy's face, sweat-soaked but still calm, was leached of colour by the harsh light. The face of a corpse. Jack forced the image away. Still no answer. Was Silver Shirt considering? Was he close to accepting Jack's offer?

"C'mon, man. Just let him go and run. I swear I won't chase you."

"I know you won't."

The words whispered out of the darkness and Jack knew what they meant.

"*No!*"

The blade flashed in the light, slashing open Sy's throat. Blood sprayed, painting the night vivid scarlet. The suspect shoved Sy into Jack's arms. Hot blood splashed Jack's face; he tasted its salty bitterness in his mouth. Sy clutched at his throat, a futile attempt to stem the blood. Jack sagged beneath the sudden weight but let Sy collapse, controlling the fall as best he could.

Sy fought Jack, not wanting to lie down. Jack shoved him to the asphalt with both hands, dimly aware he had let go of his gun. He was unarmed. Was Silver Shirt still here, waiting to spill Jack's blood? Jack was defenceless. If he died, he couldn't help Sy.

He glanced up the alley in time to see a dark man-shape silhouetted under the street lights. It darted around the corner and disappeared.

Sy clutched at Jack with a blood-covered hand. His other hand was clamped on his throat and blood still fountained up between his fingers. His face was splashed with blood, eerily bright against his paling skin. His eyes were wide with fear but still alive. Still alive.

"Calm down, Sy. Let me help you."

Jack tried to move his partner's hand, but Sy refused to let go.

"Sy, you have to let go so I can see. I can stop the bleeding. Just trust me, let go. Please, Sy, let go. Please."

Jack met Sy's eyes and the fear was under control — not gone, but controlled. Sy nodded and slid his hand from under Jack's, sliding free with incredible ease, their skin heavily oiled with Sy's blood.

Jack pressed his fingers into the wound, seeking. The blood was bright and pulsing free. The straight razor had hit an artery. If he could find it, pinch it shut, Sy would make it. Jack searched blindly. There was too much blood. His fingers were drowning in it.

He fought for Sy's life with one hand and ripped his radio free with the other. "Assist PC!" he screamed. "Assist PC! My partner's throat has been cut. I need an ambulance here now! Put a rush on it!" He released the talk button, knowing somewhere deep in his mind that if he let the panic consume him Sy was dead. Simple as that. Panic and Sy dies.

"5106, what's your location? I need your location." The dispatcher's words were steady, but Jack could tell she had heard the fear in his voice: it echoed faintly in hers.

Jack groped, feeling a pulsing flow with his fingers. Find the artery, find the cut. "In a laneway north of King," he managed. "West of . . . west of. . . ." *West of what? Where the fuck am I?* "University!" he shouted into the radio. "In a laneway off King, west of University. The suspect cut my partner's throat. I'm trying to stop the bleeding. We need an ambulance here now. Right now!"

"10-4. Ambulance on the way. Hang on, '06, hang —" Jack dropped the radio, losing the rest of her message. He added his left hand to the search.

Sy thrashed beneath him but kept his hands away from Jack's. "Sorry, Sy. I know it hurts, but I have to find the . . . the cut." *Don't say artery, don't tell him that.* "Lie still, Sy. Just lie still, please."

Jack followed the pulse of the blood as it spurted against his fingers, a pulse that was steadily becoming weaker. There! A cord that felt like a slick, muscular hose. It was the source of the pulse and he clamped his fingers to it, pinching its sides together. He could feel it throbbing, a living — living! — heartbeat beneath his fingertips. The pulse pushed against his fingers faintly. Faintly, but it pushed.

The blood in the wound receded, a terrible tide retreating. It drained away, no longer swallowing his fingers, no longer adding to the pool surrounding them.

"I've got it, Sy. I've stopped the bleeding." He leaned down and stared into Sy's eyes, just inches away. "You're going to be all right, partner. I've got you."

Sy nodded and, amazingly, smiled.

Jack grinned back. "You ain't leaving me to work with Boris."

Sy smiled again, at the feeble joke. His face was pale, a deathly white, and his mouth and chin were smeared with red.

Sirens screamed in the distance, a chorus of avenging angels.

"Hear that, Sy? Help's on the way. Hang in there, partner. Hang on."

The pulse beneath his fingers was gone. But that was okay, wasn't it? He had the artery pinched shut. The blood had nowhere to go. It would only pulse if the blood was moving, right? Right?

Sy convulsed under him, a sudden heave that arched his back off the ground. Jack almost lost his grip on the artery. He pushed down on Sy's chest with his free hand, frantic to hold him still. "Calm down, Sy, calm down. Don't move, help's on the way. Don't move, help's on the way," he chanted, not knowing he was doing so.

As quickly as it hit, the convulsion passed. Sy dropped flat and the sudden release caught Jack by surprise. His chest slammed into Sy's. Blood squirted from where it had collected under Sy's vest and splashed against Jack's hand. But Jack's grip was solid. He would die before loosening his hold on his partner's life.

The sirens were louder, almost on top of them.

"Hang on, Sy. Damn it, hang on! The ambulance is almost here."

Jack felt a shudder run through Sy. Sy raised his head, stared at Jack with eyes wide with fear . . . and knowing. His hands rose to clutch at Jack's arms.

"You're going to be okay, old man," Jack whispered. Unfelt tears washed streaks through the blood drying on his cheeks. "You have to hang on. Please, Sy. Please."

Tires screeched on pavement. A powerful light stabbed into the laneway, blasting away the darkness. Voices shouted.

A second shudder, no more that a ripple this time, quivered along Sy's body. His lips twitched in what might have been a smile, then fell slack. His head splashed in the blood puddled under it. His hands lost their grip, fell free. More splashes.

"No, Sy, no."

Jack squeezed that muscular hose harder than ever. Sy couldn't die as long as he hung on. As long as he hung on. . . .

He never knew who finally pried his hand free.

Sunday, 27 August
1400 hours

The funeral was held four days later on a searing afternoon. Thousands of police officers from across Canada and the United States defied the heat in dress uniforms to pay their respects. Officers from Britain, Australia and other countries around the world sent representatives. It was a global display of police unity, a declaration of the price all officers were willing to pay and a statement of defiance to those who would see the world in chaos.

Ranks of officers stood solemnly outside the church listening to the service over speakers; inside, people stood shoulder to shoulder with bowed heads. Friend, co-worker or stranger, they had all come to bid farewell to a fallen brother, to support those personally touched by the tragedy and to support themselves: when one officer falls, all officers feel the loss.

The day was not without its victims. Men and women, indomitable in spirit, collapsed, succumbing to the heat or to overwhelming grief. Yet, where a few fell, others, be they officers, medics or civilians, helped them to stand and, more often than not, return to the ranks to resume the vigil.

At the conclusion of the service, the same officers who had braved the heat marched to line the route from church to cemetery. Away from church grounds, citizens approached officers to offer condolences, prayers and words of gratitude. Water was freely given, gratefully accepted. On a day of tremendous grief, the union between police and those they protected was at its strongest.

Amid an ocean of solidarity and brotherhood, Jack walked alone. Sy's cap, the cloth brushed a lustrous black, the brim and badge polished to gleaming brightness, lay on a cushion in his arms as he marched behind the casket, a solitary figure. Karen was somewhere in the crowd, her parents with her to show a rare moment of compassion and understanding for their daughter's husband, but still, he was alone.

It shouldn't be his hat. He threw it in the trunk of the car every day. It should be something that meant something to him, shows who he was.

Jack had a sudden urge to fling the hat over the heads of the officers lining the road. He could picture it spinning through the air, the sun flashing off the badge. His hands twitched beneath the cushion, then were still.

The intense August sun glared down on him, burning him from above and baking the asphalt beneath him. As much as the sun punished him, it was a guttering candle compared to the firestorm of grieving guilt within him. If he had run faster, pushed himself harder, reacted quicker. If, if, if . . .

Beneath the grief, under the layers of sorrow, lay something else. It waited patiently, knowing it would have its time once the wounds inside Jack began to heal, to lose their raw tenderness. Now was the time for Jack to say goodbye to Simon. Now was the time for grief.

But soon, it would be time for rage.

Sunday, 10 September
1700 hours

Jack was on the deck barbecuing chicken breasts when Karen came back from her run. She had on a sweatshirt and shorts, but no matter how good her legs looked, she wouldn't be staying in shorts for long, as the air had a definite autumn feel to it. Not briskness, exactly, but a memory of it. Summer was on the way out, with fall eagerly awaiting its turn.

Jack liked the fall; it was his favourite time of year. Cool air, crisp nights, a welcome relief from air-conditioned life. Winter, on the other hand, he could do without. If fall went from October to April, he'd be perfectly happy. Karen would prefer summer year-round. How she had survived growing up in northern Ontario he didn't know, but it did explain her aversion to winter. Lucky for her, her parents had decided to move down to Toronto so her father could pursue his academic career.

She came over and gave him a kiss on the ear. She tugged the sleeve of his T-shirt. "Aren't you cold?"

"Not now." He wrapped an arm around her, held her close. "You know the sight of you always warms me up."

"Well, if you weren't busy playing chef, I'd invite you to join me in the shower."

"If you can wait a few minutes, these are almost done and I'll gladly wash your back and any other parts of you that are dirty." He nuzzled her neck, nipping playfully at the ticklish spot below her ear. She squirmed in his grip but didn't move away.

In the time since Sy's death, Karen had given him space when he needed to grieve privately, a sympathetic ear when he needed to vent and had been a willing partner when he needed love.

Even her parents had supported him in their own way: they had kept contact at the funeral very brief and then stayed away. No Sunday dinners, no unexpected visits. Jack could get used to that.

"Are we having company I'm unaware of?" she asked, gesturing to the half dozen breasts on the grill.

"Since the barbecue was on, I thought I'd do some extra. We can use them in our lunches at work."

She stiffened. "You're going back to work?"

"Yeah. I thought I'd give it a try tomorrow." He switched the tongs for his beer. He had been drinking a lot lately: more beer but also coffee, water, whatever was available. He found having something in his hand oddly comforting. It gave him something to fiddle with, helped keep his thoughts from wandering too far down a dark alley.

"When did you decide this?"

He set the beer down and started flipping chicken. "I've been thinking about it for the last few days. Figure it's time."

Karen stepped back, pulling free of his arm and crossing hers.

"And when were you going to tell me about this?"

"I'm telling you now. Come on, Karen, you knew I was going back eventually. I can't stay home for the rest of my life."

"I know, but it hasn't even been three weeks since Simon died." It had taken her two weeks before she could say those words to him; he knew she feared hearing them would tear open wounds not even close to being healed.

"I know that, Karen. But I can't sit around here all day with nothing to do. Now that you're back to work, I realize how big and empty this house is with you gone. I can only work out and clean so much." He smiled at his little joke and was relieved to see her smile back.

"But I've gotten used to the house being so clean." She relaxed her defensive stance, even moved closer to lay her hands on his chest. "If you think you're ready, then do it."

He kissed the tip of her nose. "Thanks, hon. I appreciate it."

"Are you going back to 51?"

"Where else would I go?" he asked, genuinely perplexed at her question.

"I thought . . ." She shook her head. "Never mind. You'll put in your transfer tomorrow, though. Right?"

Again he gave her a puzzled look. "I'm not transferring any-where."

"What?" She clutched his shirt and pulled him to face her. "You said you weren't going back there. You promised me!"

"Ouch! Careful, hon, you got some hair." He put his hands on hers. "I never said I was going to leave 51. I said I wasn't going back for a while, that I was taking some time off. That's all."

"This is bullshit!" She yanked her hands free and stalked away, her back to him, then rounded on him. "How can you go back there? Simon's dead and it could have been you!" She was angry and fighting tears.

"I'm a cop, Karen. That could happen wherever I work."

"Bullshit! You said when you were in 32 you never once

pulled your gun out. Now every damn story you tell me is either a fight or a gun arrest thing."

"Gunpoint arrest," he offered.

"I don't fucking care!" she screamed. Her tears were flowing. "Why do you want to go back there? Why?"

He shrugged. "I like it there. I feel like I'm accomplishing something instead of just writing reports or giving out tickets."

"That's bullshit and you know it," she threw at him. "It's some macho thing, isn't it? You have to be the big, tough cop, don't you? Even if it kills you."

"It's not going to kill me." He knew she was scared, but he knew better than to say it.

"Can you promise me that? You can't and you know it." She roughly palmed away her tears. "What if I say I won't be here if you go back?"

His stomach clenched. "Don't say that. Don't even joke about it."

"What if I'm not joking? Me or 51, Jack. Which is it?"

"You know that isn't even a decision. Of course it's you." He dropped his eyes and softly added, "But I'd hate that you made me make that choice."

"I know." The anger was gone, but the tears remained. "Go back. But don't bother calling me when you end up in the hospital." She walked into the house and closed the door behind her.

"Crap." Slump shouldered, Jack turned back to the barbecue and reached for the tongs; the chicken had started to burn.

Monday, 11 September
0652 hours

Jack was sitting in the staff sergeant's office — an extravagant designation for a room crowded by two desks and used primarily as a corridor from front counter to lunchroom — with the platoon's boss, Staff Sergeant O'Rourke. As far as staffs went, O'Rourke was one of the better ones. Tall and lean but with the beginnings of a desk gut, he had enough time on to have learned to let the sergeants and senior PCs run the shift. Yet he was still young enough to try to keep most of the shit that ran downhill from headquarters off his guys.

He was studying Jack, no doubt attempting to decide whether he was some of that down-rolling shit. "It's good to have you back, but I'll be honest, Jack, I'm leery of putting you back out on the road so soon."

"I know: it's only been three weeks. Trust me, I've heard that several times since I told my wife yesterday that I wanted to come back. But she's back at work, she's a schoolteacher, and I end up sitting around the house by myself. I've run out of things to keep me occupied."

O'Rourke nodded sagely. "I can appreciate that, which is why I'll let you back out, but —" he held up a cautionary finger "— on my terms. First, you go out as a special car. That way you can pick and choose the calls you want to go on. If you need some downtime, you can sit and relax. If all goes well, you can get back into the regular cars on evenings."

"No problem. I can handle that. Thanks, Staff."

Jack got up to leave, but O'Rourke put him back in the chair with a second finger. "And you go out as a two-man car."

"Come on, Staff, I don't need a babysitter."

"You ride shotgun, or you go home. No negotiating. You can pick your escort, though. Deal?"

Jack laughed. "A deal would suggest we negotiated."

"True, but . . ." O'Rourke shrugged.

"If Manny's in, I'll work with him."

That definitely astonished O'Rourke. "You want to work with Armsman?"

It was Jack's turn to shrug. "Manny's a good guy. I've done some calls with him and I like the way he works."

"It's your funeral. Oh, shit, sorry, Jack."

"It's okay, Staff. Actually, I'm getting a little tired of people treating me like I'm fragile or something." He snorted. "Maybe that's the real reason I came back: to be treated like any other copper." He paused, his hand on the doorknob. "Speaking of which, I don't think I can handle parade quite yet. All those sympathetic faces."

"I understand. I'll tell Armsman to meet you at the car. And Jack? I'm sorry about Sy."

"Yeah, me too." What else was there to say?

Jack was leaning on the scout car, sipping from a bottle of water, when Manny came out of the station. He spotted Jack and hustled over, an impossibly large duty bag banging against his leg.

"I thought only rookies carried bags that big," Jack commented when Manny dumped it in the trunk. The car settled noticeably. "What the hell is in it?"

"It's my crime-fighting kit," Manny said by way of explanation. He was sporting a shaved head — out of necessity, to judge from the faint hairline running across the top of his scalp — and a goatee. Goatees were, of course, prohibited in uniform, but beards were allowed, so Manny did what so many others did. He had a trickle of a beard running along the bottom of his jaw and up to his ears.

"No one given you flak about the goatee?"

Manny tried to look indignant. "Hey, it's a beard . . . technically."

"I guess. It makes you look like a professional wrestler."

"Gee, thanks, man." He sounded like he meant it. "Listen, Jack, the Staff told me you asked to work with me and I just want to say that I feel, you know, kind of privileged that you asked for me." He held his hand out.

Touched and a little embarrassed, Jack shook with him. "I just figure you don't deserve the reputation you've got."

"Thanks, man, but quitting time's a ways off. You might change your mind by then." Manny grinned and Jack couldn't help but smile back. Maybe it wouldn't be such a bad day after all.

"The Staff also tell you to drive?"

"Uh-huh."

"And to keep an eye on me?"

"That too."

"So you're to be my chauffeur and babysitter." Jack opened the passenger door. "Well, then, James," he decreed in a snooty voice, "once around the park and then to a coffee shop. Your charge needs his caffeine."

"Sure thing, man." Manny hopped — actually hopped — into the car. Was he old enough to babysit? "Where to, m'lord?"

Jack considered. "Any place but the Baker's Dozen at Wellesley and Sherbourne." He wasn't ready to face Sy's coffee spot just yet.

"I'll take you someplace special, then." He dropped the car into drive but hesitated before hitting the gas. "Jack, I just want to say I'm sorry about Sy. He was a good cop, man."

"Yeah, he was." God, how many more times was he going to hear how sorry people were? It was amazing how such an innocent phrase spoken in honest sympathy could hurt. He'd had enough of sympathy. Let's get over it and move on, folks.

Jack cleared them as Special 51 while Manny wove his way through morning traffic. Jack had experienced less darting and weaving on bumper cars. No bumps, though. Not yet, at least. In less time than Jack thought possible, they pulled up out front of the Second Cup at Church and Wellesley.

"This okay with you? I know some guys aren't comfortable around here. I can get you your coffee if you want."

"Relax, Manny. Gay Town doesn't scare me."

"Cool."

The wide stairs in front of the coffee shop were empty at this time of morning. The stairs, locally known as the Steps, were a popular hangout and meeting place for area residents. As Manny said, many coppers were uncomfortable — in some cases down-right terrified — about going into a coffee shop in the heart of the city's gay district.

The door was propped open to exploit the morning's relatively cool air and inside was dim and refreshingly free of conditioned air. A smattering of customers occupied a few tables, but at this time of day most people grabbed their morning commute coffee and left. As usual, two uniformed officers occasioned scrutiny and Jack caught one man giving Manny a prolonged — and favourable, if he had to guess — appraisal over the top of his newspaper. Manny didn't notice. Or chose not to.

"Ooh, a big, strapping policeman in my shop! Well, slap the handcuffs on me and call me a bad boy." The employee behind the counter pranced — pranced! — over from the pastry case to Manny. "I love the new look! Lemme feel, lemme feel," he squealed, hands out, wiggling his fingers like a hungry baby reaching for a bottle.

Grinning, Manny bowed over the counter and let the employee run his hands appreciatively over his shaven scalp. "Ooh, I love a man with a big, bald head."

"All right, that's enough." Manny laughed, straightening up. "Hey, Chris, how you doing, man?"

"Cool as always, dude, you know me."

They clasped hands over the counter.

"Chris, this is Jack. Chris is the owner here."

"They finally get smart and assign someone to keep you on a short leash?" Chris asked before reaching out to shake with Jack. "Sorry you're the one to get the job."

"It hasn't been too difficult yet."

"I'm sure it will be." Chris was short and on the stocky side, almost a squished-down version of Manny, including the clean scalp. His grip was sure and firm, completely at odds with the personality that had fondled Manny's head. "Hope we didn't frighten you back there."

Jack smiled. "Nope, but I was beginning to think I'd have to go wait in the car for him."

Chris laughed. "I keep hoping, but the man is hopelessly, utterly straight. What can I get you, gentlemen?"

"Coffee for me," Manny replied.

"The dark, right? What about you, Jack? Coffee?"

"Um, no. Tea would be good. Earl Grey if you have it." He couldn't say why, but the notion of coffee just didn't feel right. Maybe coffee on the job would go the way of the Baker's Dozen for now.

"That'll be easy to remember." Manny stiffened his voice, trying to sound authoritative. "'Tea, Earl Grey, hot.'"

"Well, at least your TV references are more up to date."

"What?"

Jack waved it off. "Never mind."

"Here you go, gentlemen." Chris waved Jack's offered money away. "No charge for our boys in blue. Or should I say black, now that you've changed shirt colours?"

Jack shrugged. "It's an old saying. Thanks for the tea. I appreciate it."

"Hey, someone has to offer the olive branch between our two communities. Might as well be me." The prance suddenly jumped back into his voice. "And if we get known as the place where the sexy policemen *come* —" he dropped a rather lavish wink "— to get their coffees, who am I to complain?"

Manny shook his head in mock disgust. "Play safe, Chris."

"I always do, sweetie. If you want, I could show you sometime." Seemed like Manny brought out the prancing side of Chris.

"You know I'm taken, man. Otherwise . . ."

"Yeah, yeah." The prance was gone. "Get out of here, you big tease."

"Excuse me, officer." The second staff member behind the counter spoke up as Jack passed by. He was tall and thin with the pale complexion of a true redhead. He had hung back timidly during Chris's banter but now hesitantly approached Jack. "I don't mean to bother you, but are you the officer whose partner was killed a few weeks ago?"

Blood, vivid and horrible, flashing through the night air.

Jack pushed the damning image away. "Yes. Yes, I am." *Don't say it. For the love of God, don't.*

"I recognized you from the news and I just wanted to say . . ." He faltered, swallowing nervously.

"You don't have —" Jack jumped in, hoping to prevent the unbearable words, but the kid found his nerve and pushed on.

"I just wanted to say how much we appreciate the work you do. All of you, I mean. I guess I just wanted to say, well, thank you."

Jack was speechless, not sure he had heard right. "Thank you," he managed after a moment. "We don't hear that nearly enough. Thank you."

The kid bobbed his head and shuffled away.

"Where to?" Manny asked when they were settled in the car.

"Cherry Beach, James. I feel like having my tea lakeside."

"Cherry Beach it is, m'lord."

The two parking lots at the beach were about as busy as the tables in the Second Cup had been. The scout car bumped through potholes that slowly eroded the dirt parking lots every summer.

"Who needs speed bumps?" Manny muttered as he tried to navigate around the larger of the craters. He found a relatively level spot, parked, and they both got out to enjoy the breeze coming in off the lake.

"It's nice down here. Almost feels like you're not in the city," Manny said.

"Yeah. There's nothing like this up in 32. The closest we had was the reservoir in Lord Ross Park. Not quite the same."

They leaned against the hood of their car and watched the seagulls and the occasional dog being walked. A few owners hastily tried to get their dogs on leashes when they spotted the cops, but Manny waved them away, occasionally calling the dogs over for a pat. One exceptionally friendly lab shared some lake water when he joyfully shook himself dry in front of them.

Jack and Manny exchanged brief personal histories like a couple on a blind date. Jack: married, no kids, house in Pickering, six years on the job. Manny: one girlfriend, not serious, renting a basement apartment in the city, three years on the job.

"How'd you end up with the nickname Manny?"

"Sy actually gave it to me. Just from my last name, I guess. Arms*man*, Manny. Not much to it."

"Figured he would have called you Army, then, not Manny."

"Army would've been cool, but someone said some other guy's already called Army. Bummer." He took Jack's empty cup and tossed it with his own into the trash. "Ready to roll?"

They rolled. The typical workday morning calls spilled from the radio, the dispatcher's voice frequently fighting static for dominance. Jack let the litany of house and business alarms, traffic accidents and drunks — it was still summertime in 51, after all, and public drunkenness had no off times — roll over him, oddly comforted by their familiarity. Manny kept off the main streets as much as he could, prowling the laneways and side streets, keeping up a pretty much one-sided conversation. He chatted about work, women, cars, work, the gym and work. Jack listened with half an ear, making appropriate noises when required.

"*5103, 5110, in 6's area. Disorderlies in the 7-Eleven at Sherbourne and Dundas. Two males refusing to leave. Time, 0831.*"

Manny looked at Jack, eagerness in his eyes. Jack nodded and Manny swerved onto Sherbourne, tromping the gas.

"Take it easy, man," Jack said. "It's just some disorderlies."

"I wanna make sure we get there before they leave." He was like a puppy tugging at the leash. A freaking huge puppy.

"Whatever makes you happy. Special 51 to radio. We're not far from that call at Sherbourne and Dundas. We'll take it; no sense tying up two solo cars on it."

"10-4, Special 51, thanks. 03 and 10, you can clear off the call, Special 51 will handle."

The 7-Eleven plaza — although "plaza" was far too grand a word for the two stores — on the southwest corner was steps up from 230 Sherbourne, home of the cockroach-toe man. The convenience store faced Sherbourne across a modest parking lot and a tiny burger shop jutted out from the south end of the plaza like an overgrown wart.

Manny pulled into the deserted lot — the plaza relied on pedestrian traffic — and they both got out, scanning the area. On the church steps across the street, several less-than-respectable-looking characters were simultaneously struck with a need to be elsewhere and casually hurried from sight.

Walking up to the store, Jack studied its interior through the glass front. Except for the clerk and one ancient woman with a walker, the store appeared as empty as the parking lot. He hadn't realized how the day was warming up until he and Manny entered the store's icy atmosphere.

While Manny checked out the aisles, Jack went to speak with the clerk. "You called?"

The middle-aged Asian man behind the counter said, "They gone now."

"Okay. What were they doing?"

"They want to buy but have no money. They want for free. I tell them to get out."

"Excuse me, officer." The elderly lady had snuck up on Jack like some hoary ninja, the rubber feet of her walker making zero noise on the tile floor. She was advancing at a pace only a sloth could envy. Jack didn't want to break her momentum, so he stepped aside.

Manny joined him at the counter as the clerk rang up her purchases — a jar of instant coffee and a carton of smokes — and bagged them, then thrust them at her with a distinct lack of civility, before dismissing her from his notice. She shuffled off, her day's ration of nicotine and caffeine hanging from the cross-bar of her walker.

Hell of a customer service. Jack asked, "What did they do after you told them to leave?"

"They call me names."

With your cheerful disposition, I can't imagine why. "Anything else? Did they steal anything, threaten you, something along those lines?"

"They call me 'fucking chink.'"

"And?"

"They leave. They go in there." He pointed through the front window at the burger shop. "You tell them not come back. Never."

"Can you tell us what they look like?"

"White, like you."

Like pulling freaking teeth. "Old? Young? Fat, skinny, short, tall? What were they wearing? Anything like that?"

"Not old. You find them in there." The clerk thrust his finger toward the restaurant again and Jack had the distinct impression they had just been dismissed as brusquely as the ancient ninja. Jack returned the favour by walking away without another word.

When the doors sighed closed behind them, Jack turned to Manny. "You, too, can meet interesting and friendly people with an exciting career in law enforcement."

Manny snickered. "We going to see if they're in there?"

Jack didn't really want to, but the puppy was still tugging at his leash and Jack figured Manny deserved a reward for his patience earlier this morning. "Yeah. Might as well see if they're planning a dine and dash."

The burger shop was a tiny affair, boasting four tables along one windowed wall facing the parking lot and two along the street side. All the tables were full and none of the patrons — a mosaic of the offensive in sight, odour or attitude — appeared police-friendly. The blue haze of cigarette smoke hanging smog-like in the air did little to improve the atmosphere.

Good thing smoking's illegal in restaurants. Jack walked up to the counter, a distance of three steps, and asked the overweight, middle-aged cook if anyone had just come in.

"I dunno. People come and go alla time." He sniffed and wiped his nose with the back of a nicotine-stained hand. "Why do ya wanna know?"

"Couple of guys just tried to make some purchases in the 7-Eleven without any cash. The clerk said they headed in here and we thought we'd save you the trouble of serving up some free food. But if you didn't notice anyone, that's okay." He shrugged to show how much he really cared. "I'm sure you'll figure out who they are when they can't pay you."

The cook's eyes narrowed as he turned toward two suddenly nervous guys sitting at a table facing Sherbourne. "Hey! You two numbnuts got the money to pay fer yer san'wiches?"

The guys in question, both young enough to be in college but ages past the possibility, exchanged uneasy glances.

"Get the fuck outta my rest'rant, ya fuckin' mooches! If I ever see ya come back in here, I'll fuckin' serve ya yer own fuckin' balls. Get the fuck out!"

They got the fuck out.

"Have a nice day, gentlemen," Manny said as he held the door open for them, an amused grin betraying his sincerity.

The cook watched them until they disappeared around the corner of the 7-Eleven. He concluded the whole unsavoury event by horking a glob of vile-coloured phlegm into the sink.

"Thanks. Ya want some coffee or somethin'? It's onna house."

Jack figured his thanks was as grudgingly genuine as the offer of coffee. "Thanks, but we just finished some."

As if the cook's phlegm had been some signal, the rest of the patrons resumed whatever conversations they had suspended when the uniforms had come through the door. As Jack joined

Manny, one of a quartet of seniors sitting at a table by the door raised a quivering hand to touch him on the forearm.

"Pardon me, officer." His voice shook more than his hand. "Me'n my friends would just like to pass on our condolences for that officer who was killed t'other week. We're sorry to see a good man go like that."

A quiet voice near the back of the room said, "I ain't. Good riddance to a fucking pig, I say."

"Who said that?" Jack roared, whirling to face the tables behind him. *"Who the fuck said that?"*

Silence dropped on the room. Everyone was studiously looking elsewhere. One prick in particular at the last table was trying extra hard to look innocent. Jack noticed a black tank top, a mangy mass of dirty hair and arms covered in skull-themed tattoos. He must have considered himself quite the badass. Too bad the hand holding his coffee cup was trembling.

Jack stalked over. "Was it you?" he growled.

Mr. Badass kept his eyes down, but his coffee was sloshing over the rim of the cup.

"Was it you?" Jack smacked the stained cup from the guy's hand. It exploded against the wall. Jack planted his fists on either side of the guy's breakfast plate and leaned in, ignoring the other three people at the table. "Come on, fuckhead. Was it you? You got the balls to say something like that to my back but not my face? Say it again, tough guy. Or are you a gutless, chickenshit coward?"

Jack waited and the silence stretched. Eventually, reluctantly, the man met Jack's eyes, then quickly looked back at his half-eaten eggs.

"I didn' mean nothing by it," he said timidly, sounding scared.

He was right to be afraid.

With one hand, Jack grabbed him by the throat and slammed him against the wall. He brought his face within kissing distance and snarled, "That man was my partner, fuckhead, and I watched him die." Jack tightened his grip on the man's throat. "If I ever,

ever, hear that you have badmouthed him again, I'll find you and I'll rip your fucking throat out. Do you understand me, fuckhead? Do you?"

The man nodded weakly as his face began to purple. Jack held on a moment longer, then released him. The man dropped to his knees, gasping hoarsely for breath. Jack shoved him back toward his table and surveyed the room dauntingly, hunting for further insolence but finding none. A chair scraped loudly in the silence as the beaten-down badass took his seat, his face still red, but from shamed embarrassment now, not lack of air.

Jack's rage was still up but beginning to cool. That could have been the end of it, should have been the end of it. But some people just never learn. Whether Badass needed to salvage whatever he could from the stinging embarrassment he had received at Jack's hands, or whether he was just stupid, it didn't matter. As Jack moved to leave, he had to have the final word, which he decided to express by spitting on the floor in front of Jack's boots.

Jack's response was immediate and brutal. He slammed Badass's face into the table. His breakfast plate broke beneath the impact. Jack held him face down in his eggs as blood began to blend with the grease and runny yolks. He yanked Badass upright. Bits of egg and congealed grease clung to his face as blood ran freely from his broken nose.

"You're under arrest, fuckhead."

With one hand clamped in his hair and the other on his arm, Jack dragged Badass unresisting from his seat and propelled him to the door. Badass's feet jerked in a parody of walking as signals from brain to feet were temporarily scrambled.

Then Jack remembered Manny standing by the door, an involuntary witness to his unseemly actions. He had placed a fellow officer, a good guy, in a compromising position because of his mindless rage, a rage which instantly vanished beneath a wave of embarrassed guilt.

But with a single sentence, Manny proved his loyalty to Sy's memory. "Anyone got a problem with that?" he challenged.

Apparently, no one did.

"Listen, Manny, I —" Jack stopped to correct himself. "Will, I owe you a huge apology and my thanks." They were out in the station's back lot, having just finished lodging Badass with his newly splinted nose and rapidly blackening eyes in the cells. "What I did was wrong and you didn't have to back me up on it."

Manny, who so rarely was called by his given name at work, looked almost offended at Jack's words. "Hey, man, you didn't do anything I didn't want to do myself. And it's Manny. Sy gave me that name and I'm proud of it."

Jack choked on his words and felt tears welling up in his eyes. And some said Manny deserved his bad reputation? With an effort, Jack composed himself while Manny pretended not to notice. "Thank you, Manny. That's about the best thing that I've heard since Sy . . . since . . ." He couldn't say it, not now, and it turned out he didn't have to.

"I know, man."

"But still, what I did was downright stupid. I went after that guy without even thinking about his buddies at the table. It was stupid and dangerous."

"No problem, man. I had your back."

One last unpleasantness to cover. "What did the Staff ask you?"

Manny shrugged. "Wanted to know why that guy was all busted up. I told him he spit on you and was going to again if you hadn't pushed his head down. He asked if I thought you had overreacted and I said you showed remarkable restraint for some-one who had just been assaulted in a vile and degrading way."

Jack laughed and shook his head. What do you say to that? As far as Jack could see, there was only one thing. He held out his hand to Manny. "If you want, I'd be honoured to partner up with you."

They shook on it.

"Jack, wait up." Detective Mason snagged Jack as he was coming out of the change room. Jack and Manny had just finished working out on their lunch hour and were getting ready to head back out on the road. "I need to talk to you for a few minutes."

"Sure, Rick. What's up?"

"Not here, upstairs in the office."

Curious, Jack followed the plainclothes detective up to the second floor, asking Deb, the platoon's civilian station operator, to let Manny know where he was.

On the way up the stairs, Mason commented, "I heard you rearranged Jesse Polan's nose yesterday."

"Little prick spit on me."

Mason raised a quizzical eyebrow. "That doesn't sound like Polan. He's a little chickenshit unless he's trying to prove something."

"Yeah, well . . ." Hell, if he couldn't be honest with Mason. . . . "He might have been upset at me for choking him out after he badmouthed Sy."

"That sounds more like him. Good going, Jack. Too many guys would have let something like that slide these days. I hear you're working with Armsman. Lot of conflicting opinions about him."

"Manny's solid. Just a little overeager at times, that's all." Jack felt he needed to add more, as if Mason's approval of his new partner was somehow connected to Sy. "I feel lucky to be working with him."

Mason nodded as if he understood. "Sy always thought he was a good copper." Those were the words Jack needed to hear. He realized Mason was making small talk, stalling until they reached the office. What was going on?

Mason led the way into the cramped office and asked Jack to

shut the door behind him. Taftmore and Tank were the only others in the room. Mason motioned for Jack to grab a seat, then sat behind his desk. The Major Crime boss scrubbed his face and heaved a huge sigh. Mason was exhausted; that much was clear to Jack. He saw the same weariness in the faces of the two detective constables.

In waters of unknown depth and current, Jack stayed quiet, waiting.

When Mason finally spoke, it was to swear Jack to silence. "What I'm about to tell you cannot go beyond this room. Period. Not to Manny, not to your wife. Can you live with that?"

"Well, to be perfectly honest, I don't know. I guess it all depends on what you have to say."

"Fair enough." Mason leaned back in his chair and fixed Jack with a penetrating stare. "We think we know who murdered Sy."

Jack was blasted by the sheer enormity of Mason's words. "Who? Fucking tell me. Who?"

Restraining hands up, Mason urged Jack to be patient. "I said we *think* we know. We need your help to confirm it." He yawned and scrubbed his face again.

What kind of hours had the unit been working since Sy's death? Did Jack think he was the only one affected by the murder?

"Before we get started, I want to thank you for your efforts with Sy. I talked to the paramedics who were there and they told me how you fought to keep him alive. They also said with a wound that severe, Sy would have had to been cut inside an operating room to have survived. You did all you could. I hope you don't blame yourself for anything."

Jack had heard that before. It hadn't really helped then and didn't mean much today.

"I've gone over your statement to Homicide and your notes and I understand your frustration in not being able to give much of a description of the suspect. He hid himself well. Homicide is focusing on the victim he killed prior to Sy. If they solve that murder, they solve Sy's. I'm interested in only one detail of your suspect description. If it pans out, we have our man."

Mason rocked forward, nailing Jack to his chair with his eyes. Jack was aware of Taft and Tank leaning in, as well. The first question was simple enough.

"The suspect was wearing gloves?"

Jack nodded. "Yes."

"Black latex gloves?"

"Yes."

"Are you sure they were latex?"

"Ye—" The fervour in Mason's voice gave Jack pause. "Why?"

"Could they have been leather gloves?"

Jack went still. "You think he did it? The guy who killed Reynolds? But that guy used a razor, not a butterfly knife."

"I know. It should have been a razor," Mason mused quietly, almost to himself.

"What do you mean it should have been a razor? I don't get it."

"Nothing," Mason said, waving it away. "I'm so fucking tired I don't know what I'm saying half the time. What I meant was, if there was any fairness in the world, it would have been a razor so we could tie the two murders together." He cocked his head at Jack. "But all we have are the gloves. You're positive they couldn't be leather?"

"No. They were too thin, too tight."

"Bear with me for a minute, Jack. I'm not talking about gloves like the type you wear, with the Kevlar lining. Think about it, Jack. Thin, tight leather. Like racing gloves. Stretched tight over his hand, could it have looked like latex?"

Jack thought back to that night, still so fresh in his mind. He could see the suspect's hand holding the knife to Sy's throat, see the steel flashing in the shadowed light, Sy's blood fanning through the air — *Focus!* Jack ripped himself away from those memories, pushed himself, fucking grabbed his own thoughts and forced them to concentrate on the glove. The glove and nothing else. Black? Yes, without a doubt. Latex . . . or leather?

"The glove had a bit of a shine to it. I thought — assumed — it was latex, but I guess it could have been leather," he admitted slowly, convincing himself. He nodded. "New enough to have a shiny finish to it. Or maybe it was sweat from the suspect wiping his forehead or something." He looked at Mason expectantly and the detective was grinning. "Yeah, it could have been leather."

"That's what we needed to hear."

A tension that had been binding the three Major Crime coppers suddenly evaporated with an almost audible hiss.

"What difference does it make?"

Mason laughed. "All the fucking difference in the world, Jack. Tank?"

The Sumo-sized copper brought Mason a file and patted Jack on the shoulder. Mason opened the file and flipped a photo across the desk for Jack to view. In the mug shot, a light-complexioned black male stared unsmiling at the camera.

"That's Gregory Johri, the first victim that night. He was a small-time dealer who suddenly disappeared from the local scene a few months ago. We all figured he had ended up dead somewhere. No big loss. But then we find out he was peddling Black to the university crowd over in 52 and, more recently, in the entertainment district. His car was parked in the same lot where he was killed. When Homicide searched the car, they found a whack of Black. Seems our man had been selling all night and was returning to his car for supplies when someone offed him."

"A rip-off?" Jack suggested.

Mason shook his head, grinning. "Nope. He still had a wad of cash on him and his car hadn't been touched. Granted, it could have been intended as a rip-off and the killer was interrupted by the witnesses who called 911."

"But you don't think so."

"But we don't think so," Mason confirmed. "We believe Johri was the victim of . . . shall we say . . . severe disciplinary action."

"He was skimming the profits?"

"Or working outside his assigned area, the university, on his own time. Either way, he was cutting into his boss's profits and was terminated, so to speak. And by the boss himself, we believe. Enter Anthony Charles, the man we think is the head of the Black organization."

Mason cracked open a bottle of water and took a long swig. "Charles is 51 Division born and bred. His mother was a local crack whore. Unlike other local shit rats, Charles never used crack, though he certainly sold it. His younger brother was a crack baby and is fucked up to this day. You've met him, by the way."

That startled Jack. "The brother? I don't — oh, fuck. The guy under the bed at the search warrant."

"Exactly. Sean Jacobs. Different fathers," he advised before Jack could ask. "Once we learned who Sean's brother was, it all began fitting together."

"So if Sean is the brother of the boss, that would explain why everyone in the apartment tried to hide him and wouldn't give up anything on him."

"Right again. Now, what did Sean like to wear in imitation of his older brother?"

"Black leather gloves. But that's a pretty big leap to make."

"Trust me, it isn't a leap. We've been working our asses off trying to track down Charles. What we have been able to learn is that the Black boss is a very hands-on type of leader, the type who would prefer to carry out the execution of a disloyal employee personally, rather than delegating the task. And his trademark, his signature if you will, is black leather gloves.

"Charles is a very disgruntled young man. He sees what crack did to his brother through their mother and he blames society. White society. He's more than happy to sell crack to white university students. He'll also sell to poor black folks. In his eyes, if you're weak enough to be a drug user, then you're only useful to him as a customer.

"None of that is new information. It's straight from court transcripts at his last trafficking trial. That was about three years ago. When he got out, he dropped out of sight and not long after, Black started showing up on the streets and Sean was suddenly sporting gloves out of admiration for his brother."

Mason fell silent and looked expectantly at Jack.

"Okay, I can connect the dots and it sounds good, but . . ." Jack said.

"Exactly: but. As in, try to convince a judge or jury. What we have is a bunch of impressive-sounding ifs and maybes. What we need is a solid fact. What we need, Jack, is you."

Jack knew what they wanted, what they needed, but he couldn't give it to them, as much as he would like to. "I can't ID Charles. I only saw a corner of his head and one eye and even less when he killed Reynolds. No one would believe an identification based on that."

"IDs have been made on less and have held up in court. Some witnesses who only saw a partial face have been able to ID a suspect based on certain features of the face but not all of it. All we need to do is take our theory to Homicide. They'll pooh-pooh it, of course, because we're just divisional grunts, not big-time homicide investigators, but I'll push for a photo lineup. What's there to lose, after all? And they'll agree, even if it's to make us look stupid. They show you the lineup, you pick out Charles and, if we're lucky, he decides he doesn't want to be taken alive."

"And if I can't ID him?"

Mason studied Jack, then looked to his officers for confirmation. They both nodded.

"What if we could guarantee you'd be able to pick him out?" Mason slid another photo across the desk, face down. He kept it pinned down with one hand. "It's your choice, Jack. If you don't want to, I'll understand and this conversation will have never taken place. If, on the other hand, you do decide to accept my help, there's no turning back. Ever. We're in this together. If one of us goes down, we all go down." He slid his hand free of the photo. "It's your choice."

A warrant for the arrest of Anthony Tyrone Charles on three counts of first-degree murder was issued later that day. Jack heard it on the news as he drove home. And smiled.

Thursday, 14 September
1027 hours

"I am not leaving until they fix my car and that's final." The defiant gentleman dressed in a suit that probably would have covered two, if not more, of Jack's mortgage payments crossed his arms and looked as if he wanted to stamp his feet.

Tired and exasperated, Jack sighed and rubbed his eyes. He'd had a headache most of the day — no doubt thanks to the weather, once again hot and humid — and if the expensively dressed man kept arguing much longer it would surely cross over to migraine status. He and Manny were handling an unwanted-guest call at a BMW dealership on Adelaide Street and they had already been there twice as long as they should have been.

"Sir, the manager has explained to you, repeatedly, that the damage to your car is not covered by the warranty. They will gladly fix it but you'll have to pay for it." *How many times does this moron need to be told?*

Jack and Manny — taking turns so neither of them punched out the idiot from sheer frustration — had laid it out to Mr. BMW several times, but he refused to budge.

"And I have explained it to you, *officer*, they *are* going to fix it and it *is* covered by the warranty. Do you not understand me for some reason?"

Pain throbbed behind Jack's right eye and he was starting to squint against the bright lights in the showroom, two sure signs his headache was cheerfully on its way to a full-blown migraine. All he wanted to do was get in the car, down some meds and try to forget this condescending prick.

It was Manny's turn. "Sir, if you have a problem with —"

Mr. BMW threw up his hands, interrupting Manny. "Of course I have a problem! My God! Have you not understood a single word I've said? I understand the qualifications to become a police officer are lenient, but I had no idea they were that substandard. It's no wonder you two ended up as policemen. If you represent the norm for those who serve the rest of us —"

"That's enough!" It was Jack's turn to interrupt and he did it like a volcano erupting. Mr. BMW may have stood taller than Jack, but right now he took a tentative step back. "I've had enough of your fucking attitude. The manager has *asked* you to leave, we've *asked* you to leave and now I'm *telling* you to leave. If you don't, I will gladly arrest you for trespassing, handcuff you and dump you in the back of my shitty North American–made police car. Do. You. Under. Stand. Me?"

Mr. BMW quickly recovered from his shock. "You, officer, have just bought yourself trouble you cannot handle. Do you know who my lawyer —"

Manny threw his hand up in BMW's face to silence him as the portables, always kept on at low volume when they were out of the car, crackled with urgency.

"CB51 Bravo in pursuit!" a female officer shouted.

Jack and Manny cranked their radios up.

"CB51 Bravo! We're chasing a male southbound through north Regent Park on a bicycle. Male black wearing a red shirt and black gloves!"

Sirens erupted across the division; Jack could hear them through the dealership's fancy glass walls. Every officer in the division knew what the gloves meant.

"Out! Now!"

Jack and Manny grabbed an arm each, wrinkling BMW's expensive suit, and ran him to the doors, not bothering to slow down when they reached the glass panels. Mr. BMW bore the brunt of the impact when they rammed open the doors. They ran to the scout car, BMW sputtering a tirade of threats and promising legal retribution; they would have dragged him if he hadn't been able to keep up. At the sidewalk, they released him, and with the abrupt freedom he careened into the side of the scout car. Luckily for his suit, they had managed to get the car washed that morning.

"Don't go back in there," Jack yelled as he ran to the passenger side. He slid in and Manny screamed away from the curb as Jack slammed his door.

"Southbound from 605 Whiteside now!"

"Who is that?" Jack wanted to know.

"Jenny, I think."

The red light at Parliament was coming up fast. Manny braked at the last instant and didn't hit the gas again until Jack yelled, "Clear!" To cut down on time at red lights — when the sirens were wailing, seconds mattered — two-man cars held the advantage over solo units; the passenger's responsibility was to check for traffic on his side and the driver had to learn to wait for the "clear" without checking. It took practice and trust. A distinct advantage for permanent partners.

In their four days together, Jack had learned that Manny was one of the best drivers he had ever seen. The guy could squeeze a scout car through a keyhole at unimaginable speeds without scraping either side of the car. Jack had ridden with one officer up in 32 who had enough titanium holding him together to qualify as a cyborg, all as a result of departmental accidents. High-speed manoeuvering seemed as natural to Manny as breathing.

"Where do you think he's headed?"

"If he was going to bail off the bike and head inside — clear! — he probably would have done it in north Regent. I bet he's planning on heading into the little streets south of Shuter," Jack said.

"Male now westbound on Shuter!" came Jenny's voice again.

"Or not," Jack admitted.

"10-4, CB Bravo, westbound on Shuter. Bravo, what's the male wanted for?" Either the dispatcher didn't understand the significance of the gloves — which Jack found hard to believe — or she was trying to legitimize the bicycle pursuit. Since the warrant for Charles's arrest had been made public, there had been five foot pursuits of glove-wearing suspects. None of them had been Charles, of course. Overnight, black leather gloves had become a fashion statement in 51.

"Possession cocaine and assault to resist." Jenny hardly sounded out of breath, evidence that those legs of hers were good for something other than being stared at.

"Any idea — wait, wait, clear! — who she's working with?"

"I think I saw her riding with Sue earlier."

"Then this guy's fucked."

Officers didn't like it when one of their own was assaulted; they tended to repay the culprit back twofold or more. When a female officer was assaulted, coppers took it personally.

The scout car screeched around the corner onto Shuter and Manny mashed the gas pedal. The car leapt out of the turn while Jack scanned the road ahead.

"Special 51's on Shuter. Bravo, where are you?" No answer. "Bravo! What's your 20?"

"The last location I had for Bravo was westbound on Shuter," the dispatcher advised.

"They probably came out around Blevins, so they have to be around here somewhere. Slow down."

Manny eased off the gas and killed the siren, but left the lights on, then drove down the centre of the four-lane road, searching his side of the street. Jack was checking between houses and straining for sounds of a fight. Suddenly, Manny goosed the car ahead.

Jack grabbed the mike. "Special 51, we've found them. Front

lawn of the Shuter Street school. All appears in order, units can slow down. All in order."

Manny bounced the car over the curb onto the sidewalk, but there was no need for hurry. The two PWs were kneeling on their suspect, who was face down and cuffed on the grass. The male faced away from Jack, but he knew immediately that it wasn't Charles; the man's complexion was too light.

"Good afternoon, ladies," Jack greeted them, walking over. "Nice day for a bike ride." The two white police bikes and a beaten-up mountain bike were lying nearby.

"Hi, Jack. Nice to see you." Jenny was kneeling on the man's back, completely at ease having a friendly conversation from that position. She flashed an enrapturing smile at him. Even with sunglasses and the bulky helmet, she was an incredibly beautiful woman.

Jack's heart fluttered for a beat or two before he could answer. "Hate to be the bearer of bad news, but —"

"I know, it isn't Charles. I saw that as soon as we got him cuffed."

"It isn't? That fucking sucks." The second policewoman was kneeling astride the prisoner's legs. She stood, unclipped her helmet and let it fall at her feet. Not as tall as Jenny, she had dark red hair — the word that popped into Jack's mind was *crimson* — and a set of lips so pouty, they had him thinking collagen.

"Sorry, Sue; seems like every sack of shit down here is wearing the gloves now." Jenny unfolded her legs and, with Manny's help, heaved her man upright. "I gave him a quick pat-down, Manny, but he could use a thorough search."

"My pleasure." He planted the man chest down across the scout car's trunk.

"Those bitches be lyin'. I ain't done nothin' wrong."

"Then why were you running, or biking, away?" Manny asked as he began his search.

"'Cause they was chasin' me! I didn' want to get Rodney Kinged."

"Isn't that phrase a little out of date? Besides, you're just upset because you got caught by two girls." In Manny's world, a day wasn't complete if he couldn't taunt at least one criminal.

"Do either of you ladies need any physical attention? Any areas of your bodies in need of examination?" Paul Townsend had cruised to a stop and called from the driver's seat.

"Dark Chocolate! Baby!" Sue lost interest in the arrest and sashayed over to his car. Her legs were nowhere near the quality of Jenny's, but she certainly put a lot of hip sway into her walk.

"I thought you were married, Officer Warren." Jenny had caught Jack looking and there was amusement in her voice.

"Actually, I was just comparing her legs with yours," he admitted truthfully.

"Really? And . . . ?"

Jack smiled at her — it was easy to smile at Jenny — and told her the truth. "No comparison."

"And don't you forget it," she cautioned him with a grin. "It took you that long to come to your verdict?"

"Nope, that was almost instantaneous. I was just thinking that my Scottish grandmother would say she had the *sheuggle* for a kilt."

"The what?"

"*Sheuggle*. Hip sway. If you like," he offered sincerely, "I can watch you walk for a while and see if you have a good sheuggle. I'm just trying to be fair."

"I hate to interrupt, but is anyone still involved in this arrest except for me?"

Jack and Jenny looked over their shoulders at Manny. "You're doing an excellent job, officer. Carry on."

"Gee, thanks, Jack. That makes me warm and fuzzy all over."

They loaded Jenny's prisoner into the back seat and his stolen bike — what anyone caught on a stolen bike called a "community bicycle"— into the trunk for the short trip to the station. In the station's back lot, they passed prisoner and bike to the ladies and decided to hang around until Jenny and Sue headed inside with him. While the bike officers waited to be called into the booking hall, Manny leaned the prisoner into the wall and planted his hand between the man's shoulder blades to keep him put. Sue stood on tiptoes to run her hands over Manny's bare scalp.

"She will flirt with anything male," Jenny declared, sounding somewhat strained.

"Trust me," Jack told her, "you'd rather see this than the guy who was feeling up his head a few days ago." Not wanting to let the conversation end, he added, "I thought you usually worked with Al." While he asked, he dug his migraine medication out of his duty bag — he tried to never be far from his drugs — and downed a pill with some water.

"Al's sick and Sue's partner's also off. Gee, Jack, that's rather ballsy of you, doing drugs where the sergeants can see you."

"It's all right, just migraine meds. I do the illegal stuff on my way to work in the car."

"Sensible. Migraines, huh? Is that why your face is all squinted up and you look like you're going to throw up all over me?"

He nodded. "Pretty much, yup."

"That's good to hear. I was beginning to think it was me."

"Oh, no," he reassured her. "You have a completely different effect on me."

"Really? Sy never told me that about you," she said with a sly smile.

"You talked to Sy about me? Interesting. . . ."

Jenny smiled, then chewed nervously on her lower lip.

If Jack had known her better, he would have said she was stalling. "Something on your mind, Jenny?"

"This may — no, I'm pretty sure it will — sound kind of nuts, but it's about Manny and you being partners. I like Manny," she added hastily, "don't get me wrong, but . . ."

"But it seems pretty soon after Sy . . . dying for me to pair up with someone. Right?"

She looked embarrassed, then nodded. "I guess it seems kind of disrespectful to Sy. I know you weren't with him for long, but for him to partner up with you said a huge amount about you to the station. I'd hate to see you throw that away inadvertently."

"Whoa. I never thought about it that way. Believe me when I say I never intended to throw away my time with Sy. It's just that . . . well, I need some stability in my life right now. I'm not sleeping well and when I do, I have nightmares about Sy. And now my wife and her parents are hounding me to transfer out of 51 to someplace safe."

He couldn't believe he was opening up like this to Jenny. Except for saying hello a half dozen times and the odd small talk she was a stranger to him. But that didn't stop him. There was something about her that made talking to her easy and natural. True, she was a beautiful woman, but that wasn't it. Talking to her just felt . . . right. He couldn't explain it, even to himself.

"And something happened on Monday, the first day Manny and I worked together, and it meant so much to me —"

"Jenny! We're up."

The sally port door was rumbling open. It was time to parade their prisoner.

"Are you coming out tonight?" Jenny quickly asked Jack.

"No. I should go home and try to smooth things over with Karen. My wife," he explained.

"Okay, but if you change your mind, we're going for wings first and then down to Cherry Beach for a bonfire. If you come, we can talk. You sound like you could use a friendly ear." She staggered his heart for a second time that day with a simple smile, then trotted off to catch up with Sue.

Manny joined him. "Yo, man, you okay?"

Jack shook himself back to reality. "Yeah, I'm good."

"Enjoying the scenery, were you?"

"Just checking for a *sheuggle*, that's all."

"Special 51, could you head back to Gerrard and Parliament? I've got another medical complainant for a collapsed male. Ambulance attending, time 1556."

"10-4, dispatch," Jack replied tiredly. "Maybe we should just camp out there with them."

The dispatcher laughed. *"Thanks, Special 51. I appreciate the help."*

"A nice, hot day," Manny mused, "and the drunks are falling like ten-pins."

Ten minutes earlier Manny and Jack had loaded a local drunk into an ambulance at the intersection of Parliament and Gerrard streets. Then Manny had headed east on Gerrard. When the second call came in, he pulled into Allan Gardens and eased into the shade of a huge oak, and both officers pulled out their memo books to write down the call and to give the second ambulance a head start.

This was a lesson Jack had learned very quickly in 51: unless it's a child, don't rush to a collapse call. Let the ambulance or fire department get there first, which they usually did anyway. People who "collapsed" the most frequently were people you didn't want to touch, let alone perform artificial resuscitation on. Drunks and drug users were typically not clean people.

Especially in Pigeon Park, at Gerrard and Parliament.

Call written down and ambulance given sufficient time to get there ahead of them, Manny slowly pulled out of the shade. The sky was a blue so clear it was almost white and the sun was merciless in its attack on the city. The park was all but empty. Even the hounds had abandoned it in search of air conditioning.

Traffic was light and the few cars on the road appeared to be affected by the heat as much as the pedestrians, moving sluggishly and without great purpose. Sluggish was just fine with Jack. He was in no rush to reach Pigeon Park, not after their visit there just a few minutes ago, when they had found a Native guy passed out in his own vomit.

"I wonder which one of his drinking buddies has gone down this time."

"I'm betting it's the one with the nose that looks like a mound of mashed potatoes shoved in a fishnet stocking. He downed that last bottle pretty quick when he saw us coming."

"You're probably right," Jack agreed. "And thanks for ruining fishnet stockings for me. Karen likes to wear them when she's feeling frisky."

"Sorry, dude."

Pigeon Park — really more of a parkette — was located at the northwest corner of the intersection. A small triangle of concrete and grass, it had a round fountain as its centrepiece. The fountain was dry — a good thing, according to Manny; it had something to do with skinny-dipping homeless alcoholics — but the park was still a favourite watering spot for some local Natives.

The heat didn't so much hit Jack as crush him when he got out of the car. The air was so thick with humidity that it was hard to breathe. How anyone could sit out in it and drink cooking wine was beyond him. It obviously took years of practice and the Pigeon drinking crew certainly had the experience.

There had been three of them left standing — or relatively upright — when the first guy had been hauled off to the hospital. Now they were down to two. The third one was face down in a flower bed and it wasn't Mashed Potatoes in Fishnets: he was still upright but tilting dangerously.

The medics had rolled the drunk over and were attempting to wake him up, but consciousness seemed to be at least one bottle beyond reach. Manny plucked an almost empty plastic water bottle from a limp hand and gave it a quick whiff. "The good stuff," he declared, dumping the last of the liquid and tossing the bottle aside.

"Cooking wine?" one of the medics asked without much interest.

"Nope. He's moved on to rubbing alcohol. Mixed with a splash of Gatorade for flavour, if I'm not mistaken."

"Wonderful. Okay, buddy. Time to wake up." The medic

placed a knuckle, safely covered in latex, on the drunk's breast-bone and rubbed hard and deep, grinding bone on bone. A hand twitched, nothing more. "Fuck, this guy's really out." The medic leaned forward, putting the weight of his upper body behind his knuckle. A small groan escaped the drunk's lips and his hands flailed weakly before flopping onto the pavement again.

"Here. Give this a try." Jack passed his baton to the medic.

"Cool," the medic said, a mischievous twinkle lighting his eyes. He placed one end of the baton where his knuckle had been and rubbed. Hard. Jack could hear the blunt metal grinding on the bone and he imagined he could feel it in his bones.

This time the drunk woke up or got as close to being awake as he was going to get. He lurched to a sitting position and the medics had to step quickly to avoid the swinging fists. The burst of animation was only that, a burst, and seconds later the guy was folding to the ground again. One medic got a knee between his shoulder blades to prop him up.

Jack took his stick back and while the paramedics tended to their patient, he and Manny tended to the conscious drunks. Both were Natives — Pigeon Park was their preferred place for drinking — and they eyed the approaching officers suspiciously.

"No need to get up, gentlemen," Manny said. They were both seated on the flower bed's knee-high wall. "We're just going to take a little look around since we didn't have enough time to during our last visit."

Stashed among the flowers and garbage they found an assort-ment of bottles and emptied five rubbing alcohol coolers.

Jack looked up to see that the medics had managed to pour the drunk onto the stretcher and were loading him into the ambulance. "You guys want us to tag along?" he asked.

"Nah, we got it. Thanks for the loan of the stick." The medic slammed shut the ambulance doors, pulled off his latex gloves and turned to Jack and Manny. "Don't know if you guys would be interested in this, but we were just in 295 Gerrard and there's a guy dealing in the stairwell. Didn't even bother to try and hide it when we went by."

With less than an hour to go on the last day of a very long day shift, Manny perked up like a puppy who had just spotted a squirrel. Jack sighed. In their few days together, Jack had learned that, when Manny saw a squirrel, all Jack could do was make sure the silly little puppy didn't chase it into traffic and get himself squashed by a car.

"What did he look like?" Manny asked.

Jack could feel him tugging at the leash.

"White guy, lot of acne, green shirt. He was selling rock to some black guys when we went by."

"Where in the building?"

"East stairwell. About twenty minutes ago."

"Thanks, man. We'll check it out."

In the scout car, Jack cranked the AC the second Manny had the engine running. Manny had the mike in his hand. "You don't mind, do you, Jack?"

Jack sighed again. "Fine. But if you get me in a foot chase in this heat, I'll kill you."

"I'll do the chasing, dude. Thanks." He was beaming like a kid with a new toy.

As Manny waited to merge with traffic, Jack watched the drunks. They were up and searching the flower bed, no doubt hoping a bottle had been overlooked. A pigeon near the scout car caught Jack's attention. It was walking along the curb on rather unsteady legs.

I'd swear the damn thing's staggering.

As he watched, the bird missed a step and slid off the curb. It hit the asphalt in a flurry of ruffled feathers. After several attempts to jump to the curb, it gave up and staggered off along the street.

Crap, even the pigeons down here are drunk.

295 Gerrard was diagonally across from Pigeon Park, a six-storey building holding down the northwest corner of Regent Park. There was no easy way to sneak up on any of the entrances in daylight, especially in a scout car, so Manny took the direct approach and parked on the grass in front of the building.

"You got something against parking on the street?" Jack asked as they got out of the car.

"It's rush hour, man," Manny explained. "Don't want to mess up traffic. Besides, this way we'll have shorter to walk with our prisoner."

"Like he's still here," Jack commented as Manny ducked around the building to use the rear entrance. Jack took the front.

From the outside, all the buildings in Regent Park were similar. Same brick colour, same design, same worn-down, despairing appearance. Inside, they were identical, right down to the depressing shade of paint and the stench of old urine. Jack wasn't looking forward to the smell in this heat. Mounting the front steps, he tried to see into the building, but the door's glass was reflecting the sun and everything beyond it was hidden.

This guy better be gone, or I'm gonna be pissed.

He yanked open the door and came face to face with the dealer, green shirt, zits and all. There was a split second of shocked immobility; then the dealer bolted, Jack hard on his heels. Who was the puppy now?

The dealer ran with the speed only true fear can inspire and hip-checked open the stairwell door. The door swung closed behind him and through the door's window Jack could see him pounding up the stairs.

Jack hit the door in full stride, throwing out his left arm to slam it open. His arm passed through the emptiness where the glass should have been and his head rammed the metal edge of the window frame. He crashed through the door into the stairwell and ended up on his ass at the foot of the stairs. He grabbed the railing to haul himself up, but the cinderblock walls were spinning too fast for him to stand, so he eased himself onto the steps and hung his head between his knees. That's where Manny found him moments later.

"Jack! What's wrong? You okay?" Manny squatted in front of him.

At least Jack thought the blurred image in front of him was his partner.

"Jack, you're bleeding. I'll get an ambulance."

Jack groped blindly in front of himself and managed to catch Manny's hand before he could key his radio. "I don't need an ambulance." He gingerly touched his eyebrow and felt the sting of a cut. He hoped he wouldn't need stitches. God, this was embarrassing enough without having to go to the hospital.

Who had to stop whom from running into traffic?

Jack raised his head and was happy to find that the walls were stationary and Manny was in focus. "I'm only going to tell you once what happened and then we are both going to forget it ever happened. . . ."

Thursday, 14 September
2130 hours

Jack was fast asleep on the living room couch, a well-thumbed copy of Stephen King's *The Stand* — the unabridged version, naturally — open on his stomach. He had retired, or retreated, depending on the point of view, to the couch and the world of Trashcan Man and the Walking Dude after a rather strained dinner with Karen. His return to work, to 51 in particular, continued to be a source of conflict between them, an irritant in their daily lives, and he had hoped to give her time to cool down. Instead, he had fallen asleep.

The doorbell rudely jerked him from his slumber. He lay quietly, wondering if he had dreamed the sound of the chimes. He decided on dream chimes and his eyes were sagging comfortably shut when the bells tolled again. He swung his feet to the floor as he checked his watch, confirming what the twilit sky was saying.

"I'll get it, Jack," Karen called as she thumped down the stairs to the front door. How someone so delicate could thump so loudly always amazed him.

"Unless it's a kid selling good chocolate, tell whoever it is to go away and call first next time." Jack resumed his napping position, squirming his shoulders into the cushions piled behind him. He cracked open his book as a huge yawn cracked his jaws. "Sorry, Steve. Maybe later." He deposited the book on the glass coffee table and folded his hands on his stomach.

He heard voices from the front hall but tuned them out; Karen was handling it, he could go back to sleep. Unless, of course, they had company.

"Jack! Don't go back to sleep; my parents are here."

Oh. Fucking. Joy.

"Did we wake you, Jack?" Evelyn was her normal resplendent self in a green silk blouse and slacks; she blew into the living room like some fairy something-or-other from the Emerald City. And, wherever the fairy mother-in-law was, Jack's favourite bridge-troll-in-law couldn't be far behind.

"Jack, good to see you." George Hawthorn was ultra casual tonight. A sports jacket and no tie? Jack was tempted to look outside, convinced he would see the Four Horsemen of the Apocalypse bearing down on the house.

Hawthorn stuck out a hand and Jack shook, noting — with petty enjoyment — a fleeting twinge across his father-in-law's face. And Hawthorn was man enough to admit it as he rubbed his hand. "Quite the grip you've developed, Jack. All that time in the gym must be paying off."

"Oh, it certainly is," Evelyn agreed. "Jack, you're growing like an adolescent boy. Pretty soon you'll be bigger than that Arnold fellow."

"I've got a long ways to go before that happens, Evelyn."

Her eyebrows twitched — in surprise or annoyance? — at the use of her first name. It surprised Jack as well. He hadn't intended to call her Evelyn; it just slipped out. What the hell, she'd been asking him for years to drop the Mrs. Hawthorn thing.

Guess she never figured I would.

"Sorry about the greeting. If I'd known you were coming, I'd have cut the nap short."

"Jack," Karen scolded him, "I told you at dinner my parents were coming over for coffee and dessert."

"Oh, sorry. I guess I forgot."

"Perfectly understandable, son —" *Son?* "— I imagine you have a lot on your mind these days now that you are back to work."

"That's no excuse, Dad, and he knows it. And just for that, Jack, you can help me with the cheesecake."

In the kitchen, Karen busied herself with the coffee and cups while Jack got out plates for the dessert. The cheesecake, a behemoth of chocolate, occupied centre stage in the fridge.

I must have been tired to miss that sitting there.

"Did you catch that?" he asked her in a hushed whisper as they arranged everything on trays. "Your dad called me 'son.'"

"Well, you called Mom 'Evelyn.' I think it's nice. Maybe the three of you are finally getting closer."

"Maybe," he conceded, hoisting a tray. *Yeah, right.*

They were sipping contentedly on coffee after the first round of cheesecake had been reduced to scraped plates. Jack was the only one who had opted for seconds.

"So, Jack, how's 51 Division treating you these days?" Hawthorn asked with all the subtlety of a hammer applied to a stubborn nail.

Jack paused, a fork full of cake halfway to his mouth. "Fine," he replied, suddenly on guard. He finished his dessert and swapped the empty plate for his coffee mug. Mug, not cup, and it all fell into place. His in-laws just stopping by for dessert. On a weeknight? Their casual — casual for them, at least — mode of dress. Karen's homemade chocolate cheesecake, his favourite. An oversized mug for him when everyone else had a cup. No way would Karen let that pass, not with her parents visiting. And no way would she have let him wear the jeans and T-shirt he had worn home from work.

He looked at the sitting arrangement. Karen next to him on the couch, between him and the front hall, and her parents opposite them in chairs, blocking the exit to the kitchen. He was cornered. Had they pinned him in purposefully? Or had it just happened? Either way, he was trapped and now that the chocolate bait had been taken, they were going to close the trap on him.

Evelyn leaned forward to pat his knee. "We'd like to take this opportunity to express our condolences to you again for your loss and to remind you we're here for you, for the both of you. If you need anything, all you have to do is ask."

"That's awfully kind of you, Evelyn." No surprised twitches that time. "But we're doing okay."

"That's not what we hear, son." Hawthorn had his hands folded on crossed legs, the picture of an understanding adult ready to hear his child's woes. Was that how he looked when his students grovelled for extra time on assignments?

"It isn't?" Jack eased back on the couch, mug in hand. This was his house and no way was he going to let Hawthorn play the adult. He turned to Karen. "I seem to be at a . . . disadvantage here, hon. Maybe someone can bring me up to speed?"

Evelyn spoke. "Jack, we're all worried about you. Karen has told us all about it. How you're not sleeping well, your nightmares. . . ."

"Gee, Evelyn, I guess watching my partner have his throat slit open in front of me might have something to do with that. Or maybe it was trying to stop him from bleeding to death by

shoving my fingers *inside* his throat. Either one, I would imagine."
He sipped his coffee.

Evelyn flinched.

"Don't you see, Jack? This is exactly what we need to talk about," Hawthorn said earnestly, no doubt seeing the perfect segue to his argument. "Before you transferred to 51, you would never have spoken to Evelyn in such a tone. What happened to your partner was a tragedy, without a doubt, and you witnessing it is an ordeal we can only imagine. But the changes in you were occurring before that tragic night."

"So, am I to understand this is some kind of intervention? You want me to realize 51 is destroying my life?"

Karen scooted over next to him and took his hand in hers. "Jack, I love you and I'm worried about you. My parents are worried about you."

He relinquished his mug and wrapped his hand over hers. She was the one he needed to convince, not her parents, so he spoke only to her. "Karen, what happened to Sy could happen anywhere in the city. Yes, 51 is rougher than 32 and other divisions, but I've told you, that can actually make it safer in a way. I'm more aware now of my surroundings at work and my own safety than I ever was in 32. I was complacent up there. Now, I'm not." He laughed bitterly. "And besides, the odds of something like that night happening to me again in my career are astronomical. I could probably spend the rest of my career working naked and nothing would happen to me."

He smiled at his feeble attempt at humour, hoping for a smile in return, but he got nothing.

"It isn't just that, Jack, although I never laid awake at night worrying about you when you worked in 32."

"I told you, hon, I'm safer now than ever before."

"It's not just that!" She snatched her hands away and clutched them in her lap. She began to cry. "You swear more, you spend every day at the gym like you need to become some huge, scary animal and that's what I'm afraid will happen. It is happening! You told me that Simon warned you about the division, how it could change good men into criminals, how it could ruin lives. I don't want that to happen to you! To us!"

"What would you have me do, Karen?" he asked quietly. "Quit? I'm a cop. It's all I know. It's the only thing I'm good at or qualified for."

"I'm not asking you to quit," she argued through her tears. "I'm proud you're a cop; I just don't want you to be a 51 cop."

"Oh." What was there to say to that?

Karen wiped away her tears and, for a wonder, her parents didn't jump into the silence.

"Karen, would you do something for me, then?"

"Of course," she sniffled.

"Stop teaching grade school. Become a university professor like your parents."

"What? Why? What are you talking about, Jack? I don't want to be a professor."

"I know. And I know why." He took her hands again. "You love teaching the kids, reaching out to young minds and helping them learn. You admit being a professor would be easier —" he saw her parents stiffen "— and it pays more, but that's not why you became a teacher. I would never ask you to stop doing something you love."

"I hardly think Karen's decision to teach grade school is the same as your desire to work in 51. If any —"

"But it is!" Jack snapped, cutting Hawthorn off. "It *is* the same. Karen, you love being a teacher because you feel like you're contributing to the world, making a difference. Well, I feel the same way about being downtown. In 32, I wrote traffic tickets, took reports and arrested shoplifters. Once in a while, I did something valuable. For the city or an individual person. In 51, I do that every day."

He wanted to stop, to collect his thoughts, but he couldn't.

Any opening, no matter how small or brief, and one of her parents would jump in with both feet.

"Do you know what I did just this week? In the last four days?" He spoke to all of them, hoping to convince all of them. "I put two husbands in jail for beating their wives, another for beating his child. And I don't mean just a little slap here and there. These guys *beat* their families. One of them used a belt. The seven-year-old girl ended up in the hospital with broken ribs."

Jack could have left it at that, but they needed to see, to believe. "We caught a crackhead breaking into a woman's home. He was stealing her jewellery. Most of it was cheap, but it had belonged to her grandmother and losing it would have crushed her. The crackhead probably would have sold all those memories for less than a hundred dollars."

He squeezed Karen's hands. "And the best? I identified Sy's murderer on Tuesday. A warrant has been issued for his arrest. He'll spend the rest of his life in jail."

"You did? That's wonderful." She threw her arms around him and hugged him tightly. "Why didn't you tell me?"

He laughed at her exuberance. "I didn't know if it was something you wanted to hear. The job hasn't been exactly a comfortable topic between us these last few days."

Then Hawthorn opened his mouth and ruined the moment. "That is wonderful news, Jack, but it doesn't solve the problem. You're putting your work and yourself ahead of Karen. A man doesn't do that to his wife."

Jack slowly released Karen and turned to his father-in-law. "No offence, George, but I really don't think what happens between Karen and me is any of your business."

"Of course it's our business," Hawthorn scoffed. "She's our daughter. Her happiness is of the utmost importance to us." He tried to calm his voice. "You're a good man, Jack, and —"

Whatever he had been about to say was drowned out by Jack's shocked laughter. "A good man? Get off of it. When have you ever treated me like I was good enough for Karen? From the day we started dating, you were looking to break us up. Every chance you got, you put me down. I was never good enough in your eyes. My upbringing, my family, my education, my job. Nothing I was or did ever met your standards. So, please, don't try that tactic with me."

George and Evelyn looked dumbfounded. Jack wished he could take a picture, capture their shock at the son-in-law's sudden turn.

"Jack. . . ."

"Sorry, hon, but it had to be said." He turned to his in-laws. "Maybe you are right. Maybe 51 is changing me and that's what worries you. You're afraid you'll lose your docile punching bag and have to come up with some other form of entertainment at Sunday dinners."

Silence. It filled the room, a tangible presence.

"Jack, that's not fair."

"It's all right, dear heart," Hawthorn comforted. "We understand Jack didn't mean it. He's been under a terrible strain lately, but now that he has identified his partner's killer, he can leave the division with a clear conscience."

"What do you mean by 'clear conscience,' George?" Jack asked slowly, dangerously.

Perhaps Hawthorn didn't hear the menace in his son-in-law's voice, or perhaps he was just eager to trade Jack back for his earlier comments. "It's obvious you feel guilty about your partner's death. It doesn't take a trained psychologist — although I have discussed your case with one — to see that you blame yourself for his murder. You can provide a variety of reasons to stay in the division: fulfillment, job satisfaction, personal feelings of accomplishment, but you're using them to mask the true reason for staying: guilt."

"Dad, please —"

Jack blindly reached out and placed a calming hand on

Karen's leg. "No, hon. I want to hear this."

Hawthorn beamed with approval. "Thank you, Jack. As I was saying, you feel guilty because you couldn't stop the culprit from killing your partner. You feel guilty because you let him escape. You feel guilty because you couldn't save your partner's life. All of this is eating at you, but you don't have to shoulder the entire responsibility alone. A goodly portion lies with your partner."

Karen tried one more time to stop her father. "Dad, don't. This isn't the time or place. Please."

But Hawthorn didn't heed her warning. Possibly, Jack figured, he didn't even hear it. This was between him and Jack now, and in no way was the bridge troll going to let such a golden opportunity to slam the unworthy, uneducated commoner who had dared to sully his daughter pass by.

"As much as you hold yourself responsible, your partner must accept a share of the blame. What was he doing in that laneway alone? How did he allow a lone man, armed only with a knife, to overpower an armed police officer? You see, Jack, you are not the only one to blame. But that can all change now. Now that you have identified your partner's killer, you can leave the division free of guilt and a need for vengeance. After all, didn't you say the killer will spend the rest of his life in jail? And aren't you responsible for that because you identified him? And if he is foolish enough to request a trial to refute the allegations, then you will play a pivotal role in that trial. It will be your testimony that convicts him.

"So you see, Jack, your vengeance is complete. All you need do is allow others to carry it out. You have done all you can to lay your partner's ghost to rest." Hawthorn smiled. "I'm sure if you could summon up his spirit and ask your partner —"

"His name is Simon, you asshole! Simon!" Jack was on his feet, his fists clenched in fury. "He was my friend and he was more of a man than you could ever dream of being, you worthless shit. He has a family and friends. He was more than a name you happened to read in the paper.

"Do I feel guilty? Of course I do. Only a heartless bastard like you wouldn't. If I could have, I would have killed that fucker *before* he had the chance to kill Sy. And if I hadn't been trying to save Sy's life, I would have gladly gunned him down as he ran away from me. You want to know something else? My vengeance isn't complete, far from it. I pray to God I'm there when he's arrested, because I swear to you, I'll blow his fucking head off without a second thought."

Jack stormed out of the room, grabbed a coat and his car keys, walked out of the house and slammed the door behind him.

Karen caught up to him in the driveway. "Where are you going?" Her voice was cold.

"I don't know. But I'm not staying in there with them. With *him*." He jabbed his finger at the house, as if she needed further clarification.

"That *him* is my father, Jack." She folded her arms and pinned him with a piercing stare. "Tell me, Jack, honestly. Were you serious in there? Would you really kill him if you found him?" No need to clarify whom she meant.

Jack faced her squarely, his face expressionless. As were his words. "In a heartbeat."

She dropped her eyes and shook her head. "I don't know who you are anymore, Jack, but I do know one thing." She lifted her gaze and it was her turn to speak impassively. "It's appropriate your shirts at work are now black. They match the man you've become."

Karen turned and walked into the house. Jack watched her until the door shut behind her, then got in his car and drove away.

Jack had no idea where he was going when he pulled out of the driveway, but it was no surprise when he headed into the city. The drive was a complete blur; he functioned on autopilot as a suppressed anger shattered its social chains and, with a roar of ecstasy, broke free.

Who the fuck did they think they were? Her father, especially. Laying all that guilt shit on him, acting concerned and friendly when Jack knew all Hawthorn wanted to do was break them up. Nothing would please that smug, righteous prick more than Karen leaving Jack and coming home to Daddy. It would be the ultimate put-down, the final confirmation that Jack wasn't good enough for George fucking Senior's daughter and never had been.

And Karen, sitting there, taking her father's side against him! "'Leave 51, Jack,'" he mimicked. "'It's changing you. I don't know you.' So, I have a black heart, do I?" He angrily wiped away a stray tear. "What am I supposed to do? Run away like a coward? Run away while that murdering whoreson is still out there? Fuck that!"

Before he realized it, he was exiting the Parkway onto Richmond Street. He stopped at the red light at Parliament and wondered where the platoon would be. It was pushing eleven o'clock, so the beach party would probably be warming up.

The light changed and Jack took his foot off the brake only to have to hammer it again as three young thugs sauntered in front of his car against the light. He laid on the horn and the one nearest him, a young white guy with greasy hair and ridiculously baggy jeans hanging more than halfway down his ass, gave him the finger . . . with a hand wearing a black leather glove.

Jack slammed the car into park. He was going to make that piece of shit eat those gloves. The three gangster wannabes jumped when he flung open the door.

Jack was halfway out the door when a horn blared behind him, penetrating but not banishing the red haze that saturated his thoughts. He had one foot on the pavement, the other still in the car. His intended targets were staring at him nervously from the sidewalk.

The horn sounded again and Jack cast his red-stained scowl at the other driver. The driver lifted his hands and sunk down into his seat. Jack stalked up to the wannabes and stopped inches from the one with the gloves. The kid was tall; he could have towered over Jack, but he shrank from the rage in Jack's eyes.

"Why are you wearing those gloves?" Jack snarled, his jaw barely moving.

"Huh?" the kid squeaked. His buddies had retreated a few steps.

"Why are you wearing those gloves?" Jack repeated.

"Ev . . . everyone's wearing them," he said tentatively. It's . . . it's cool?" The last word squeaked out as a question or a plea, as in *Please don't hurt me, I don't know what I'm doing.*

"The gloves. Give them to me."

It wouldn't be till later, when his buddies were relating the story to others, at his pride's great expense — although they would manage to avoid having to say what they were doing during the whole confrontation — that the similarity to the opening scene of *The Terminator* would be discerned. Luckily for them, all Jack wanted was the gloves, and he didn't rip anyone's heart out.

The kid stripped off the gloves — cheap imitation leather — and handed them to Jack with a trembling hand.

Jack took the gloves and held them up to the kid's face. "Do you know what these signify?"

The kid shook his head, his eyes locked on Jack's, fear welding their sight together.

"The gutless coward who wears these — the person you're idolizing by wearing them — killed a police officer, a good man. Killed him from behind like the coward he is. Do you think it's a good idea to make a hero out of someone who cuts a person's throat from behind? Someone too fucking cowardly to face a real man? Do you?"

The kid shook his head again and managed to get out a mousy "No."

"Then tell everyone you know who wears these gloves they are making a hero out of a fucking, ball-less coward. His name is Anthony Charles and if you ever meet him tell him I'm looking for him. Tell him he won't be able to hide behind anyone next time and when I do find him, I'll kill him. And if I ever see you wearing these again —" he slapped the kid's face with the gloves "— I'll shove them so far down your throat, the doctor will have to go in through your ass to get them out. You got that?"

"Sh — sure thing, mister. Uh, thanks?"

Jack stepped back, favoured the kid's cronies with a glare that sent them stumbling, threw the gloves in the car, got in and drove off.

Crossing the first drawbridge on Cherry Street south of the Lakeshore, Jack left the city behind him. Down here, on this man-made splat of land jutting into Lake Ontario, high-rises and towering office buildings ceased to exist. Most of the structures along the grid of roads south of the drawbridge resembled the land on which they sat: flat and broad. There was always talk of developing the area; the Docks nightclub had opened, but beyond that there was nothing much new.

Jack crossed the second drawbridge, a much more massive affair than its conservative cousin up the street. The water beneath the bridge was calm as his tires hummed over the steel grating that made up the bridge's body. At this hour, on a weeknight, the district was all but deserted. Jack didn't come across another car as he headed for the beach.

Instead of driving straight into the beach's parking lots, he hung a left on Unwin Avenue and plunged into the perfect setting for a horror movie. The narrow, two-lane road was paved, but it might as well have been dirt considering the condition it was in. Stunted scrub brush lined the road's southern flank, hiding a twisted warren of bike trails and footpaths, some official, most not. The other side of the road was a stereotypical slasher-film backdrop: old, shuttered buildings, mostly abandoned, poorly quarantined from the world by rusting chains and decrepit fences. Not far down the road, a solitary smokestack jutted into the night sky like a skeletal finger flipping off the distant city.

The brush opened up briefly on his right to reveal a dirt road — a driveway, really, to a little boating association clubhouse — stabbing arrow straight into the darkness. The streetlights along Unwin were intermittent; the tiny dirt road was nothing but a darker scar upon a dark landscape.

He turned into the darkness and flicked on his high beams. Faint red dots jumped back at him and grew brighter as he approached: the tail lights of parked cars, letting him know he wasn't too early for the beach party. Being too late had never been a concern; it wouldn't be the first time for the platoon working day shift to get calls from early morning joggers complaining about the vagrants passed out on the beach. Vagrants with badges. If they only knew. . . .

He tucked his aging Ford Taurus in behind someone's Lexus — bought with paid duties or a pile of court appearances, no doubt — and climbed out into the cool night air. It was a little chilly by the water and he was glad he had brought his old jean jacket. Karen hated the threadbare embarrassment and kept threatening to toss it into the nearest incinerator. Jack pulled its comforting familiarity around him and set off for the beach.

He returned to the car to retrieve the gloves he had seized from the kid. Or would that have been, technically, a robbery? Whichever. He tucked the gloves into his back pocket and went off to find his friends.

It didn't take long. Before he could see the leaping flames through the thinning bush, he could hear the familiar sounds: laughter, clinking bottles, classic rock playing in the background. It felt like coming home. The anger he had felt when the kid had given him the finger crept back into its lair deep inside him. It went willingly and without complaint; once free, it would never be shackled again. It could now come and go at will.

The natural barrier of brush separating road and sand gradually thinned, then disappeared just before the road came to an abrupt dead end. The secluded cul-de-sac was a choice parking spot for lovers. Except when the cops were having a beach party, that is.

The bonfire was a blazing beacon and Jack trudged through the soft sand to its siren's call. Silhouetted figures ringed the fire, drinking and laughing like modern-day pagans performing a sacred rite. And, in a way, they were. After-work platoon get-togethers — beach party, wing run, breakfast after night shift, a simple drink-fest at the nearest cop-friendly pub or bar — were a time-honoured police tradition. And a necessity.

Where else could you go to blow off steam about a job no one understood or tried to understand? Where else could you laugh at the criminals, the botched suicide attempts, the every-day violence? Who else but other cops could appreciate such black humour? If you didn't let loose once in a while, vent the mounting pressure, then you ended up a burned-out cop who didn't give a shit about anyone or anything.

"The Jacker's here!" Paul Townsend was the first one to spot him and hailed him gustily.

"The Jacker?"

"It's perfect for you," Paul declared, throwing a tree trunk of an arm across Jack's shoulders. The big guy wobbled a bit as he spoke. Seemed Paul had been venting for a while. "You're a Batman fan, aren't you?" He didn't wait for Jack's agreement. "The Joker, the Jacker. See?"

"Makes perfect sense. Maybe I should get a mask to go with it."

Paul stared at him, drunkenly perplexed. "Sue!" he hollered, brightening instantly. "Here comes your Dark Chocolate!" He staggered off in pursuit of the redheaded PW. Jack grinned and made a mental note to keep an eye on the big guy, make sure he didn't try driving home.

The heat from the fire was baking his skin before he got within ten feet. The flames were stabbing well over six feet into the starry sky, feeding off a new batch of wood. He surveyed the turnout. Most of the platoon was there — hell, even Boris was in attendance — as well as the officers from the CRU.

"Glad to see you made it, partner." Manny sidled up beside him, a bottle of Strongbow cider in hand. "Does that mean things went well or ill at home?"

Jack pointed at the cider. "You got another one of those?"

"Ooh, that good, huh? One medicinal cider coming up."

Manny was as good as his word and within seconds Jack was twisting off the cap and tossing it into the consuming flames. The cider, sharp and cold, hit his throat like ambrosia.

Manny waited for him to get down that all-important first slug before raising his bottle. "To . . . ?"

Jack considered for a moment. He looked about him and back at Manny. "To friends. To friends who understand."

"I'll drink to that." They clinked and drank and, wrapped in the warmth of the fire and friends, Jack felt the evening's shit melt away.

"I've got a case of those in the cooler over there by the picnic table," Manny informed him. "Help yourself. I'm not going to finish them; I've already promised to drive Paul home."

"Good man."

"Paul said you're a Batman fan. Guess that makes me Robin, huh?" Manny didn't sound pleased with the sidekick role.

"You sure as fuck ain't Batman."

Jack let the party flow around him and carry him where it would. He listened to and shared stories, laughed, cried bullshit when some stories grew too fantastical to be real. He was awarded best gross-out of the night with his cockroach-toe man. Sy had been right about that one; it was a keeper.

He kept an eye open for Jenny but never saw her. Surprisingly, he felt a pang of disappointment. He tried to analyze it, figure out why he, a married man and happily at that — most of the time, anyway — was disappointed that a woman, married as well, a woman he barely knew, wasn't there. It wasn't like there were no attractive women on the beach. In fact, 51 had a startlingly high number of good-looking PWs. Either that, or he was drunk already, which he doubted, having just cracked open his second cider.

Sue, Jenny's partner that day, was there, her crimson hair hanging in loose ringlets past her shoulders. She was wearing tight — no, exceptionally tight — jeans and no jacket and her Toronto Police T-shirt was cut off just below her breasts. She certainly was popular, flitting from male to male, but he noted with a critical eye that her belly-baring days were a few six-packs past their prime.

"Looking for another shaggle?"

Jack jumped. "Damn it, Manny. That's the second time you've snuck up on me tonight. How the hell do you do that?"

Manny smiled smugly. "Ninja training. Shh, don't tell anyone. So, does she have a good shaggle?"

Jack laughed. "*Sheuggle*, not shaggle. *Shew-gul*. It's Scottish for swagger, as in the *sheuggle* for a kilt."

"How do you spell that?"

"I have no freaking idea."

Manny tipped his bottle, just a Coke, toward Sue. "She has quite the reputation as a party girl."

"Tsk, tsk, Manny." Jack waggled his bottle reprovingly at his partner. "I would have thought you of all people would know to look past a person's reputation."

"There's reputations based on opinions and rumours and then there's Sue. You can ask her and she'll tell you. Hell, she'll show you."

"I'm married and besides, I like my women a little leaner."

"Hey, nothing wrong with a little padding." Manny patted his own padding affectionately. "So, you're saying, even if you were single and the opportunity arose, you'd turn her down."

Jack gagged on his drink and had to spit some of it back into the bottle. "Hell, no, I'm not saying that. *If* I was single and *if* the opportunity presented itself . . ."

Manny clapped him on the shoulder. "I got news for you, partner. *She* doesn't care if you're married — she actually prefers it — and she's been eyeing you all night." He released Jack and hurried off, mumbling something about needing to water the lake.

"I'm surprised to see you here."

Again, Jack jumped, but this time it was Jenny next to him and being startled never felt so good.

"A little jumpy, are we?" she teased.

"You must go to the same ninja school as Manny. Can I get you a drink?"

"One of those would be nice." She gestured to his cider, then followed him to the cooler.

Jack cracked open a fresh one and passed it to her. "They're actually Manny's, but he told me to help myself. He has to stay sober to drive Paul home."

"I hope he knows that being Paul's designated driver also means keeping him out of the lake."

"You're kidding, right?"

"Nope." She laughed, then sampled the cider. "Mmm, that's good. A lot of people think a beach party isn't a success until the SS Townsend sets sail."

"I hope he brought a change of clothes," Jack commented, eyeing the big man across the fire. Whatever Paul was explaining to Boris and a couple of rookies, it involved dramatic arm flailing.

"Oh, not to worry." Jenny smiled again. "He doesn't need a change of clothes when he goes swimming."

"Why not? Doesn't — oh, I see. I don't know if I want to be around for that."

"Take it from someone who has seen Paul skinny-dip on pre-vious occasions: if you have a fragile male ego, you don't want to be here when it happens." She waited for Jack to tilt his bottle up. "And that's when the water's cold."

Jack sputtered and lost some cider. He wiped his lips while he laughed. "Okay, my ego may not be fragile, but . . ."

She joined him in the laugh. "Kind of like me standing top-less next to Dolly Parton."

Taking the opportunity, Jack gave her an appraising once-over.

Her jeans weren't nearly as tight as Sue's, but they definitely had a comfortable look to them, a look that made Jack wonder what it would feel like to run his hands over the curves hinted at beneath the fabric. Her T-shirt — did all cops wear tees on their off time? — was unaltered and hung loosely on her lean frame, but it couldn't hide the fact that she was small-breasted. Her hair fell in a thick, wavy black mass over her shoulders. His blatant assessment finished where it began, with her wonderful smile.

Jenny was eyeing him expectantly, lips quirked. "Well?"

"I'd take you over a dozen Dolly Partons any day."

"Why, Mr. Warren, if I didn't know better, I'd say you were flirting with me."

"I am flirting with you," he admitted. He tapped his wedding ring against the bottle. "I'm married. I'm allowed to," he explained earnestly.

"I'm not sure I follow you on that one. You'll have to educate me." She tilted her head to drain the bottle.

Jack watched the curve of her throat working as she emptied the bottle. God, how he wanted to feel that skin beneath his lips. "Because I'm married, it won't lead to anything, so I'm allowed to flirt. And since you're married —" he indicated her ring "— with children, it makes it doubly, if not triply — is that a word? — allowed. And anyway, there's no way I could flirt with you if I was single. If I thought I had even the slightest chance of succeeding, I'd have embarrassed myself a half dozen times over by now and you'd be walking away thinking I was the world's biggest jerk."

"Ah, I see now." She nodded sombrely. "And if I wasn't married? Would you still be allowed to flirt with me?"

He pursed his lips, considering. "Yes," he decided, "but I would have to flirt with caution."

"Then you'd better proceed with caution, Jacker —" somehow that sounded so much better coming from her than it did from Paul "— 'cause I'm not married." Jenny tapped her bottle against his chest and winked.

"And the ring?"

"I got tired of being hit on by horny firemen."

"And the kids? I heard you say you have kids. Or are they a ruse as well?"

"Nope, they're real. That's why I was late. I had to go home and get them."

Shocked, he looked around. "They're here? Where are they?"

"Knowing my boys, they're probably swimming right now."

He cast her a look from the corner of his eye. "We're not talking about human kids, are we?"

"I never said human," she said in all innocence. "It's not my fault you assumed they were human."

"I'm a little disappointed." He hung his head and toed the sand.

She slid up to him and ruffled his hair. "Are you sad 'cause you think I lied to you? I didn't, you know."

"It's not that," Jack replied in mock seriousness. "I was going to tell you that you have an amazing and sexy body for a woman who has had children. Now all I get to tell you is that you have an amazing, sexy body."

She laughed and punched him in the shoulder. "You don't stop, do you?"

He looked up and grinned. "Not really, no."

"Why are you carrying around gloves? Expecting a cold front to come through?"

"Gloves? Oh, those. I forgot I had them." Jack pulled the wannabe's gloves out of his back pocket. As he slapped them idly against his hand, he cast a suspicious eye at Jenny. "Were you checking out my ass when I went to get the drinks?"

"Not at all," she replied, offended. "I just happened to notice them flapping around when you were walking over to the cooler ... as I checked out your ass."

"That's better." He handed her a fresh cider and sat down on the picnic table next to her. The fire had died down some and they had dragged the table close to the flames, but the party was far from dying. If anything, it had grown in size as E platoon, the shift just starting evenings, had joined the party after they had finished for the night. Since this was E's first day back, they had just learned that afternoon that Jack had identified Anthony Charles as Sy's killer. Several officers from the shift, including one of their sergeants, Don Pembleton, had stopped to congratulate Jack on the ID.

"So how is it? My ass, I mean."

"It's okay, I guess." That sly smile he was beginning to appreciate belied the casualness of her words. "The gloves? When I asked you about them, you got this amused smile on your face. There a story to go with it?"

"A story or a robbery confession, depending on which way you look at it."

"Now you definitely have to tell me." Jenny turned to him on the bench and propped her chin on her hand.

"Well, you know how the shitheads have started wearing the gloves since Sy was killed?"

"Yeah, the little bastards are honouring a fucking cop killer."

It was easy, looking at her, to forget that Jenny was a cop, but she belonged at this beach party as much as anyone.

Other officers standing nearby heard the comment and added to it. "Yeah, we saw pukes wearing them all over the place tonight."

"Is that what they mean? Fuck that."

"No way should we let them get away with that shit."

"You take those off someone, Warren? Cool. What happened?"

Jack had an audience, and he was suddenly uncomfortable, worried they'd see him as a loose cannon or a nut job, set to explode at any time. He needn't have worried. He finished his story to a rousing cheer and Jenny wrapped him in a delicious, congratulatory hug.

"That's what we should do this week," one E officer suggested. "Grab every fucking pair of gloves we see. We can burn them all at the next beach party."

That idea got another round of enthusiastic approval; then Sergeant Pembleton pushed forward and quashed the excitement by yelling for everyone to shut the bleeding fuck up. Pembleton was not a small man and his voice carried, catching the attention of those who had drifted away from the fire. When everyone had wandered in to listen, he raised his voice again. He was a respected sergeant, was seen more as a senior PC who just happened to have stripes on his shoulders than an actual supervisor, and when he spoke, people listened.

"For those of you with cow shit jammed in your bleeding fucked-up ears —" he was also known for a love of profanity "— Jack Warren here identified the soulless motherfucking craven coward who stole our brother from us."

Another swell of applause and calls of "Jacker! Jacker!"

When the praise faded, Pembleton continued. "Simon Carter was a God-blessed fucking great cop." More cheers. "Jack lost a partner. We lost a brother. This shithole of a city and its spineless, good-for-fucking-nothing whoresons of politicians lost a good cop." Pembleton paused and Jack was astounded to see him wipe away a tear, openly and shamelessly. When next he spoke, his voice was choked with emotion. "And the world lost a great man! To Simon!"

"To Simon!" the gathering echoed, and Pembleton was not the only one holding back tears.

The sergeant leaned toward Jack and asked, "May I?" with a quiet politeness Jack never would have guessed he possessed. Jack handed over the gloves and Pembleton held them high. "If we are fucking going to do this, we do it bloody right!" He brandished the gloves like an insane matador waving a red flag to rile up a herd of bulls. "This is not a God-fucking-damned contest to see who can bloody well get the most shit-smeared gloves. This is for Simon and for us! When a motherless, sister-fucking puke wears these, he's bloody well spitting in our fucking faces!"

Veins bulged and throbbed in Pembleton's temples. He scrutinized the pack of officers, a warlord judging if his troops were fit for battle. They were.

"I will talk to the other shifts, you bloody fucking well better believe I will. No fucking tickets, no piss-useless traffic stops. As long as one vile, putrid, shit-smeared, cocksucking puke dares — dares! — to wear a motherfucking pair of these, nothing — goddamn *nothing!* — matters. Do you motherless whoresons hear me?"

They did and roared with approval.

While the thunderous cry echoed across the still, dark waters, Pembleton formally returned the gloves to Jack. "Jack, the honour is yours." He gestured to the fire.

Jack stood and the throng fell silent. All eyes were upon him as he stepped up to the flames. The heat seared his face. He looked at Jenny and wasn't surprised to see tears streaking her face. Others were crying as well, and he finally comprehended that he was not the only one who had suffered a loss when Sy was murdered. As Pembleton had said, they had all lost a brother.

He fingered the gloves, rubbing the cheap, coarse fabric between his fingers. With the blaze scorching his skin, he held the gloves over the flames. He realized this was what he had intended to do when he had returned to his car for the gloves. It was where they belonged. Only fire could burn away this disease. He tossed the gloves into the heart of the inferno.

Somewhere at the back of the horde it began softly, mounting in strength as more voices picked it up, adding their fury to it, until it roared from scores of throats to batter at the heavens above.

"No more gloves! No more gloves! No more gloves!"

"No more gloves!"

Jack was struck again by the image of a pagan ceremony. Pure and heartfelt. Its emotional intensity unadulterated by civilized restraints.

War had been declared.

The fire was nothing but a heap of charred wooden bones and iridescent sparks flaring up on the heated air to blink out of their fragile existence. The embers still held more life and power than the distant sun that was just beginning to stir on the horizon.

The air had grown cold and damp as the night stretched toward day and the picnic table was all but straddling the remains of the bonfire so Jack could catch the last of the fleeting heat. He was sitting on its top, his feet on the seat. The wood was unyielding and sore to sit on for any length of time, but he had no desire to move, not even to rub his bare arms against the cold.

Jenny had passed out on the table about an hour earlier, too tired to drive home. She was wrapped in his jacket and using his lap for a pillow. He stared down at this woman he barely knew and wondered what the hell he was doing. He was married to an amazing woman but had, in a sense, just spent the night with another woman. If her head resting on his thigh as she slept was the extent of the physical interaction between them, then why did he feel guilty?

Jenny stirred, murmuring softly in her sleep, and Jack carefully brushed a strand of hair from her cheek. Such incredible hair. He hadn't known until he viewed her from behind that those mesmerizing waves cascaded down to her waist. He allowed his fingers to linger, soaking up the feel of her skin like a thief making off with a priceless treasure.

There weren't many party survivors. Bodies, asleep or passed out, littered the beach like chunks of driftwood washed up by the morning tide. Jack was the last of his platoon; even Paul had succumbed to the late hour and alcohol, allowing Manny to bundle him shivering and damp — yes, the SS Townsend had sailed — into his car. That had been around four.

A car door slammed and one of Jenny's cohorts from the CRU

strode onto the beach, remarkably wide awake. He had two take-out trays of Tim Hortons coffee balanced in one hand and a bulging Tim's bag in the other. He roamed the beach, squatting down whenever he found another casualty of the festivities. Jack was reminded of a medic searching a battlefield for survivors, administering aid in the form of caffeine and pastries.

The beach medic reached Jack and kept his voice down when he saw that Jenny was asleep. "I just grabbed a bunch of black coffees with sugar and milk on the side. That okay with you?"

"Okay? My God, man, you're a saint." Jack recognized him as one of the younger officers in the foot patrol and figured his training officer had done a hell of a job. Getting coffee while working was one thing, bringing coffee to the beach was above and beyond.

The young officer blushed faintly at the praise and handed Jack a coffee. "Muffin? All I've got left —" he peered into the bag "— is carrot and raisin bran. What do you think your girlfriend would like?"

"She's not ... picky. Why not leave one of each? How much do I owe you?"

The copper scrunched up his face as if Jack had spit in it. "My treat, Jacker, for everyone. Someone has to look after these bozos. Besides, I like Jenny and it's about time she found herself a good guy." He set a second coffee next to the muffins and moved on, a morning angel come to earth to heal the afflicted.

"So, I'm your girlfriend, am I?"

"You heard that, did you?" Jack lifted his arm out of the way so she could sit up. "And if you were awake, how come you didn't correct him?"

"Because I'm not picky, remember?" She accepted the offered coffee. "Except when it comes to muffins. I'll take the carrot." She took a healthy gulp of coffee. "Oh, that's good." Another gulp. "And maybe I liked the sound of that — your girlfriend, I mean."

Jack nearly dumped his coffee in the lap Jenny had so recently vacated, and she broke out in peals of laughter, startling some curious seagulls into panicked flight. "Oh, my God, Jack. You should see your face." More guffaws, then she continued. "Relax, I'm just joking. You are a good guy, but I'm not a home wrecker."

He composed himself while checking for coffee stains. "That's good. You had me scared for a second there. I mean, just because we slept together tonight . . ." He let that one linger.

"Slept together? I know I slept. Did you?"

"No, not really."

"Then we didn't sleep together. I'm not a slut, thank you." She tossed her hair indignantly, and even uncombed, with grains of sand and a few fluffs of ash, it was beautiful.

"Ah, I see. *We* didn't sleep together, but *you* slept with *me*," he pointed out.

"Oh, fuck. I *am* a slut." She laughed.

He slipped an arm around her for a comforting hug. "I still respect you."

She stretched but not enough to dislodge his arm. "Where are the kids?"

"Over there."

Beneath a wind-warped pine, a cuddled mass of black and brown fur snored peacefully. Her Rottweiler, Hammer, and Mugsy the pug had crept off to bed after swimming with the SS Townsend.

A thin, golden light was peeking at them through the trees. "Don't tell me that's the sun."

"I won't, but it is."

"I'd better get going. I have to be up for court in a few hours." She stretched again, a full-blown, arms-in-the-air stretch this time.

Jack reluctantly relinquished his hold on her. "Glad I'm not you, then."

She shrugged out of his jacket. "Thanks for the loan. Are you going to be okay?"

"No problem. I'll grab some more coffee with breakfast somewhere before I do the drive home."

"No, not like that." Her voice was serious. "I mean with your wife. Sounds like you left on bad terms last night and I can't imagine you not coming home would make it any better. Did you call her?"

He shook his head. "I have my phone with me, but I never did. Guess I was still a little too mad to call." *And I guess she wasn't concerned enough to call. Let's call it even, shall we?*

Jenny turned to face him. "I know we don't really know each other, but I've seen enough cops spend the night away from home and it usually means there's trouble. Is everything okay?"

Jack paused. Was everything good with him and Karen? If it was, would he have spent the night on the beach? "I guess it isn't," he admitted.

She sipped her coffee, waiting for him to expand on his answer, and when he didn't, she nudged his leg with her knee. "And?"

"And? Hell, where to begin?" He ran a hand through his hair and blew out a frustrated breath of air.

"The beginning's always a good spot."

He eyed her speculatively. "You sure you want to hear about this? Don't you have court?"

Jenny shrugged. "Court can wait. C'mon, spill it."

Jack told her what Karen and her parents had done.

"She wants you to go back to 32?" Jenny asked.

"32? Hell, she wants me to quit. Her and her parents."

"That doesn't sound good."

"Trust me, it isn't. They ganged up on me last night, saying I'm being selfish staying in 51, that I should quit and get a nice, safe job where Karen wouldn't have to worry about me all the time."

"What do you want to do?" Jenny asked.

"Stay in 51," he said instantly. "I couldn't go back to 32."

"And if she gives you an ultimatum, 51 or her, what then?"

"There's no question. It's her."

She studied him for a moment, then surprised him by stepping in and giving him a quick kiss on the cheek. "A lot of guys would have chosen the job. You're a good man, Jacker."

"Please, just Jack." He smiled.

She smiled back, and it was brighter than the dawn. "Jack it is, then."

Thursday, 21 September
2217 hours

The rain was pelting down, a falling flood the car wipers could barely keep up with. Jack was nauseous from another burgeoning migraine and Manny had surrendered the wheel after Jack explained that driving was easier on his head and stomach than being a passenger.

"Why not just go home sick if it's getting that bad?"

Jack grimaced. "Let's just say home isn't a very pleasant place these days. Besides, I popped some meds and they should be kicking in soon."

"Things still not good with Karen?"

"Not even close. The latest fight started Friday when she got home from work and ended this morning when she left for work. And I'm afraid that was just the first round."

"That sucks, man."

"That's an understatement. And it's the same fucking argument every day. She's worried the division will change me into some kind of asshole racist cop. She says it's already started, that I'm mad all the time."

"Dude, your partner was murdered a few weeks ago. Of course you're mad. Anyone would be."

"Try telling that to her."

The leather glove fashion trend was virtually gone. Over the past week, the 51 cops had waged a war on anyone daring to support a cop killer. And it wasn't just 51. Officers from other divisional foot patrols plus the mounted unit and other Major Crime officers had swamped the division to reinforce the blue wall. Twenty-four hours a day, cops were smothering the streets, searching the halls and stairwells, smashing down the doors of crack houses. God help anyone found wearing black leather gloves.

The word had gone out: 51 wanted Charles, and the shit kickings, shakedowns and tune-ups would continue until he was found. The low-lifes were learning the price of aiding Anthony Charles. People were hauled off to the cells or commanded to carry the message that the division would remain in permanent lockdown until Charles was found. Preferably alive.

One veteran officer said he'd never seen the division so quiet for so long. "It's like the angel of death has passed through and laid waste all the criminals, first-born or not." Except the angel of death would have had a gentler touch. But despite the pressure, Charles was still free and flaunting his fame as a cop killer. He had been spotted several times and chased twice, but he kept eluding capture, primarily because he was getting help from citizens.

"It's like he's Robin Hood or something."

Jack looked at his partner. "Who's like Robin Hood?"

Manny had a habit of making abrupt topic changes and if Jack wasn't paying close attention, he got lost.

"Charles, man. He's like this hero to the villagers and whenever the sheriff gets close to him, they all help hide him away. It ain't right, man."

"No, it isn't." On parade they had learned that Charles was making a point of showing himself in the division, to both the public and the police. Mason had told them Charles's control of the downtown crack trade was nearly absolute, despite the extra police pressure. It was only a matter of time before he got his hands on all of it. The fuck was getting rich on Sy's blood.

Jack gripped the wheel hard enough to temporarily drown out the pain behind his eyes. "I know he'll get caught eventually. I want to be there when it happens. I pray to God I'm there."

And sometimes God answered prayers.

"5105 in pursuit of male wanted for homicide!" A siren shrieked in the background. Jack held his breath, waiting for the words he needed to hear. "It's Anthony Charles! Northbound on Parliament from King, driving a black Honda SUV...."

Jack didn't wait for the licence plate number. He stomped on the gas as Manny hit the lights and siren. They were just south of King on Jarvis, two major streets over. Jack headed north, paralleling the pursuit. If Charles cut west, they'd have him. If he went east, they were just a few seconds behind him. Units from across the division were responding to the pursuit and cars from 53 Division, which shared the radio band with 51, started blasting down from the north.

"5105, keep up your location and road conditions."

"Still northbound Parliament, passing Queen. Single male occupant. Just blew through a red at Queen."

"Is that Boris?" Jack asked incredulously.

"I think so. He's working with Paul tonight."

"5105, what are the road and traffic conditions?"

Boris hesitated and Jack's opinion of him actually went up a bit. The rain was still pelting down and if traffic on Parliament was anything like it was on Jarvis, which was too fucking busy for a Thursday night....

A new voice, a no-nonsense voice, got on the air. *"5105, this is Sergeant Bragado of Communications. You will advise of the road and weather conditions immediately, or this pursuit will be terminated."*

"Don't you dare, don't you dare, you cocksucking prick," Jack muttered.

A slight pause and then, "Still northbound Parliament passing Dundas, suspect's speed is —" Jack could picture Boris leaning across the seat to get a look at the speedometer, which meant a few more seconds for the pursuit to last "— approximately seventy kilometres an hour. Not bad for road and traffic conditions." Just the blaring of the siren for a few seconds, anything to delay an answer. Damn, Boris was acting like a real cop. "Approaching Gerrard. It's raining, traffic is . . . light. Now eastbound on Gerrard app —"

Sergeant Bragado, monitoring the pursuit from a detached, uninvolved position, issued his verdict: *"5105 and all units. This pursuit is terminated due to unsafe road and weather conditions. I repeat, this pursuit is terminated. All units abandon the pursuit."*

"Fuck you." Jack braked hard, then swung hard onto Gerrard, the Crown Vic's ass end sliding wildly on the flooded road. Once the car was righted, he bore down on the gas, urging the worn car to even greater speed, its abused engine screaming with effort.

"5105, suspect just crashed at Gerrard and Sackville! Suspect has bailed and is running northbound. My escort is in foot pursuit."

"Get him, Paul. Get the little fucker."

Jack hit a green light at Sherbourne and added a bit more speed. Manny looked at him as if he was wondering when Jack was going to start driving fast. Red light coming up at Parliament. So close now!

Boris's huffing, strained voice kept up the pursuit. "Still northbound. . . . Suspect wearing black Tor . . . ah, God . . . black Toronto Raptors jacket." The last was spit out as Boris's brief involvement in the foot pursuit ended in pained gasps.

Jack swung into the oncoming lanes to dodge the stopped cars on Gerrard. "Clear!" Manny shouted and Jack goosed it, forcing a southbound driver to hammer on the brakes as he peeled through the intersection. An angry horn was batted away by the siren's urgent scream.

Paul's voice, strong but hurting, took over the pursuit. "Eastbound Spruce! Eastbound Spruce!"

Gerrard and Sackville was a clogged mess. A white sedan, its front end a crumpled ruin, lay across the eastbound lanes of

Gerrard; a black SUV had a telephone pole buried halfway up its engine block on the southeast corner. 5105, its emergency lights still flashing red and white in the rain, was just south of the SUV.

"Looks like Paul expected him to run into the Park," Manny commented as Jack mashed the brakes.

The tires burned away the water to find a grip on the pavement; when he had dumped enough speed, Jack was off the brake and steering into the turn. As the car came out of the corner onto Sackville, Jack was back on the gas and they were flying up Sackville in a matter of heartbeats.

"Nice turn, dude."

"I've lost him!" Paul yelled over the air. "Suspect last seen northbound through the Spucecourt schoolyard. Damn it!"

Sergeant Rose was on the radio instantly and — God fucking love her for a man-hating, fuck-you-over-in-a-second bull dyke — took the situation by the balls and made it dance to her tune.

"5151, I want a perimeter thrown up now! This is the last time that puke runs from us. Townsend! Where are you?"

"On Spruce by the school. He hasn't cut back south."

"Everybody listen up!" Rose barked. "I want units on Spruce, Sackville, Sumach and Wellesley. Keep your roof lights on and get out of your cars. I don't want to hear anyone bitching about the rain. I want him to know he's caught. Let's force him to go to ground. Dispatch, do we have enough units for the perimeter?"

There was the slightest of pauses as the dispatcher consulted her screen. *"10-4, Sergeant. I have units from 51, 52 and 53. 54 and 55 are offering if we need them."*

"Good. Get as many over here as possible. I want a fence of uniforms and cars around this area. I'll be using the school on Spruce as the command post. Townsend, I'll meet you there."

"10-4, 5151, command post at Sprucecourt school. K94 advises he is on the way, ETA, fifteen minutes. ETF is also responding."

Units began advising radio of their locations and Manny grabbed the mike. "5108, we're at Sackville and Carlton."

"10-4, '08. Sackville and Carlton."

Jack parked just north of Carlton. "Manny, you go to the intersection, I'll take north up Sackville."

The rain was still pummelling the ground and Jack watched as bands of heavier rain swept across the street. He had his radio on, hearing but not paying much attention, waiting for shouts of discovery or another foot pursuit.

Within minutes they had the residential area cut off from the rest of Cabbagetown. The trees were old and mature, the houses well taken care of and cherished. Renovations had not spoiled the community by bringing anything too modern to its family-friendly streets. Within the chaos of 51, Cabbagetown was an oasis of small-town life.

The roads were laid out with grid-like precision, though there was a confusing blend of two-way and one-way avenues. But within the grid, precision gave way to a labyrinth of emaciated streets, choked lanes and elongated driveways. A thousand places to hide, a thousand places for someone to miss Charles.

Jack stood on Sackville Street, a one-way southbound artery through the neighbourhood. Parked cars lined the west side; the remaining lane was almost too narrow for trucks. Bulls in china shops had nothing on moving trucks in Cabbagetown. The homes on the street had postage stamp–sized front yards but also enough trees and well-manicured bushes to offer a fleeing felon a choice of hiding spots.

Jack stood at the end of Sackville Place, a narrow one-lane alley that ended at its heftier namesake. He kept his eyes moving north and south, determined that Charles would not slip past him. The scout car, sitting between him and Manny, painted the houses and falling rain with strobes of red and white.

Sergeant Rose's human fence was in place. In a few minutes, they would send in a dog and the ETF and Charles would be taken into custody. Nice and civilized.

Better than the asshole deserves.

The rain fell. The radio quieted as units settled in for the siege. There was no fear of anyone giving up on the perimeter. The city could go to hell right then, and none of the officers would budge. This was Charles's last stand.

"K94, exiting the 401 to southbound Parkway. I should be there in about ten minutes."

"10-4, K9," Rose acknowledged. "ETF is already here. They're suiting up and will be ready for you when you get here."

Jack listened to the exchange with mixed feelings. Until Charles was arrested, the officers on the perimeter would remain wet sentinels. This was Robin Hood's last chase. But Jack wanted to be there when he went down. Preferably in a hail of bullets.

Minutes passed, marked by the oscillating car lights. Partial seconds ticked away in flashes of red and white.

The rain continued to fall. Jack shifted his feet, feeling the water squish in his boots. A raincoat would have been nice, but his was in his locker; he rarely brought it out with him. Hell, he would even appreciate his hat, just to keep the rain out of his eyes. He was contemplating going back to the car to get it when movement down Sackville Place caught his eye.

A shadow stepped onto the slender street, a street light shining on its rain-slick surface. The shadow, man-sized, paused, looking back the way it had come. The shadow's jacket was hooded, but rain and poor light made further details impossible.

Jack's hand fell to his gun. Another shadow joined the first, a small, four-legged one. Jack grinned at his nerves, but his hand felt comfortable on the gun and he left it there.

Hide in plain sight. I wouldn't put it past the bastard. Ambush some poor schmuck out walking his dog, take his raincoat and dog and walk casually past the line of police officers. Hell, even give them a wave and thumbs-up as he passed them.

The shadow walked toward Jack, his shoulders and head hunched. Against the rain or to hide his face? Jack snapped open his holster.

The man stopped not twenty feet from Jack. Had he finally noticed the flashing lights? Had he heard the faint warning snap of Jack's holster? The dog, a little fur mop with its own raincoat, stopped as well for a sniff and a piss.

Jack drew his gun and held it down by his leg. He wiped his eyes free of rain. He announced his presence with a firm "Evening, sir."

The man jumped and the little fur mop was forced to hop with him. "Oh, officer. You scared me." The man held one hand, a white hand, Jack noted, theatrically against his chest.

While the man composed himself, Jack slipped his gun back into its holster.

"Is there something I should be worried about?" the man inquired, shooting puzzled glances up and down the street.

"We're just looking for someone, sir. That's all."

"Not a black fellow in a Raptors jacket, is it?"

Jack's stomach clenched. "You saw him? Whereabouts?"

The man pointed down Sackville Place. "Back on Flagler. He was near some cars when I came out with Jasper. He waved at me like he knew me, but I didn't recognize him. Is that who you're after?"

"Could be," Jack replied indifferently. "I'll pass the info along. Thank you, sir."

Jasper led his owner off into the rain. Jack reached for his radio but paused. He stared down the tiny street and the flashes of red rain became a spray of blood in a dark alley.

Nice and civilized. Sy's blood, hot and flowing between his fingers, stealing his friend's life away.

Better than he deserves.

Jack's hand fell away from his radio. He drew his Glock and slipped away from the flashing police lights.

Flagler Street was a driveway with a superiority complex. It ventured north from Sackville Place for a hundred feet or so before ending at a tall wood fence. A solid row of townhouses lined the west side, the front steps of each home touching down on the street. There were no yards, no trees, no parked cars. Nothing to hide behind.

Halfway up the east side, another driveway branched off to the east, running behind the houses that sat on the north side of Sackville Place. Those houses also grew right up to the street. No street parking; was there parking behind the houses?

Jack stood by the first townhouse, searching the rain-soaked night for Charles. He could only see a slice of the driveway leading east from Flagler Street. If he wanted Charles, he would have to go down its throat.

He stepped from cover, gun in front of him, angled down. He knew what he was doing was wrong, dangerous. He moved up Flagler anyway.

The house to his right had an SUV parked nose in beneath a second-floor deck at the rear, creating an open-sided car port. Jack moved up to the SUV, then squatted by a rear tire. The north side of the driveway was lined with flat-roofed garages; the only illumination came from the streetlight on Sackville Place.

But it was enough light to see Charles.

He had his back to Jack, not thirty feet from him, tucked into a tiny niche made by the first garage and a wood fence that jutted out a foot or two past the garage. Charles was trying to climb the fence, but the rain-soaked wood and sodden ivy along its top defied his fingers. His leather-clad fingers.

Smart. Climb to the flat roof of a garage. The dogs can't follow and cops forget to look up. Wait for them to pass, make a break for Regent Park. Robin Hood lives to embarrass the police again.

Jack smiled grimly in the rain.

Not this time.

He stepped away from the SUV and quietly cut the distance between him and Charles, staying under the edge of the connected carports. He wiped rain from his eyes and forehead. Charles had been too lucky for too long.

Jack stopped when less than fifteen feet separated them. He could hear Charles cursing softly as his hands slipped on the fence. Jack raised his gun. The basketball logo on Charles's jacket made an ideal target.

But that would be too easy for Charles.

Keeping his gun levelled, Jack whispered a word into the rain. *"Charles."*

Charles froze, his arms stretched above him. Slowly he turned around. He looked surprised when he saw only Jack, a lone officer. He smirked. Water washed down his angular face, dripped from his unconcerned brow.

"Are you going to arrest me now, officer?" He kept his hands raised, still smirking. "How you going to do that on your own?"

Jack stared at him down the sights of his gun. He was taller than Jack remembered, but he wasn't cowering behind a human shield this time and Jack could picture that hard face taunting him from behind Sy's shoulder.

"What're you going to do if I decide to run away, officer?" He took a step to his right. Jack followed with his Glock. "You going to shoot an unarmed man in the back?"

"Like I should have the night you killed my partner?" Jack's voice was soft, but at his words Charles halted. "You don't remember me, do you?"

Charles stared at Jack, the smirk gone. Jack saw a trace of fear in his features. "I didn't kill your partner. I didn't kill any cop."

"Lies," Jack snarled, his voice barely more than a whisper. "You slit his throat and laughed."

Charles's face showed real fear as the importance of Jack's words sank into him. His hands, which had begun to fall, darted skyward again. "I didn't kill your partner!"

"Then die with that lie on your lips," Jack hissed. Then, louder, "Drop it! Drop it now!"

Charles thrust his hands out, begging, pleading. "I give up! I give up!" he screamed, but Jack roared over him, ordering him to *Drop it, drop it now.*

Jack's finger slid onto the trigger and he saw the realization of death in Charles's eyes. Jack smiled.

When you look into the abyss, the abyss looks into you. Sy's words sounded clearly in Jack's head, as clearly as if Sy were standing next to him.

This is for you, Sy. But Jack could picture his partner, his friend, shaking his head in sorrow. Sorrow for Jack.

Charles stood frozen, his hands above his head, his lies and pleas silent in his throat. Jack stared at the monster who had so unfeelingly ended a good man's life. He deserved to die. Imprisoned, he would be a hero, admired. Dead, justice would be done.

Whoever fights monsters should see to it that in the process he does not become a monster. Jack's words back to Sy.

Charles stared at him, rigid with fear. A perfect target. A simple squeeze of the trigger, once, twice. Done.

This isn't justice, it's murder. Sy's voice or his own?

I don't know who you are anymore. Karen.

Jack almost staggered from the force that whispered memory carried. She had asked him if he would kill Charles, given the chance, and he had sworn he would. *In a heartbeat.*

I don't know who you are anymore.

Charles deserved to die, but not at the price of Jack's soul. Keeping Charles covered, Jack reached for his radio. "5108 to radio. I have Charles in custody."

Friday, 22 September
0317 hours

Jack quietly closed the front door. Slipping off his shoes and dropping his jacket, he tiptoed up the stairs, not bothering with the lights. He stood in the bedroom doorway, watching Karen sleep. She was wearing an old sweatshirt and had kicked off the covers. He smiled; he'd never had to complain about her hogging the sheets. He breathed in the sight of her, relishing the stillness of the moment and the love he felt for her.

He knew how close he had come to losing her since the night of Sy's murder. He had gone beyond grief and sorrow, had let the guilt consume him until there was nothing left in him but a mindless rage. Sy had warned him, tried to steer him away from that abyss, but in his need for vengeance Jack had become what he fought.

But tonight, thank God, he had stepped back from the abyss. He had to see if he'd turned aside in time.

He sat on the edge of the bed and laid the flowers — a poor selection of blooms from an all-night convenience store and already beginning to wilt, but where else could he get flowers at three in the morning? — next to Karen. She stirred, touched the flowers and looked up at him.

"Jack?" Sleep gave way to puzzlement. "Why are you sitting in the dark?" She reached up to touch his cheek and found it wet with tears. "Jack?"

"It's over, Karen." He scooped her up in his arms and pulled her to him, laughing through his tears. "It's over."

Monday, 25 September
1627 hours

"5103 on the air?"

"Not even giving us time to sign on today."

"Dude, you're a hero. People can't wait to talk to you. That's what you get for taking the weekend off, man. Your adoring public missed you."

It was Jack's first day back since arresting Charles. He had been under strict orders from the Staff to "disappear for a few days and celebrate." He and Karen had taken off for a three-day weekend at a spa resort. Although the trees had been spectacular with colour, they had rarely made it out of their room.

"This is '03, dispatch. We're just in the process of signing on."

"10-4. Is this PC Warren?"

"See, dude? I told you."

Jack made a *yeah, sure* face at Manny as he keyed the mike. "10-4 again, dispatch."

"Detective Mason needs to see you in the Crown's office at College Park Courts as soon as possible. 10-4?"

"10-4. Mark us heading over." Off radio, he asked, "Wonder what that's all about?"

The scout car roared to sluggish life. "Probably wants to discuss what type of award you're getting."

"No need to be jealous, Manny. I'll be sure to point out that you were in the car that night."

"Gee, dude, thanks."

The courthouse at 444 Yonge Street was a bit of an oddity as far as courts went. First, it was on the second floor above retail stores, not in a building of its own, and there was no parking anywhere around it. Granted, parking at most of Toronto's courts sucked, but at least there was some. Manny parked on a side street that, during the day, was lined with police cars, both marked and unmarked. There were no police cars at this hour.

They dodged the rush-hour traffic crossing Yonge and made it inside unscathed. "I'm going to head downstairs for something to eat. Meet me there, okay?"

"Sure. I can't imagine I'll be long." Jack punched the elevator button while Manny disappeared down the stairs to the basement food court.

The second floor featured metal detectors and a wide central corridor, which during the day was filled with criminals and cops, defence lawyers and Crown attorneys, mingling and hammering out plea bargains or stubbornly waiting for trial. It was neutral ground, a watering hole where an uneasy truce held sway over the natural adversaries.

In the late afternoon, only a few stragglers occupied the hard wooden benches lining the walls; justice was a nine-to-five — more like a ten-to-four, actually — job.

From the elevator, Jack headed down a side hallway to the police office, hoping someone knew where Mason was. It was fine to say to meet him in the Crown's office, but which one? Every Crown had his own. Mason saved him the trouble by meeting him in the hall; the detective did not look happy.

"Jack. Thank fuck you're here. We've got a problem."

Jack didn't have time to ask before he was steered into the closest room, a library. Heavy tomes — legal texts, Jack assumed — filled the shelves lining much of the four walls. A small conference table was squeezed in between the shelves. Two men, one young, the other not, rose when Mason ushered Jack into the room.

"Officer Warren?" the younger one asked. He was a tiny fellow with metal-framed glasses and a receding hairline. He stuck out his hand. "I'm Daniel Stevens, head Crown attorney. This is Judge Warren. No relation, I trust?"

"No, none." They all shook hands and took seats, an anxious-looking Mason next to Jack. The judge and lawyer sat opposite the two cops and Jack felt like he was sitting at a negotiating table between a union and the company employing its members, a union and a company with a history of bad blood.

"I'll get straight to the point, officer." Stevens folded his hands on the table and leaned forward, fixing Jack with what he guessed was supposed to be an intimidating stare. "We have a problem with the case against Anthony Charles."

"A problem? What kind of problem? Is he lodging some bull-shit complaint about the arrest?"

"I'm afraid it's much bigger than that. It's regarding your identification of the accused. I was uncomfortable with it and that's why I've consulted with Judge Warren about it."

"Uncomfortable with it? Detective Mason had a suspect, he went to Homicide with it and they had me view a photo lineup. What's the problem?"

Instead of answering, Stevens asked another question. "Did Detective Mason ever discuss the accused with you prior to the photo lineup?"

"Yeah," Jack responded matter-of-factly. "He told me his office had a possible suspect and he wanted to know if I would be able to pick him out in a lineup. I said I didn't know. That's it." Jack knew better than to look to Mason for confirmation.

"I see. Had you ever met Mr. Charles prior to the arrest?"

Mister Charles? "Yeah —" again matter-of-factly "— on the night he slit open my partner's throat."

Stevens blanched and the judge murmured, exchanging a knowing glance with Stevens.

"We've been over this already," Mason interjected.

Whatever was going on, it sure as fuck didn't feel good to Jack. It was his turn to fold his hands and lean into the discussion. "Maybe you could skip the bullshit cross-examination and just tell me what the fuck the problem is."

Stevens pursed his lips before settling back in his chair. "Your ID won't stand up in court." He tossed a sheaf of stapled papers onto the table. Jack recognized them, even upside down, as photocopies of his memo book notes. "In your notes from the night of Officer Carter's homicide, you state you only saw part of the suspect's forehead and one eye. His right eye, if I remember correctly."

"That's correct. That night I said I saw the *suspect's* eye, forehead and scalp. Now I can say that I saw *Charles's* eye, forehead and scalp. I don't see a problem."

Mason gave him an approving thump on the shoulder.

But Stevens wasn't convinced. "In a dark alley, with poor lighting, after having just run for several minutes, you are confronted by a suspect in an extremely stressful situation. A good defence lawyer will pick that to pieces. And believe me when I say there is a lineup of good lawyers willing to take this case. Successfully defending an accused cop killer is one hell of a way to make your reputation."

"Isn't it your job to see that doesn't happen?"

That hit a nerve. Stevens came up out of his chair to lean across the table. *I guess when you're that small, you rely on grand gestures to make up for the lack of size.* "It's also my job to see that the Crown's office doesn't get ass raped before the media. And this will be a media frenzy."

Mason added his say to the argument. "Then it's your chance to make your reputation by successfully prosecuting an accused cop killer."

Stevens glared at him, then looked at Jack. "And then there's the matter of the gloves. In your notes, you describe them as ..." He picked up the photocopies and began searching through them.

"As black latex gloves. Don't bother; I know what I wrote."

"All right, then," Stevens challenged, throwing down the notes. "How do you explain the sudden change from latex to leather? A small point, I'm willing to admit, but a good defence lawyer will make a fucking mountain out of it. Do you remember the O.J. Simpson case?"

Instead of answering, Jack pulled on his search gloves. "Will you hit the lights, Rick?"

Nodding in approval, Mason got up and doused the lights, restricting the room's illumination to what came through the partially closed door. Jack made a fist and tucked it under his jaw. Next, he clicked on his flashlight and angled the beam across the back of the tightly stretched glove.

"Bad lighting, a foot chase and a stressful situation. You tell me: leather or latex?"

Mason hit the lights and Jack stowed his flashlight away.

"Thank you for the dramatic demonstration, officer. But all

theatrics aside, it still won't fly. Charles has a solid alibi for the night of the murders."

Jack scoffed. "And which one of his criminal friends is providing it?"

"He was seen by many people, several of them not associated with him, at a nightclub in Scarborough." Stevens looked smug, the way a defence lawyer would probably look when producing the airtight alibi. Jack didn't think that expression should be on the face of the man assigned to prosecute the case.

Mason threw up his hands. "We've been over this. That nightclub is a major location for the sale of narcotics, including the Black that Charles sells. There are no video cameras to confirm he was there or what time he left, if it turns out he was actually there. And the witnesses? Come on. He's got enough money at his disposal to buy the Pope as a witness."

Stevens shook his head in resignation. "Doesn't matter. The gloves, the ID, the alibi. There's no case."

"That's bullshit and you know it!" Mason pounded the table and Stevens flinched. The judge watched the proceedings impassively. "If this was a cop accused of murder, this office would be turning itself inside fucking out to tear apart the witnesses and the alibi."

"Got that right," Jack agreed.

Stevens sighed. He studied them both for a moment, then looked to the judge for confirmation. Judge Warren nodded once, and once was enough.

"Like I said: the ID, the gloves, the alibi. There's no case and I'm withdrawing the charges against Anthony Charles."

Tuesday, 26 September
1644 hours

"I still don't understand why he dropped the charges. So what if he's got an alibi? Dude, it's the Crown's job to prove it's a lie."

Jack shrugged. Manny wasn't saying anything Jack hadn't said or thought a thousand times already. "Welcome to the Canadian legal system. The best system in the world. If you're a criminal, that is."

"It's not right, man. It's not fucking right. What about him killing your snitch in the street? They didn't drop those charges, too, did they?"

"As quick as loose shit. The fucking wimp of a Crown said my ID on that one was even worse than when he killed Sy. So Charles walks free."

They were heading to the Second Cup for the evening's first hit of caffeine. They hadn't cleared with the dispatcher yet and as far as Jack cared they could stay off her screen all night. Manny was usually gung-ho enough for both of them, but this afternoon even he seemed unmotivated to do police work.

"Why bother? Why fucking bother?" Jack swept his hand to encompass both sides of the street. "Why do we risk our lives to arrest these assholes when the courts, the politicians, the media never support us? Hell, our own command officers don't support us. They'd rather stand by and do nothing while the SIU fucks us over every way they can, destroying our lives, our marriages, our jobs by laying bullshit criminal charges even if there's evidence proving we're innocent. They'd rather wait until the trial's over and say, 'See? We knew our officers were innocent.' Never mind that for the last two or three years the coppers' lives have been put on hold and they've been fucked over by a bunch of civilians who've probably never been in a police car. Fuck!"

Jack fell silent, brooding out the open window. "I don't know why we do it, Manny. I really don't."

"Because somebody has to," Manny replied softly.

Jack gave him a quizzical look. "What are you babbling about?"

"We do it because someone has to. We're not the type to sit back and complain about a problem. We do something about it.

It's what we do." He looked at Jack, his face grave. "'With great power comes great responsibility.'"

Jack burst out laughing. Not at Manny but in release. It was either laugh or cry and he'd done enough crying these last few weeks. He patted Manny on the shoulder. "At least your references I understand. God, you remind me of Sy."

"I do? Gee, thanks, man. That means a lot to me." Manny beamed like a kid who had earned his first A on a test.

"But just for that, you're buying."

"Dude, no problem."

The visit to the Second Cup was subdued. Chris offered his congratulations to Jack for catching his partner's killer, then his condolences for the guy's release when he heard the update. "We were robbed here, once," he said, all flamboyance aside. "You guys caught him, but every time we went to court it was put over, put over, put over. Either his lawyer couldn't make it, or he couldn't make it. Then, the one day I couldn't make it, his lawyer wanted the trial and the charges got thrown out." He shook his head in frustration. "I don't know how you guys do it. I really don't."

Jack smiled a small, sad smile. "Somebody has to. Right, Manny?"

"You got it, dude. Thanks for the coffee, Chris."

"Hang on a quick sec, guys." Chris bagged a couple of the shop's extra-large, extra-chewy oatmeal cookies. "On the house. It isn't much, but it's something." He shrugged apologetically.

"Thank you," Jack said, accepting the gift. "It's more than we usually get."

They were cruising down Church — Manny seemed to be instinctively staying away from the 51 streets for the time being — when Jenny called out for Jack.

"Is PC Warren on the air? Warren on the air in 51?"

"Things are looking up, man. First a free cookie, now a call from your girlfriend."

Jack grimaced at him, then spoke into the mike. "Go ahead for Warren."

"Jack, can we see you at Moss Park Armouries? Shuter entrance."

"10-4, Jenny." He glared at Manny. "My girlfriend?"

"Sure, dude. I heard about you and her getting all cuddly at the beach party."

"Uh-huh." Jack sat back and dunked his cookie into his tea.

Moss Park Armouries was a brooding thug of a building on the west side of Moss Park, squaring off against the community centre to the east. A playground, baseball diamonds and a soccer field held the no man's land between them. Jenny and Al were waiting in the parking lot behind the Armouries off Shuter Street, their bikes on their stands. They were still in bike shorts but had donned their yellow jackets in acknowledgement of the cooling weather.

Jack and Manny got out to join them. Jack offered Jenny half his cookie. She gladly took it, but her face remained grim. When he asked what was up, she pointed to a group of males loitering on the soccer field.

"Sy would probably make some quip about the Six Million Dollar Man, but my eyes aren't bionic. Who is that?" Jack asked.

"Charles," she said quietly.

A wave of cold, icy anger swept through him. "What does he want?"

Jenny sighed. She looked at Jack with those beautiful eyes and they were filled with pain. "You," she whispered. "He wants you."

"Dude, he's challenging you. I say we go over there and kick his fucking teeth down his throat." That was Manny: *Attack my partner, attack both of us.*

"What do you mean, he wants me?"

"We were riding through the park when one of his little ass lickers came over to us," Al explained. Jenny seemed too distraught to speak. "Little fuck said Charles knew you were working and wanted to talk to you. Alone. Says he'll meet you in the baseball diamond."

"Dude, you're not going, are you? Not alone?"

"I'll see what he has to say." Jack stuffed the last of his cookie into his mouth and softened it up with tea. Around the wad in his cheek, he said, "Can't hurt, can it?"

Crossing the parking lot, he headed for the far diamond. Al, Manny and Jenny fell in behind him. As he walked, he saw Charles and his entourage begin to drift toward the diamond as well. When Jack reached the infield, the three officers behind him stopped, keeping a watchful eye on the approaching group. Charles left them at the field's edge. Jack and Charles moved on alone, two kings of opposing armies meeting for a parley before the battle.

Jack stood at home plate, sipping his tea unconcernedly as Charles swaggered up to him. He wore another Raptors jacket, leather this time and new by the look of it. And the gloves. Always the gloves.

Charles stopped about an arm's length from Jack and looked him up and down. "Not so big when you aren't hiding behind your Glock, Officer Warren."

Jack sipped his tea, eyed Charles back. "Any time you want to meet, let me know and I'll leave the gun behind."

Charles laughed, a light chuckle. "You cops are all the same: big talk but no balls."

"This coming from the man who kills people from behind, then runs and hides whenever the police come near."

Charles sucked his teeth at Jack. "I told you, I didn't kill your partner. Not that I'm afraid to dust a cop, but I don't like taking credit for someone else's work."

Jack took a drink. Concentrating on calmly drinking his tea was the only way he could stop himself from killing the little fuck right now. "Seems to me you've been taking a lot of credit for it, though."

Charles laughed again. "If word gets around that I offed your partner, then who am I to contradict that story? I figure I'm owed some payback, anyway. I just found out you're the one who broke my brother's nose."

"Your brother's lucky I didn't kill him. Rather irresponsible of you to let him play with toy guns." Jack looked over Charles's shoulder. Sean was there, wandering slightly apart from the rest of the group and no longer sporting a splint on his nose. He was wearing a Raptors jacket similar to his brother's. Sean saw Jack looking and waved at him. "How nice of you to give him your hand-me-downs. Does he know he's wearing the jacket you had on when you shit your pants in fear?"

Charles smiled; he was not about to be baited. "You break my brother's nose, try to frame me for three murders, then shove your gun in my face." He stepped close, getting right up into Jack's face. "You owe me and I mean to collect."

Concentrate on the tea. Up slowly, sip, down slowly. "I didn't kill you in that lane because I was trying to save my partner. I didn't kill you last week because I thought it wasn't the right thing to do. Give me another opportunity and I won't make that mistake again."

"We ain't finished, you and me." Charles's words were soft, meant for Jack's ears only. Smiling, he eased back, adjusted his collar. He paused to admire his gloves, even held them out for Jack's inspection. "Like 'em? I got them to match my new jacket, in celebration of my release from prison. Wanna know how much I paid for them?"

Sip. Jack crumpled his cup and flicked it at Charles. It bounced off his shiny new jacket, leaving a slight spray of drops on the leather. "Next time you want to talk to me, have something useful to say." Jack turned his back on his partner's murderer. He had taken only a couple of steps when Charles's words stopped him dead.

"They was pretty expensive. Three pair cost me probably as much as you pay each month on that shitty little house out in Pickering."

Jack slowly turned. The ice that had held him in control was melting beneath a fury burning up from his gut.

"Oh, yeah. I know all about you, Officer Jack Warren."

Jack advanced on him, fists clenched at his side, but Charles held his ground, coolly adjusting his gloves. Jack grabbed him by the lapels of his new leather jacket and slammed him against the chain-link barrier behind home plate. "If I catch even your smell near my house, there'll be no place on Earth for you to hide."

Charles stared impassively into Jack's eyes. "Like I said, *Jack*: I've got some payback owed to me, but I'm willing to forget it if you fess up to framing me. I'm even willing to make it easy on you, Jack, 'cause I'm betting my old friend Mason's behind the whole thing. Since his little game backfired and I got this new bad rep out of it, I'm willing to call things even. All you or Mason gotta do is tell those Homicide dicks that been hounding my ass you were wrong about me, now that you seen me face to face. You do that and I won't have to visit that sweet little blonde wife of yours."

Jack shoved Charles harder into the fence. "You go near her and I'll kill you the next time I see you. I won't care who's watching." Jack gave him a final heave against the chain link, then let him go. "I swear to you, I see you near her, I'll kill you." He stalked away.

Charles called after him, his voice friendly and light. "You remember my offer, Jack, and we'll get along fine."

"What was that all about?" Manny asked as soon as Jack reached them. "What did he want?"

"I need to go to the station. Now."

On the short ride, Jack kept muttering, "I should have killed him when I had the chance. I should have killed him."

"Dude, what's going on?"

"He knows where I live!" Jack snapped. "He knows where I live, he knows I'm married. He knows what Karen looks like!"

"Then we kill him, dude. Simple as that."

Manny's open trust and loyalty stunned Jack. "I don't think it can be that simple, Manny. I wish it was."

At the station, Jack took the stairs two at a time to the MCU. The office door was closed. He didn't bother knocking. Mason was there with his usual team: Taft, Tank and Kris. Didn't anyone else work in this office?

Mason looked up from his desk. "Jack, good to see you, but until you're part of this office you may want to knock in the future."

Jack looked around the office. The four of them were at their desks, doing paperwork or typing on computers. What difference would knocking make? He planted himself in front of Mason's desk. "He knows where I live. He knows I'm married."

"Who knows — not Charles? Fuck!" Mason leaned back in his chair and blew into cupped hands over his mouth and nose. "Sit down, Jack."

"Boss." Taft jerked his head toward the door. Manny was standing in the doorway.

"Armsman, maybe you should —"

"Manny's my partner," Jack cut in, earning a withering look from Mason. He ignored it. "He can hear whatever you have to say. Fuck, he's already offered to kill Charles for me."

Mason looked at Manny with a new eye, as if he was judging him by a new set of principles. "All right, he can stay. There isn't much we can do right now anyway."

Manny sat on a desk near the door. Later, Jack would realize Manny was able to watch all the other officers from that position.

"Who else have you told?"

"No one else. What the fuck do I do, Rick?"

"First, you tell us exactly what he said. All of it, word for word. Don't leave anything out."

Jack related the conversation — how could such an experience be labelled as a simple conversation? — as best he could. When he was finished, he sagged back in his chair, drained.

Mason sat back, too, thinking. "Sounds like he's not planning on doing anything right away. So we have time to figure this out."

"What did he mean by 'my old friend Mason?'" The Major

Crime officers all looked at Manny.

Mason was glaring at him. "It means I've been trying to put his ass in jail ever since he started dumping the Black shit on the streets."

"I thought you only found out he was behind the Black recently," Jack said.

"That's right, not until after Sy was killed. But we've been trying to put that whole organization out of business since it started. ID'ing Charles just gave us a specific target."

"So what do I do? Ask for surveillance on Karen, my house? For how long? I can't have this hanging over us for the rest of my career or until he decides I'm not co-operating."

"Give me a couple of days, Jack. Let me talk to Homicide. I've also got a couple of buddies at Mobile Support who could help out, maybe keep an eye on Karen. Don't worry, she'll never know they're there. Give me a couple of days," he repeated, "and we'll have an answer for you. Okay?"

"And what do I do till then? Stay home? I could call in sick."

Mason considered for a minute. "Unless you can guarantee Karen won't figure something's up by your attitude, I wouldn't. Come to work, do your job. Your shift finishes tomorrow, right? I'll have your answer by then."

Jack got up and walked to the door. "I'm trusting you with the most important person in my life, Rick."

"I won't let you down, Jack. I promise."

Jack looked like he wanted to say more, needed to say more, but he gave a silent nod and walked out. Manny shut the door behind them.

Wednesday, 27 September
1400 hours

Last day of shift. Mason's promised day of delivery. The day before had been sheer hell and Jack knew Mason had been right about coming to work; there was no way he could have kept this secret from Karen. The shift hours had helped. He saw her briefly when he rolled in after three in the morning and again a few hours later when she got up for work. A quick "Hello" and "How you doing?" passed between them.

But today was the last day and it was training day, to boot, which meant the shift started early and Jack would be off early. If he went straight home after work — and there was no way he could go out for drinks that night — she'd still be awake and no amount of acting on his part would hide the truth from her.

And if it wasn't settled — and how the hell did Mason plan on fixing it? — didn't she have a right to know?

"Jack! You with us?"

"Sorry, Sarge."

"As I was saying," Johanson carried on, "Warren and Armsman, 5108, eight o'clock for lunch." He finished reading out the assignments, then set the sergeant's clipboard aside. "All right, listen up." He leaned on the little podium, his bushy grey eyebrows furrowed into one long hairy centipede. "It's been a hell of a week and I know you're all anxious to go out tonight and get pissed." A hearty cheer confirmed his thoughts. "But first we have to get through tonight."

The platoon settled down; Johanson was not the type to drag parade on for no reason.

"First, our own Officer Warren identifies a cop killer —" a round of applause "— then he has to go and make the arrest on his own —" heavy applause and whistles "— which, if he ever does again, I will personally kick the brains out of his ass. And, no, I don't believe that bullshit about your radio not working. It was a stupid, dangerous stunt to pull, Warren. We could have ended up with another dead cop. Good job, though," he added quietly.

"For those of you who don't know, the Crown decided to withdraw the murder charges against the suspect." Jeers, boos and a chorus of "Fucking lawyers." "I imagine the charges from the pursuit will also be eventually dropped. So, the suspect is out on the streets. Which brings me to my last point. Midnights had a homicide at Sherbourne and Dundas last night after we finished. The victim hasn't been identified yet, but I've been told he is black with a shaved head and was wearing black leather gloves."

Another burst of applause saluted the news. Johanson waited for the ruckus to die down on its own before continuing. "The victim will probably be ID'd tomorrow during the autopsy by fingerprints."

"Why can't Jack just go look at him over at the morgue?" someone threw out from the back of the room.

"Because the victim's face is missing. Apparently, someone put a shotgun to the back of his head and removed the front half of it. We'll have to wait for the results. In the meantime —" the sergeant cracked a very rare grin "— I think we might be able to celebrate a bit tonight."

More cheers.

"You buying, Sarge?"

"Fuck you, Townsend. All right, that's it for now. Take ten, then get your asses back here for training. Jack, stay put."

Once the room was clear, Johanson got serious. "You go home last night, Jack?"

"Yeah."

"You married?"

"Yeah. Sarge, what —"

"What time did you get in?"

"After three. Why —"

"Can she confirm that?"

"I guess. What diff—" Then it hit him. "You're shitting me, Sarge."

Johanson put a hand on Jack's shoulder, an act of physical contact even rarer than a grin. "I don't think so, no, but a lot of people will. And some of those people will be looking at you very closely. I know this is good news to you, it's great fucking news, but all I'm suggesting is that you shouldn't act too happy about it."

Jack nodded. "Thanks, Sarge. I won't."

"You don't own a shotgun, do you, Jack?"

"No."

"Even better. See you back here in ten."

Jack headed upstairs to the report room, a tiny, cramped room — was there any other type in the station? — off the front desk. A day-shift officer was pecking away at a keyboard.

"Were you at the homicide scene today?" Jack asked without preamble.

The officer looked relieved to have a break from his blistering two-finger typing. "Yup, I was."

"Did you see the body?"

"Fucking right I did." His face brightened. "You shoulda seen it. Everything from here up —" he placed his hands just below his nose "— was missing. It was fucking awesome."

"Was he wearing a Raptors jacket?"

"Yup, he was." The officer suddenly looked worried, his *Aw, shucks, ma'am, 'tweren't nuttin'* country-boy face pale. "You didn't know him, did you?"

"No, not really. Last question: was the jacket leather or nylon?"

"Lemme check." The officer flipped through his memo book, searching, searching . . . searching. Jack wanted to rip the book from his hands and look himself. "Okay, here it is. Leather. It was a leather jacket." Officer Country Boy looked at Jack hopefully. "That what you wanted to hear?"

Jack didn't know if he should laugh or panic. "I guess so, thanks."

Next stop: Major Crime. The door was closed and this time he remembered to knock. No answer, and the door was locked. "Damn."

"Looking for me, Jack?" Mason stepped out of the stairway down by the Youth Bureau. He had a Subway sandwich bag and a full paper cup in one hand while he dug in his jacket pocket for keys with the other. "Come on in," he invited when he got the door open. "I was expecting a visit from you today." He set his lunch on his desk and shrugged out of his well worn leather jacket.

Mason settled behind his desk and took a long gulp of his drink, the ice cubes rattling clearly in the room's stillness. "I know what you're going to ask, and, no, we had nothing to do with killing Charles."

Jack sighed in relief. "I'm sorry, Rick. It's not that I really thought you —"

"But you weren't exactly sure, either." He smiled perceptively around a mouthful of sub. Swallowing, he added, "Shit, man. If I was in your place, I'd be thinking the same thing."

"Then who?"

Mason shrugged and bit into his sub greedily. Talking as he chewed, he speculated, "Could have been anyone, really. Charles made a lot of enemies downtown with his push to take over the crack trade. It was only a matter of time before someone took a shot at him. I'm just surprised it was done so well. Normally, these mumble-fucks would drive by and empty a clip in his direction, hoping to get lucky. Whoever did this was determined not to miss."

"Johanson talked to me on parade, implied I might need someone to vouch for my whereabouts last night."

Mouth too full to speak, Mason nodded, a cynical frown on his face.

"You think I need one?"

Swallowing, Mason wiped mayonnaise off his lips. "Well, you certainly have reason to kill him and you were working last night, right? Now, the guys from Homicide aren't all idiots and they'll know there's a whole host of suspects out there, but in order to appear impartial and open-minded they'll have to take a look at you, if for no other reason than to cross you off as a suspect." He chewed on his sub for a few seconds. "Karen was home when you got in last night, right?"

Jack nodded.

"Went straight home from work? No side trips to the girl-friend's or anything like that?"

"Straight home. Got there around quarter to four."

"And Karen can attest to that? Not that a wife's word is the greatest alibi, you understand. Somewhat of a biased position. As long as the marriage is still good, that is." A cocked eyebrow changed that last bit into a question.

"Yeah, we're good."

"All right. Let's see. . . ." Mason hunted through some papers and came up with a printout of a radio call. "Here it is. A call for the sound of a gunshot came in at 3:27. Almost half an hour after you booked off work. Someone could argue that gave you plenty of time to drive around, find Charles and surgically remove his head from his shoulders with a shotgun. Drive home like a demon and still be in bed by four or so."

He tossed the paper back onto the pile. "You didn't tell any-one else about that little meeting you had with Charles, did you? If Homicide found out about that little tidbit, you'd jump to the top of the suspect list. Shit, you'd be the *only* name on the list."

Jack shook his head emphatically. "Just the people who were here. No one else."

"What about Manny? Could he have mentioned it to anyone?"

"He said he'd keep it to himself and I believe him. I'd trust him with my life."

"Don't say that too lightly — you just might be." Mason leaned back in his chair and sipped his pop, using the straw this time. He abruptly banged the chair back down on its four feet. "Tell you what: after work last night, you came here and we shot the shit for a while. You left around 3:30. It's better than relying on Karen's statement and it puts you at the station at the time of the shooting."

"Thanks, Rick, I appreciate it, but why are you doing this for me?"

Mason waved away the thanks. "I know what it's like to have Professional Standards or Homicide sniffing around you. It's a pain in the ass you can do without. If they ask, tell them we talked about the charges against Charles and why they were dropped 'cause you were still pissed off about it."

Jack smiled. "But not pissed off enough to go kill him."

"You're a smart lad. Now fuck off and let me work. Oh, and Jack?" he called when Jack reached the door. "Two things: first, this conversation never took place and, second, now you know why you should knock before coming in."

The shift passed by in a swirl of emotions, the headiest being relief. Charles was permanently out of the picture and along with him went the threats against Karen. True, she would be royally pissed if she ever found out a threat had existed, but he figured he could justify his silence.

Manny was ecstatic over Jack's good fortune and never complained when Jack stood mutely at calls, his thoughts clearly elsewhere. As the hour of eleven approached, they asked for and got the okay to go one and one — taking an hour of time off at the end of shift in lieu of banking the lunch hour they had not been able to take — and made a beeline for the station.

Jack grabbed the duty bags while Manny unloaded the shotgun. Between his duty bag, lunch cooler, soco kit and camera and taking out a shotgun, Manny had to make at least two trips to load and unload the car if he was working solo. Jack held the door open for his partner, who trundled past like some overloaded, clanking Sherpa.

Jack ran into Jenny outside the report room.

"Coming out tonight?" she asked. "Reason to celebrate."

"Not this time. Think I'll just head home and share the good news with Karen."

"In shape, intelligent and considerate. Why are all the good ones taken?" she mourned.

"Maybe we just seem that much better because we are taken," he suggested, shrugging.

"Maybe," she agreed reluctantly, a mischievous twinkle in her eye. "But you'll let me know if you ever become available, right?"

"Absolutely," he promised and darted into the change room when he felt himself blushing. Jenny's laughter chased him in.

The lights were on when Jack pulled into the driveway just before midnight. He would have been home earlier, but he had stopped along the way to pick up flowers again. Same store, but this time the flowers looked fresh. He sat behind the wheel listening to the engine ticking as it cooled off in the autumn air. *How do I break good news like this? Great news, hon! Guess who was murdered today at work?* Jack laughed at himself. *Probably not the best approach. Screw it, I'll wing it.*

Stepping inside, he called out, "Karen? You upstairs or down?" He kicked the door shut behind him and toed off his shoes. "Karen?" He took two steps into the front hall and sharp pain exploded behind his right ear and everything went black.

His eyelids flickered and the pain greeted him enthusiastically. Groaning, he rolled onto his stomach and felt carpet beneath his hands. When he tried to lift his head, his belly heaved as the pain radiated in great nauseating waves from a spot behind his ear. Clamping his teeth shut, he fought the urge to puke and waited for the pain to subside to a more manageable level.

Jack thought he heard someone calling his name. Karen? Maybe, but everything sounded fuzzy, as if she was phoning from far away and there was a really bad connection. Gritting his teeth and telling himself he would not puke, he pushed himself onto his hands and knees, his head hanging between his arms.

Slowly, he opened his eyes to a world of vague and distorted images. Were those his hands? He wiggled his fingers, and the shadowy blobs moved appropriately. He felt the carpet under his hands. Carpet meant the living room. He remembered being in the front hall when . . . when what?

He could hear Karen calling his name. She sounded like she was crying, but he couldn't focus his thoughts. What was going on?

Something smashed into his ribs, lifting him off the floor and dumping him on his back. His head seemed to hurt less with this new agony in his ribs. Jack clutched his side and stared at a spinning ceiling, willing it to slow, to stop.

A dark shape blocked out the revolving ceiling. A face? It had to be a face because words came out of it. The words were fuzzy, but he could understand them.

"I'm surprised you're awake so soon. You must have one fucking thick skull."

Hands grabbed his shirt and hauled him to a sitting position. His head and ribs tried to outscream each other.

"Get up, you murdering son of a bitch. Get up."

Whoever was behind him was pulling on his shirt and Jack helped as much as he could; he sure as hell didn't want to fall down. When he reached his feet, he was spun around on wobbly legs and thrown backward. He braced for a painful impact but landed on the couch. It still hurt, and he cried out, but he could have landed on the floor or coffee table.

That dark shape was in front of his eyes again. "Wake up, motherfucker." Something hit the side of his head. A slap. Another slap, this time from the other side. "I said, wake the fuck up!" Two more sharp blows in quick succession.

Jack's vision cleared. The pain in his head was still trying to burn conscious thought from his mind, but his eyes slowly cleared. And he could see who was slapping him.

Anthony Charles.

"Surprised to see me, motherfucker?" He gripped Jack by the hair and jerked his head back. "Thought you killed me, didn't you? Well, I got fucking news for you, motherfucker. I ain't dead, but pretty soon, you will be. You and your little bitch here."

Charles moved aside and there was Karen, duct-taped to a dining room chair between the two wing chairs. She was terrified, and rivers of tears coursed down her cheeks, red from where Charles had hit her. She was wearing one of his old blue police shirts.

Oh, God, Karen, you were waiting up for me!

Jack tried to soothe her. "It's okay, honey. Everything's going to be fine. Trust me."

Then Charles was between them. "Trust you? Why should she trust a murdering fuck like you?"

Murder? "I don't know what you're talking about." Slowly, carefully, Jack swung his head side to side, the closest he dared to shaking it.

Charles leapt at him, smashing something hard against Jack's head. Jack cried out and crumpled sideways onto the couch. Charles hauled him upright again. His vision was spinning wildly, and he felt himself slipping away, but Charles wouldn't let him go. He grabbed Jack by the throat and pinned him to the back of the couch. With his other hand, he jammed a gun against Jack's cheek.

At least I know what he hit me with. A morbid little voice deep inside Jack chuckled at the thought.

"Don't lie to me! Don't fucking lie to my face!" Charles ground the gun barrel into Jack's cheekbone. His eyes were wide and wild, beyond reason. "You killed Sean, you fuck! You killed him!"

Sean? Suddenly everything made sense to Jack. Everyone, even Jack, thought it was Charles who had been killed. The gloves, the leather Raptors jacket.

"He was wearing your jacket," Jack mumbled, his mouth not wanting to work properly.

"I gave it to him, you fuck! I gave it to him 'cause he liked it so much, and you killed him!" Charles howled, a pain Jack understood all too well choking his cries.

"I didn't kill him. I didn't even know about it till this after-noon when I got to work. Why would I kill him?"

"'Cause you thought it was me! Me!" Charles dug the gun in again, forcing Jack's head back.

Staring along the barrel, Jack said as calmly and clearly as he could, "I didn't kill Sean."

"Yes. You. Did." Charles punctuated every word by pressing the gun harder and harder against Jack's cheek. Jack could feel the bone grinding beneath the metal and the warm trickle of blood as skin gave way. "But now, I'm going to make things even." Charles tore the gun away and walked over to Karen.

"No, don't. Please," Jack begged, but Charles only smiled, an evil smirk, and placed the barrel gently against her temple.

"You killed my brother, I kill your bitch." He cocked the hammer back and for the first time Jack recognized the gun as a revolver, a big one. There would be no surviving a shot from that range.

"I didn't kill your brother!" Jack yelled. He lurched forward on the couch, his ribs crying out and his head threatening to burst. He made it as far as sitting up straight, then slid off the couch to his knees. His hands on the coffee table were all that kept him from collapsing face first onto the carpet. Or so he wanted Charles to think. The pain in his head was excruciating, but he could handle it; he'd had worse with his migraines. He could fight through it.

"You think I'm going to believe your lies, motherfucker?" Charles was still distraught but seemed more in control of him-self. Jack didn't know if that was good. "First you frame me, then you almost shoot me in the back and now you want me to believe your lies?"

Karen was silent, an unwilling witness. Her life hung on her husband's actions and words.

"You did kill my partner. I saw you."

Charles laughed. "Just like every fucking other cop. If you can't catch a brother one way, just make up some lies. You're like every other fucking white motherfucker out there — can't stand to see a brother doing good for himself and his family."

"Doing good? By selling crack?" Jack straightened his arms, then sagged, as if too weak to stand.

"I'll sell to anyone who wants to buy. White, black, chinks, I don't care. If a nigger's stupid enough to use that shit, then he ain't no good to me."

"Your mother smoked crack."

"Yeah. She was a stupid bitch. Five years old and I knew better than her, asked her not to, but she didn't listen. Didn't care. Just kept turning tricks for her rock. And look what that shit did to my brother. She did that to him by smoking that shit! Nobody cared. All they saw was a knocked-up nigger getting high. You think if she'd been white nobody woulda cared? Shit! Child Services woulda been all over her, 'for the sake of the baby.' But she was just another fucked-up nigger."

"So you sell to your own kind?" Jack's hand went to the growing lump behind his ear and came away bloody.

"If niggers are stupid enough to smoke it, I'll sell it to them."

Jack laughed, a hoarse, ragged sound. "Your mother smokes crack and fucks up your brother, makes him a retard, and you blame society." He laughed again, baiting Charles, taunting him. "And you fucking killed him by selling that shit."

"What the fuck did you say?" Charles swung the gun toward Jack.

Jack drew himself upright on one knee, swaying, one hand on the coffee table to steady himself. *Come on, fucker. Closer.*

"You killed Sean by selling that shit. You think you could just come in and take over without pissing anyone off?" He barked a laugh, scornful and demeaning. "Somebody was bound to come after you and they got Sean by mistake. I didn't kill your brother. You did. You killed Sean."

"Fucker!" Charles came at him, gun held stiffly out at arm's length as if he intended to spear Jack with it.

Jack lunged, driving in his legs with all the power he could muster. There was a red-orange flash, a deafening blast, and something hot and hard punched into his right shoulder. An instant later he crashed into Charles, taking him around the stomach. They toppled into the chair his father-in-law had so recently berated him from, and then onto the floor.

Jack landed on top, and they grappled for the gun, its barrel wavering dangerously between them. Jack seized Charles's gun hand with his left then dropped an elbow down into that smirking face. The elbow landed square but pain flared from Jack's shoulder, robbing the hit of any real power. It distracted Charles long enough for Jack to go for the gun. With his left hand still clamped around Charles's wrist, Jack grabbed the gun hand with his right hand and pushed down, but again he lacked power. He dropped his chest on the back of Charles's hand. It had to hurt.

Charles's free hand went for Jack's face, raking at his eyes. Jack twisted his face away and bore down on the gun hand until it popped open and the gun fell onto Charles's chest. Charles bucked and heaved and flipped Jack off his chest. They scrambled to their feet and faced off over the fallen gun.

Charles darted for it and Jack rushed him, driving a knee into his chest. Charles fell back against the fireplace, knocking over the wrought iron implements. They clanged shrilly against the stone. Jack stumbled, caught his balance and swung a backhand, catching Charles flush in the side of the head. Jack's shoulder screamed and his fist bounced impotently off Charles's head.

Jack closed in, pinning Charles against the mantel. He snapped a quick head butt, but Charles took it on his cheek. Charles latched a hand onto Jack's injured shoulder and dug his fingers into the wound. Jack tried to pull away from the shrieking pain, but Charles held him tightly and drove a fist into his ribs. The first punch doubled Jack over, the second buckled his knees. Charles knocked him back with a knee to the chest, and Jack sprawled on the carpet.

Karen was screaming for help when Charles knelt down and picked up the fireplace poker. He grinned maliciously as he swung it before him, testing its weight. "Shut the fuck up, bitch." He whacked her across the back of her head with the poker, and her cries snapped off, her head lolling limply from her shoulders. "That's better." He turned his attention to Jack.

Where was the gun? Jack rolled onto his stomach and frantically searched for it, then spotted it just out of reach. He crawled for it, but Charles saw where he was going.

"Not so fast, motherfucker."

Charles swung the poker and it thudded into Jack's back just above his right hip. Jack ignored the pain and lunged for the gun. Metal smashed into his injured ribs, and he screamed.

Charles knelt beside him. "How's that feel, you fuck? Bet it doesn't hurt as much as it did for Sean when you shot his head off. But I'm going to fix that, you hear me?"

Jack reached for the gun. Charles let him wrap his left hand around the butt before stepping on it. He ground Jack's hand beneath his boot. "What should I do, motherfucker? Kill you while she watches or kill her while you watch? After I fuck her, of course. Yeah, that's it. I'm gonna fuck all her holes and let you watch."

Charles bent over to pick up the gun and as soon as the pressure came off his hand Jack rolled to his left, ramming Charles's shins with his back. Off balance, surprised, Charles crashed backward into the dining room table. Jack groped for the gun and came up with it at the same time Charles reared up with the poker held high for a skull-crushing strike.

Jack fired, and the recoil nearly tore the gun from his hand. The bullet punched Charles in the abdomen, and he grunted, staggering back a step. Surprised, he looked at the gun in Jack's hand, then placed his own hand to his stomach. It came away bloody.

Jack was leaning on his left elbow, the gun propped on his thigh, pointed at Charles. In the sudden silence, Jack could hear distant sirens coming closer.

"Hear that, fuckhead? It's over."

"Then I guess you gotta arrest me, Mr. Policeman." He let the poker tumble from his hand. "But this ain't over between us. I still got payback coming to me." He raised his hands and smiled.

"Like fuck," Jack said and shot him twice in the chest.

Friday, 29 September
1000 hours

"There's the man. Still in one piece, I see."

"Hey, Rick. You didn't have to drop by." Jack propped himself up in his hospital bed carefully; broken ribs were a bitch.

"Are you kidding? They're restricting the number of visitors you can have. Otherwise, the whole station would be down here. You're quite the hero."

"I'm no hero. I just got lucky."

Mason dropped into a chair beside the bed. "You don't look so lucky, unless you compare yourself to the dead guy." He pointed a finger at Jack, waving it up and down the length of his body. "What's the official tally, anyway?"

"Two broken ribs, a fucking big dent behind my ear, I forget how many stitches in my shoulder and an assortment of cuts and bruises."

"The bullet missed the bone?"

"Yeah. Like I said: I got lucky. It just tore a chunk out of the muscle. I won't be doing shrugs in the gym anytime soon."

"Well, you look like shit, wrapped up like a mummy like that. I didn't know what gift to bring, so —"

"You didn't have to bring me anything," Jack protested.

Mason overrode his objections. "Don't worry, we didn't spend any money on you. I bring the gift of good news. Charles's organization is already falling apart. If his lieutenants aren't fighting each other for control, they're heading out on their own, and the other dealers, the ones Charles forced out, are swarming back to 51." He snickered derisively. "I never thought I'd be happy to see so many dealers back out on the streets."

"What about the charges against Charles?"

"As far as Homicide is concerned, and I agree with them, Sy's murder is solved and his killer is dead. They don't give a fuck what the Crown says. They're looking into his brother's murder, but that list of suspects goes around the fucking corner."

"They're not looking at me?"

"Nah. They came around and chatted with me and it's all good. They been in to see you yet?"

Jack groaned. "If I'm not being poked and prodded by the doctors, then it's either our Homicide guys or Peel's or the SIU. I wish someone would restrict *their* visits."

Mason stood up and shook Jack's left hand. "Don't sweat it, Jack. You're the hero and they're just going through the motions. You take it easy."

Jack waited until Mason was almost at the door before voicing the question that had been on his mind for the past two days. "Rick, did Charles kill Sy?"

Mason gave him a perplexed look. "Of course he did. Why are you asking that?"

Jack gave a one-shoulder shrug. "Just something that's been bothering me. When I fought Charles, I was doing pretty well against him even though I was shot and banged up."

"So? You're tough, strong, and you were fighting for your life and your wife's. You probably could have kicked Tank's ass that night."

"No, that's not it. He wasn't overly strong or skilled at fighting. How'd a guy like that get the drop on Sy and get him in that hold? It doesn't seem possible."

Something flashed across Mason's eyes so quickly Jack wasn't sure he really saw it. "This may sound harsh to Sy's memory, Jack, but sometimes shit just happens. Maybe Charles got lucky. Maybe

Sy got careless. It happens to guys with that much time on. They get complacent, overconfident. Maybe Charles just got the jump on him."

"Yeah, I guess. Thanks for stopping by, Rick."

"No sweat. Take it easy and rest up. I'll see you when you get back to the station."

Jack watched the door swing shut, thinking how wrong Mason was to say Sy could have been careless. Sy had watched his back when he'd gone to get a coffee. No way would he have been careless chasing an armed suspect.

Jack's thoughts were pleasantly derailed when Manny burst into the room with Jenny right behind him. Manny had a giant bouquet of flowers and Jenny was carrying a tray of drinks from the Second Cup.

"Earl Grey with honey, right?"

"Thank you, from the bottom of my stomach." Jack took the offered cup and appreciatively breathed in its aroma. "The tea they give you here is like dishwater and the coffee's worse."

"Our pleasure. If no one's told you, there's a Second Cup downstairs." Jenny settled onto the bed next to his legs. That wondrous mass of hair was hanging loose, draping her back and one side of her chest. He wondered what she would look like wearing nothing but the hair.

Manny intruded on that pleasant thought. "The tea's from here, but these —" he produced a paper bag with a flourish "— are from Church and Wellesley. Chris sends his best and prayers for a speedy recovery." Manny distributed the giant oatmeal cookies and plopped down in the chair. "They looking after you well?"

"Take a look." Jack used his head to gesture at the room while he transferred the tea to his immobile right hand and pried the lid free. The walls were covered with get-well cards. There were three giant-sized cards: one from 51 and another from 32, both crammed full of signatures and best wishes; the third one was from the rest of the service, signed by every officer who'd been able to get to headquarters since Thursday morning. The cards were taped to the walls because every horizontal surface was chock full of flowers. There were flowers on the floor, and Manny's behemoth arrangement had taken over the window sill.

Jack dunked a piece of cookie in his tea and popped it into his mouth. His sigh sounded almost orgasmic. "You have no idea how good that tastes after two days of hospital food."

"Dude, if I'd known that, I would've grabbed a pizza or something. Any idea how much longer they're going to keep you?"

Jack shrugged his one working shoulder. "Day or two," he mumbled around a mouthful of cookie. "Oh, man, that's good. Now, if I could only get laid, another few days in here wouldn't be so bad."

"If you want, I can go stand guard at the door for a while." Manny made to get up. "Give Jenny some time to help you out with that."

"Very funny, smart guy." She reached over and smacked Manny in the head. "Something tells me Jack's wife might object." She gave him a look that twisted his stomach into a wonderful knot.

She said Karen might object, not her. "Yeah, I don't think that would go over too well with her."

A silence, not uncomfortable, drifted in then, and they all took the opportunity to finish their cookies. Manny slam-dunked his coffee cup, then slapped his forehead. "I forgot. Dude, I'm supposed to pass on an unofficial compliment from the firearm instructors on your grouping. Three in centre mass."

"Well, at that range, it was kind of hard to miss."

"Although," Manny pointed out, "I'm a little disappointed that your third shot dropped down into the stomach. Tsk, tsk."

"Hey," Jack objected, "I was shooting with a bad arm. Give me a break."

"Okay . . . this time."

"Enough of the macho crap," Jenny complained. "Changing the subject, how is Karen?"

"Good. Bit of a concussion. They kept her just the one night."

"I guess this means the end of your time with us?"

"What?" Manny gasped. "You're not coming back?"

Jack shrugged again. He was getting good doing it one-shoul-dered. "I'd love to stay. I want to stay. The work is great and the people, those present definitely included, are amazing."

"But?" Jenny prompted.

He sighed. "But . . . I think Karen would divorce me if I stayed. Seriously."

"Dude, that sucks. Who am I going to work with?"

Jenny patted him on the head. "There, there, it's all right. Maybe when I get out of the foot patrol I'll let you work with me."

Manny beamed at her. "Can I be Batman?"

She snorted. "In your dreams."

Jack smiled at their banter, enjoying the camaraderie. It was just one of the things he would miss if he left 51, and in his gut he knew he had found his calling in being a 51 copper. He hoped he wasn't finished with the division.

"Do you guys know anything about Mason?"

"I know he says hello to me now. He never used to."

"I'm not sure what Jack had in mind," Jenny told Manny, "but I'm pretty sure that's not what he meant."

"Nothing really. Sy once told me that everything from Mason comes with a price. He never elaborated on it and I'm just won-dering what he meant."

"Has Mason offered you a spot? That'd be cool, dude."

Jack shook his head. "He did, sort of. But not right away."

"All I know," Jenny volunteered, "is that he's very picky about who gets into his unit. And he has that inner circle who get to do all the real interesting stuff."

"You mean Tank, Kris and Taftmore?"

She nodded. "Why the questions about Mason? He say something to you?"

Jack slowly shook his head, not sure why he was asking. "I feel like Sy was trying to warn me about him. Whether to be careful around him or stay away from him entirely, I don't know."

But it was too late for that, wasn't it? He was already tied to the MCU boss by a rigged photo lineup. A thought hit him and his stomach clenched.

"Jack, are you all right?" Jenny leaned forward, concerned.

"Yeah; guess my stomach's not used to decent food."

Had Charles killed Sy? Or had Mason used Jack to settle an old score?

That secret glint in Mason's eyes.

Jack suddenly knew, regardless of what he wanted, 51 wasn't finished with him yet.